ROAD
TO
OMALOS

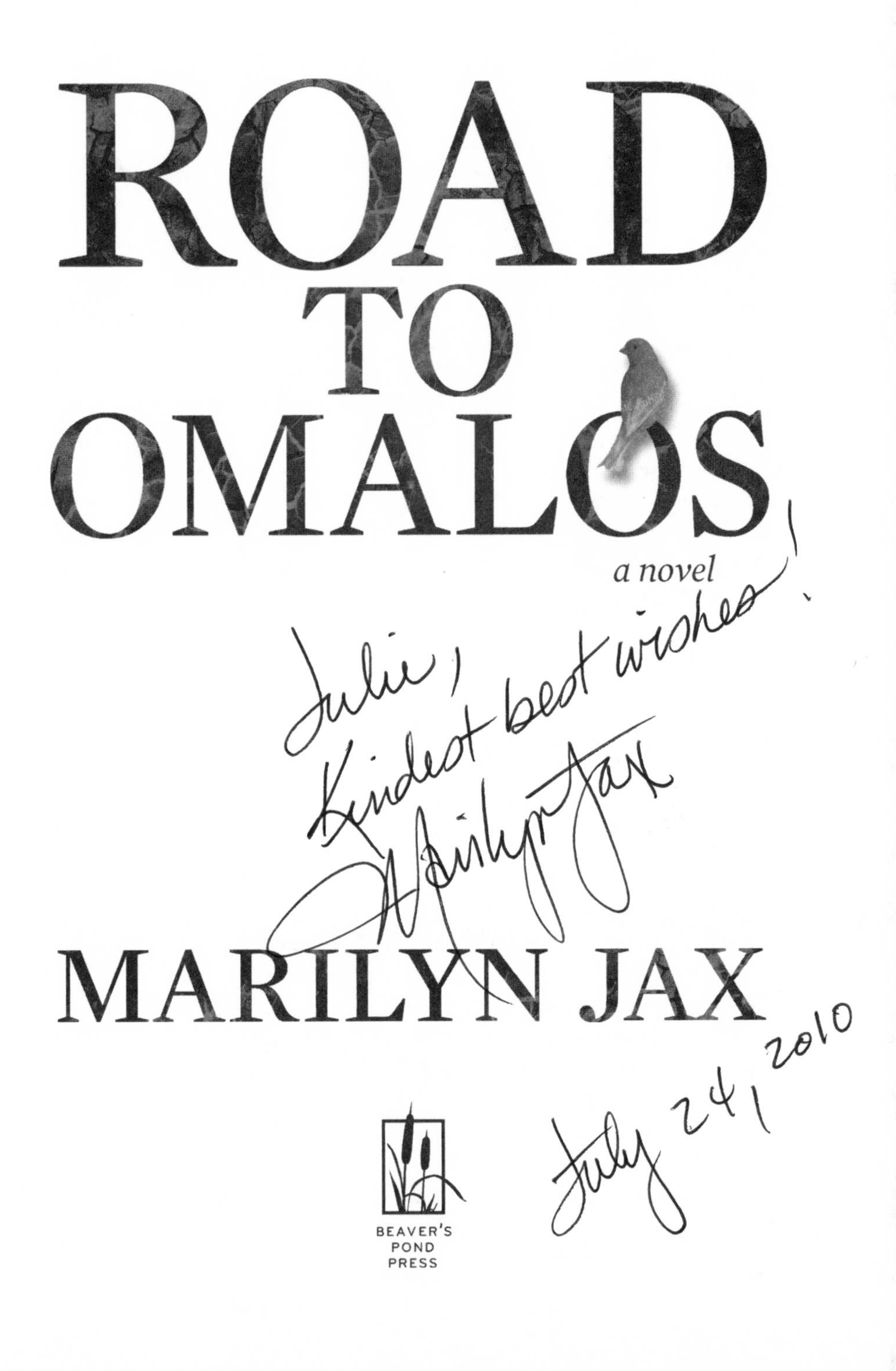

ROAD TO OMALOS

a novel

Julie,
Kindest best wishes!
Marilyn Jax

MARILYN JAX

July 24, 2010

BEAVER'S POND PRESS

This book is a work of fiction. Names, characters, places, and incidents either are products of the author's imagination or are used fictitiously. Any resemblance to actual events or locales or persons, living or dead, is entirely coincidental.

ISBN 10: 1-59298-329-4
ISBN 13: 978-1-59298-329-2

Library of Congress Catalog Number: 2010927647

Printed in the United States of America

First Printing: 2010

14 13 12 11 10 5 4 3 2 1

Author photograph by Patrick Broderick.
Cover and interior design by James Monroe Design, LLC.

Beaver's Pond Press, Inc.
7104 Ohms Lane, Suite 101
Edina, MN 55439-2129
(952) 829-8818
www.BeaversPondPress.com

To order, visit www.BeaversPondBooks.com or call (800) 901-3480.
Reseller discounts available.

Dedicated to my mother,
with everlasting love

ACKNOWLEDGMENTS

A special thank you to the countless readers of *The Find*, and to relatives and friends alike, for their encouragement and gentle but constant urging through phone calls, e-mails, and in person, to complete *Road to Omalos*. You are loyal fans and I appreciate each one of you so very much.

Many thanks to my beloved, Daniel, for his ever-present love, friendship, and support throughout the writing of this novel. You fill my heart with happiness.

And a sincere note of gratitude to my amazing editor, Michele Bassett, for her editorial guidance and praise that made this second book sing, to my expert proofreader, April Michelle Davis, and to my gifted designer, James Monroe. Also, a heartfelt thank you to my dedicated managing editor, Amy Cutler Quale, and the others at Beaver's Pond Press who helped this novel become a reality.

PROLOGUE

One year earlier . . .
Miami, Florida

RETALIATION LOOMED IN the lightlessness. The golden opportunity to strike was about to be realized—a time to level the playing field, to effect redress and satisfaction. The old Sicilian proverb, *Revenge is a dish best served cold*, would once again play itself out. Emotional detachment was ideal for the distribution of punishment. After methodical and painstaking planning, and then waiting for the precise set of circumstances, the time had arrived to avenge a hideous wrong.

Sounds from an approaching vehicle heightened animal instincts in the group of four men, and they poised internally for battle. Shrubbery planted near the perimeter of the horseshoe-shaped drive provided close cover and allowed for strategic vantage points to better eyeball the target. Semi-automatic pistols being slid back into firing position interrupted the hush of the evening.

Rigid outstretched arms crisscrossed at chest level for balance, and legs stood unbending with feet positioned as far apart as necessary to enable an even distribution of weight. The moment neared to eliminate evil beyond redemption. Leather-gloved hands fiercely gripped devices capable of firing one cartridge with every pull of the trigger. As each man grasped his pair of weapons—one in his right hand, the other in his left—sweat dripped from skin pores. Like lionesses hunting in a pack, the prey would soon be surrounded.

Trepidation abounded tenfold.

A sleek, black extended limousine rolled into sight after inching its way along the lengthy driveway toward the elegant house situated so majestically on the private property. A powerful motion light simultaneously activated like a flash, hurling nearly blinding light outward onto the asphalt road.

The foursome, dressed completely in black, wore black hoods with holes cut out for the eyes and a larger hole for the nose and mouth. Their weapons of choice were black oxide finish, single-action .45 caliber Kimber firearms, complete with luminous tritium sights for precision shooting in low-light conditions and threaded screw-on silencers attached to the extended gun barrels to suppress the sound of impending gunfire. Both hunters and weapons blended sufficiently into the darkness of the nighttime sky so as to go completely unnoticed.

As usual, the element of surprise would work its magic.

The car came to a full stop as it neared the garages, and the chauffeur opened the driver's side door and exited the vehicle. He walked around to the back passenger door, gently pulled it open, and extended a hand to assist his boss. As the two began the short walk from the luxurious automobile to the mansion's front door, the passenger stopped suddenly and unexpectedly, mid-step, hesitating for a mere split second. His guard dogs did not bark. This shocking realization produced a fleeting moment of horror as he realized what was about to happen.

In an instant, a rainstorm of cylindrical, pointed metal bullets filled the air, seemingly coming from all directions, pelting and penetrating the flesh of both men until neither breathed the breath of life. Without skipping a beat, the shooters ejected the empty magazines, stuffed them into their pockets, and rearmed the guns.

Streams of red liquid pooled around the crumpled bodies of the victims and began to run onto the driveway. Fast and fatal, the hit was finished. The irrepressible smell of death caused one of the shooters to bend over, hold his stomach, and force back vomit.

Taking out the driver had been unfortunate but necessary to ensure no witness to the crime. The passenger, the intended object of the strike, would victimize society no longer. The plan of the vigilantes had been executed without a hitch.

Pistols drawn, the four quickly searched inside the limousine for other passengers, but found no one. Then, without delay, they vanished into the shadows of midnight.

ONE HOUR later, two well-dressed gentlemen boarded commercial airliners—one bound for Tennessee, another for Arizona. The third drove north toward a city on the east coast of Florida. The fourth man lit a cigar and poured a brandy at his home in Miami Beach. The following day, each would return to a most respectable life and profession.

1

Miami, Florida
Life can change in an instant . . .

A VIOLENT EXPLOSION rocked a vintage two-story building in an industrial section of Miami, blowing it to smithereens. The many cracks and gaps in the old structure provided ideal spots to insert the off-white, clay-like plastic explosive used to guarantee monstrous devastation upon detonation. The sudden, burgeoning blast completely leveled the factory within several short moments, setting the surrounding atmosphere aglow with its impact and shooting a mushroom of concrete, mortar, piping, and debris upward, high into the nighttime sky.

A figure stood on the sidelines watching the deafening display of destruction. He smiled at his handiwork. Then, without delay, the man ducked into a dark sedan parked nearby and sped away from the scene, leaving behind a collapsed mound of blazing rubble. Minutes later, sirens from approaching emergency vehicles resonated in the near distance.

Two months later . . .

Office of Caswell & Lombard, Private Investigation
Collins Avenue
Miami Beach, Florida
10:15 a.m.

CLAIRE CASWELL sat up straight and glanced at the wall clock. This promised to be a strange day. Something soon would roll, pitch, toss, lurch, reel, and list her world. She did not know precisely what the new challenge would be, but the fact that an intriguing mystery was heading her way seemed undeniable. That little voice within her—the one she could not ignore, the one she relied upon heavily in her investigations, the one that never let her down—screamed out the announcement again and again.

Whenever an inkling of this nature took hold of her, it became more than difficult to concentrate. She stood. She sat. She rocked. She stood again. The tailored crimson suit she had dressed in that morning showcased her shapely figure, and while Claire Caswell worried that it made her appear five pounds heavier, she could not help but notice the frequent gazes Gaston "Guy" Lombard, her partner, threw her way. Strawberry blonde hair pulled back into a ponytail, and adorned with a wide, deep-red headband, made

Claire's baby face appear much younger than her age, and today her eyes sparkled with excitement—even more so than on other days.

She walked to the water dispenser, pushed the red spigot downward, and filled her pink flamingo-decorated mug with steaming water. Continuing to hold the ceramic cup with her left hand, she used her right to dangle a peppermint tea bag into the hot liquid. The aromatic leaves at once began to steep, filling the surrounding air with the penetrating, distinguishable scent of menthol. Peppermint tea always calmed Claire, and she often did her best thinking while sipping it.

A veteran government investigator for the State of Florida, she had put in years working up difficult, multi-issue cases. At times, sitting back and pulling herself away from the surrounding mounds of paperwork and evidence, giving her intellect a break, and letting her natural instinct on an investigation take over, had been the key to her successfully solving the most puzzling and problematic files.

Claire Caswell was born with an innate sense of extrasensory perception, and had always enjoyed a consciousness and awareness of things others did not see. A trait inherited from her grandmother, now deceased, Claire's seemingly amazing insight had distinguished her as an investigator extraordinaire throughout her sterling years with the government. Because her sixth sense had been a part of her for as long as she could remember, she rarely even noticed it anymore. But others did. And one of those others was Guy Lombard.

As she turned and walked the few paces back to her desk chair, she glanced over at him. Her beloved in life, and her partner in business, he sat, deeply engrossed in a file, at the only other desk that occupied the office. Sinking back into her chair, she studied him intently. He looked elegant and dignified, even while fully enveloped in his work. She liked the fact that his salt-and-pepper hair seemed to be turning a shockingly pure white with each passing year. It looked dashing on him.

She smiled to herself as she took sips of the inviting hot beverage and pondered her life with Guy. A better investigative partner she could never have found. Guy was an ace legal expert, and former long-time Miami–Dade state attorney. His legal mind rivaled any in the field, a significant asset to the private investigation business the two had together opened only a few months earlier.

A natural-born lawyer, the one-time ace criminal prosecutor detested those who committed crimes and hindered the otherwise well-greased workings of society. Viewing criminals as the weeds of the earth that needed to be plucked from life's garden to allow for the whole to prosper, he had committed his life and career to seeking out the perpetrators of illegal, immoral, and harmful acts, making certain that those responsible were confined to cramped, uncomfortable cells, looking out from behind vertical bars. He believed in the American legal system to the very core of his being, and although not flawless, he considered it the best in the world.

Whenever he observed a guilty person walk free, however, due to a mere loophole in the law, it contributed to his ever-growing, now deep-seated anger. Over the years, the anger had basically turned into perpetual rage—a fury his professionalism helped to suppress most all of the time, but one that showed its ugly face on occasion. And as much as his rage acted as a catalyst to drive him to work extraordinarily hard to solve complicated cases, that element of Guy Lombard concerned Claire Caswell to no end.

The life the two shared outside of the office was everything she had ever wanted. It was a partnership filled with passion, love, respect, and friendship. And even after eight years of being together, sex was steamy. Yet, she had put off answering Guy's proposal of marriage months earlier because of her unfounded fear of the institution, and also due to her equal trepidation of the anger Guy kept contained so tightly just below the surface. What if one day he could not keep his indignation in tow? What would happen? On the flip side, what if she never gave him an answer to his proposal? What might he do? These *what if* questions haunted her so.

Claire leaned back and took a steady, long sip of tea. Guy glanced up at her for a fleeting second, and their eyes met and locked. He quickly returned his gaze to the work that sat before him. She smiled again, keeping her attention focused directly on her partner. She loved this man beyond measure and knew that he felt the same about her. Drawing in a deep breath, she exhaled slowly, savoring the perfume of life, taking in its characteristically multifaceted aroma—at times, positively overwhelming in its richness. Work was good, plentiful, and challenging, and she enjoyed so much the business she and Guy had created. It was a pleasure to be part of a team that made a positive difference in society. Fighting for justice had become the powerful common thread—the essential condition that interlaced the two of them into an unstoppable and productive team of investigators. In business, as in life, the two fit together like puzzle parts.

That afternoon
1:20 p.m.

A WOMAN barged into the lobby of the small, meticulously kept office of Caswell & Lombard, Private Investigation, rudely and awkwardly interrupting an otherwise normal afternoon.

"I'm here to see the owners," she bellowed.

Claire looked up at the woman, a bit startled by her unconventional entrance.

"I'm Claire Caswell, one of the owners, Ms. … ?" She stood up to greet the roaring woman. "What is it we can do for you?"

"I've heard about the two of you and would like to hire you immediately. As a matter of fact, right now!" she boomed.

"Come in, please. Sit down," Claire said. She motioned to a chair in front of her desk. "This is Gaston Lombard, my partner." She introduced him as he made his way over to shake the trembling hand of the obviously emotional lady who had now garnered his full and absolute attention.

"Your name?" Claire persisted.

"I'm Hillary Stewart Otto … *Mrs.* Otto, and I'd like to hire your investigative firm. Sergeant Massey of the Miami–Dade Police Department referred me to you. When I told him what I needed, he told me to contact the two of you. I don't have much time. What are your fees?" As she spoke, she pulled a checkbook and ornate Montblanc fountain pen from her Louis Vuitton handbag.

"Whoa. Slow down a minute, Mrs. Otto, will you?" Guy broke in. "Why don't you start from the proverbial *beginning.* Assume we know nothing at all about your situation, and fill us in from that point forward. Please." He paused momentarily and smiled slightly. "Go ahead."

"Very well then," she started, clutching her checkbook tightly in hand. "But brief, I will be. I'm afraid I do not have the luxury of time, as I said." She glanced furtively over her shoulder every few seconds as she spoke.

Claire had assessed the demeanor of this woman from the moment she stepped through the doorway. Looking to be in her late fifties to mid-sixties, she dressed conservatively. Her stringy, shoulder-length dark hair showed an inch or two of gray re-growth, and she appeared overly fatigued, with dark, puffy circles pervading her lifeless eyes. A heavy layer of makeup caked her ill-at-ease face. Remnants of classic red nail polish, all but chipped entirely off, dotted her short, bitten fingernails. Nervousness and impatience possessed her, and she seemed unable to control the persistent shaking of her hands. In short, she appeared to be a troubled woman who had not cared about her physical appearance in quite some time. Claire could not help but stare at the nickel-sized, irregularly-shaped brown mole, so prominent on the woman's left jaw line. It was impossible to ignore, and Claire found her eyes involuntarily darting to the raised blemish often, despite her attempts not to look at it.

"I need you two to find out what *really* happened to Billy," Mrs. Otto began. "He's missing, and we must find him. Things are not right without him." Her eyes misted as she spoke, and her sincerity seemed undeniable.

"Billy *who*?" Claire asked.

Out of the blue, a man in a charcoal gray suit burst into the lobby. His eyes hurriedly scanned the scene and fell squarely on Mrs. Otto. He moved brusquely and forcefully in her direction.

"There you are, Hill," he said, attempting to mask the edginess and irritation so evident in his voice. "I've looked everywhere for you. I turned to plug the meter and *poof*—you were gone. You vanished into thin air. Now it's time to come along, dear. And apologize to these nice people for taking up their valuable time." He grabbed the woman vigorously by the arm, hoisted her from the chair, and hurriedly began to steer her toward the door.

"But I ..." she stuttered. "I..."

Just before being pulled completely from view, her strained face turned back toward Claire, a look of pleading in her pathetic and penetrating eyes. And then, just as abruptly as she had appeared, she was gone.

"What do you make of *that*?" Guy asked, obviously puzzled.

"Not sure," Claire said. "I'll be right back." She got up and raced from the office. Quickly, she spotted the couple and followed behind them at a distance not close enough to be noticed, but near enough to hear their conversation.

"What exactly did you think you were doing in there, Hillary?" the man asked, jolting her arm assertively. He eyed her like a vulture ready to pounce on its freshly caught prey. Continuing to grasp her arm too tightly, he coerced her with his physical strength to walk alongside him on the sidewalk. It was clear she had no chance of breaking free.

"Do you hear what I'm saying to you? Did we forget to take our meds today?" he demanded sharply.

An unresponsive stupor seemed to own Mrs. Otto, leaving her unable to speak.

"Hillary, I'm talking to you!" he persisted piercingly. He jerked her arm in an unpleasant manner. "Are you trying to get us *all* killed?"

She remained mute as he forced her along the walkway.

"We're going home, and I will not take you out again for quite some time, of that I will assure you." He uttered a low, short, guttural grunt. "Understand?"

No audible sound emanated from Mrs. Otto. Claire thought it clear the woman had no intention of responding to the belittling man.

Reaching a late-model, green Lincoln Town Car, the unidentified man rushed Mrs. Otto into the front passenger seat. At once, he clasped the seat belt in place around her struggling body. Without delay, he ran to the driver's side of the automobile, jumped in, and sped off, but not before quickly glancing around in all directions.

Peering out from behind a nearby boulevard palm tree, Claire took it all in as she went unnoticed by the agitated man. As he squealed off, she memorized the license plate number on the departing vehicle. She sprinted back to the office, grabbed a scratch pad, and jotted furiously.

"Let's run this plate, Guy. Something is clearly amiss here," she said. "The man muttered something about 'getting us all killed' to the poor woman. What do you suppose this is all about?"

"Not a clue," Guy said. He raised his eyebrows.

Claire got busy on the computer. In no time, she determined that the car was registered to a Chadwick Warren Otto at a local Miami address. She ran a preliminary computer background check on both Chadwick Warren and Hillary Stewart Otto and discovered no helpful information. Claire probed further, checking other online sources, and learned some sparse facts. Mr. Otto had owned and operated a plastics factory in a now marginal section of Miami, and had been in the business for close to forty years. No employment record showed up for Mrs. Otto, and there was nothing suspect about either. Claire sought to uncover more information, and learned that an explosion and fire had ravaged the plastics business only two months earlier. She then brought up and scanned several archived newspaper articles in the *Miami Herald* that had covered the tragedy.

"Guy, they lost their one and only child, William Otto, in the explosion," Claire said aloud. "According to the paper, he was the accountant for the business and was working overtime in the early morning hours on the day of the disaster. Says here his body was never recovered. And no cause or motive for the explosion and subsequent fire could be established for certain, so the insurance company will not rule out foul play on the part of the Ottos and has refused to pay on the claim—pending further investigation, of course. As if they'd blow up the factory with their son working inside. Brilliant thinking on the part of the insurance investigators . . . simply brilliant."

Guy Lombard listened with keen interest as Claire continued to fill in the blanks.

"Apparently Mr. Otto did not trust banks and kept his life savings in a standing vault at the factory," she said.

"That's interesting," Guy said.

Claire looked very solemn. "The Ottos lost everything, Guy—their child … business … lifetime savings … and no insurance payments to help them out. Poor things. Explains a whole lot, doesn't it?"

"Bad scenario. Real bad," Guy said. "No wonder the lady's a basket case. Looks like she hasn't handled this at all well—not that anyone could."

"Yeah. I agree. And she said she wanted us to find out what *really* happened to *Billy*—that's got to be William, their only offspring, no doubt. Sounds like she's not convinced he's dead."

"That's the hope, or should I say the denial, of a mother in its purest form, isn't it? It's easier not to face it at all, I'm sure."

"I don't know," Claire said. "She seemed earnest to me. Maybe I should call her and see if I can get more information. Maybe there is something we can do for her."

"Claire, from the looks of it, her husband—and I'm assuming that was *Mr.* Otto who snatched her away—surely didn't appear to want *any* help from us. He made that abundantly clear, wouldn't you agree? You need to back away."

"That's not going to happen," she said. She looked him squarely in the eyes. "I think I'll wait awhile and give her a call. It can't hurt."

"Well, I know better than to attempt to dissuade you when I see that look of bold resistance gushing from your eyes. Really, though, I don't think it's a good idea to stick our noses where they don't belong, do you?"

"No. And, yes." She paused. "That's precisely what we do best, isn't it?" She gazed at him introspectively. "Maybe something is wrong with the story, after all. It wouldn't be the first time things are not as they seem."

"Well, if you do find out anything of interest, let me know."

"Of course." Her intent appeared unshakable.

Hours later, Claire retrieved a phone number for the Otto residence and dialed the number. There was no answer. She would try again later.

THE FOLLOWING morning, Claire attempted to call Mrs. Otto a second time.

After several rings, a low female voice exuding sounds of great fatigue answered. "Hello?"

Claire strained to hear her. "Mrs. Otto? Is that you?"

An even fainter reply came from the woman on the other end of the line this time. "Yes. Who is this?"

"It's Claire Caswell, Office of Caswell and Lombard, Private Investigation, calling. We met yesterday when you came to our office. I'd like to talk with you further, if now's a good time."

There was a pause.

"Never call here again," Mrs. Otto whispered. "*Never.*"

"Okay, but…"

Mrs. Otto hung up.

2

SEVERAL DAYS PASSED, and Claire was consumed by the pressing work of open investigations. Yet she could not seem to shake the looming image of Mrs. Otto's distressed face. She told herself time and again that they could only get involved if and when Mrs. Otto re-contacted them and expressed an interest in hiring Caswell & Lombard, Private Investigation, but that reminder provided Claire with little or no solace. The lingering look of raw despair on the face of Hillary Otto haunted Claire. Mrs. Otto needed help. There was no doubt about it. But were Claire Caswell and Guy Lombard the two to provide the suffering woman the assistance she needed? Or would psychological counseling be more appropriate to help her deal with such a horrific loss? As the woman's misery continued to eat away at the investigator like vinegar on a fresh wound, she remained unsure.

One week later, at precisely eight-thirty in the morning, Claire unlocked the front door of their office and stepped inside. Guy shadowed her in, holding a bag of fresh chocolate croissants and two black coffees. Opening bell for the sleuths was nine a.m., and this particular morning they had hoped for a half-hour of private time to eat a quick breakfast and glance through the newspaper. And while they usually did not answer the telephone if it rang before nine, this morning Claire did. Her craving for chocolate would just have to wait.

"Caswell and Lombard, Private Investigation, Claire Caswell speaking," she answered. Her eyes grew large as she listened carefully to the caller's soft, confidential words.

THE FIRM of Caswell & Lombard, Private Investigation was a dream come true for Claire. After numerous years as a Florida State enforcement investigator, performing her job with extraordinary skill, she had been ready for the next step, and partnering with Gaston Lombard to open a private investigation firm had proven to be a brilliant decision. The business suited the two of them to a tee, and word spread like wildfire throughout the greater Miami area that the firm was open for business and that Claire Caswell and Gaston Lombard would *get the job done.* Clients had poured in almost immediately. Money was good, work presented one intriguing challenge after another, and not long after opening, the two sleuths found themselves overburdened with cases. In fact, it became imperative to turn away many potential clients in order to ensure the exceptional handling of the investigations currently underway.

The most perplexing matters—the ones requiring unusual and highly honed skills to resolve, those involving victims hurt to the greatest degrees—these were the cases Caswell & Lombard, Private Investigation concentrated on and excelled at solving, be it a murder investigation or another type of matter entirely.

No sleuth, detective, investigator, or private eye in the entire Miami area could vie with the level of competence offered by Claire Caswell and Gaston Lombard—the dedicated duo. Soon, requests to hire the remarkable pair began to arrive from all over the state of Florida, and before long the entire U.S., and even abroad. Demand for the firm's services rose quickly. Stunned by the unforeseen whirlwind in popularity, Claire Caswell and Gaston Lombard felt a great responsibility to perform.

"CLAIRE, IT'S Hillary Otto," the caller said in a voice so low Claire could barely make out her words. "Meet me at two o'clock this afternoon at the Solo Café on the lobby level of the Fontainebleau Hotel. *It's urgent.* Come alone."

The voice of a man sounded in the background and the line went dead.

Claire hung up and grabbed the cup of coffee waiting at her desk. She took a sip and filled Guy in on the strange call.

"Want me to tag along when you meet her today?" he asked.

"Thanks, but no. I think it's best if I go alone. I get the idea she may be more comfortable talking with a female."

"Okay. But be careful, Claire. Her husband's a live wire!"

"Of course."

Claire worked until it was time to leave for the afternoon rendezvous at the famous Miami Beach hotel. She felt anxious and a bit uneasy on the drive over, but couldn't identify why. When she arrived and walked into the lobby, her eyes first scanned the scene before walking toward the café—located thirty feet to the right of the check-in desk. Once inside the Solo Café, her eyes quickly drifted from table to table searching for Mrs. Otto. But she was not there. Being a few minutes early, Claire opted to sit down at a semiprivate corner table, where she could keep an eye out for the woman, and ordered a mocha latte with skim milk. Claire finished the entire espresso drink, whipped cream and all, and still Mrs. Otto had not appeared. She was twenty minutes late. Where was Mrs. Otto? Perhaps tied up in traffic?

After consuming two additional cups of regular coffee very slowly, Claire became quite concerned. Hillary Otto was now one hour late. This seemed exceedingly unusual, considering she had requested the meeting. And Mrs. Otto had used the term "*urgent*" in her call to Claire. To make matters worse, she did not feel at liberty to contact the Otto residence and check up on the woman—especially after Mrs. Otto's previous admonition about calling her at home. Claire pulled out her cell phone and called Guy at the office to see if Mrs. Otto had phoned to change the meeting time or to say she couldn't make it.

"I would have let you know if she'd called," Guy said. "Wonder what's going on with that lady?"

"I don't know," Claire said slowly, "but I'm worried." Her mind drifted. Something had obviously prevented Mrs. Otto from attending the meeting. What was it? Claire would have to wait for Mrs. Otto to make contact again. No other choice was available. "I'm on my way back to the office. See you soon."

"I'll be here," Guy said.

A DAY passed. And another. No word came from Mrs. Otto. Then, on the third morning after the no-show meeting, Guy and Claire sat eating breakfast in the kitchen of the condo they shared in

Aventura, North Miami Beach. Guy finished two slices of toast and sipped orange juice as he browsed through the *Miami Herald*. Suddenly, something roused his attention.

"Claire. Is this the woman who came to see us? Mrs. Otto? The name is right, but the face doesn't seem to be." He pushed the obituary page toward her.

Claire perused the very short entry for a Mrs. Hillary Stewart Otto, age sixty-two, who had died "unexpectedly." Guy was right. The photo, although appearing to be fairly current, did not seem to resemble in the slightest the woman who had come to their office seeking to hire the investigators. The photograph in the obituary portrayed a well-groomed woman, tasteful makeup in place, and hair pulled back off her face—a woman wearing a pleasant smile, her eyes filled with life. Claire stared at the photo. There, on the woman's left jaw line, was the not-to-be-forgotten mole. Claire gasped.

"It's her. It's Hillary Otto. She's dead. Take a longer look and you'll see it. It's unbelievable what stress did to this poor woman." She passed the section back to Guy, and thought for a long moment. "I want to attend her funeral. Will you come with me?"

Claire picked up the phone and dialed the Miami–Dade Police Department.

"Sergeant Massey? It's Claire Caswell. I need a favor. I'm interested in learning more about the cause of death of a Mrs. Hillary Stewart Otto." Claire spelled each name she uttered. "Her obituary is in today's *Miami Herald*. It states that she died *unexpectedly*, but I need details. Can you check it out and get back to me?"

"Yeah, yeah, yeah. Okay, okay," he replied gruffly. "I'll do what I can."

Sergeant Jack Massey was the same crusty, cantankerous man he'd always been, so the apparent lack of eagerness in his voice to accommodate her simple request did not surprise her in the least. Yet she knew he'd come through for her. In the end, he always did. She heard the familiar cracking of his knuckles before he hung up. Old habits die hard.

Later that very afternoon, she received a call back from the sergeant. "No apparent cause of death is noted in the Medical Examiner's report," he informed Claire. "And there are no notes in the file to indicate any suspicions on his part. Can't help you any more than that. Sounds kind of strange, though, I have to admit. Did you know this dame?"

"We met only briefly," Claire said. "The woman came to see us a while ago, seeking our help, but her visit was abruptly cut short. She said you referred her to us. She was the mother of William Otto, the young man who purportedly died in the explosion of the plastics factory off I-95 in Miami, a couple of months ago. Anyway, as always, I appreciate your help. Thank you."

"Not so fast, Claire Caswell. Now that you mention the circumstances, I seem to recall that broad. She came in to see me saying that her son was *missing*. She would not accept his death. Certifiable, if you ask me. A real loony. Needed professional help in my humble opinion. Yeah, yeah, yeah. It's all coming back to me. I referred her to you to get her off my back." He cracked his knuckles. "Thought you could do something for the woman, if anyone could."

Claire's professional relationship with Sergeant Massey was bittersweet—more bitter than sweet. She was never certain why he seemed to have a chip on his shoulder when dealing with her, and all other females for that matter. Working together on previous investigations, usually out of necessity, he seemed well aware of her crack investigative skills. But Claire was a member of the opposite gender, and he could never verbalize even a modicum of praise to a woman. He had mentioned once that she reminded him of his daughter. Claire often wondered what the relationship was like between the two of them.

Out of professional need, however, Claire Caswell and Sergeant Jack Massey now exchanged information whenever such opportunities arose, and even referred victims, or clients, as the case may be, back and forth when appropriate. And Claire thought she experienced fleeting moments, on rare occasions, when he almost let complimentary words regarding her sleuthing talents slip through his lips, but he always caught himself before that happened. Nevertheless, the private investigator and the Miami–Dade police sergeant had established a business relationship that seemed to work.

THREE DAYS later, Claire and Guy walked into the funeral chapel minutes before the service for Mrs. Hillary Otto was to begin.

"Look, over there," Claire said. "That's the man who pulled her from our office. People are in line to greet him. Let's extend our condolences."

As they approached, they could hear others greeting the man as *Mr. Otto,* or as *Chadwick*, and some even called him *Chad*. The couple in front of Claire and Guy took turns embracing Chadwick Otto, and separately agreed aloud that Hillary had never returned to herself after the tragedy.

"We feel so very sorry for you, Chad," the gentleman of the couple said. "If there's anything we can..."

"Thank you," Mr. Otto muttered. "She died of a broken heart. There was nothing I could do to make things better."

The couple sighed and slowly walked away, nodding in agreement.

Chadwick Otto then turned his gaze to Claire and Guy.

"We're here to express our heartfelt condolences, Mr. Otto," Guy said.

"I have to apologize," Mr. Otto said. "I do recognize your faces, but I'm afraid I can't place the two of you. Forgive me. It's a tough time."

"Gaston Lombard and Claire Caswell—the private investigators your wife stopped in to see the other…"

"Of course," he broke in. "How forgetful of me." Nervously, he glanced around. "Thank you for coming," he said mechanically, and then turned his full attention to the people next in line, engaging them in quick conversation, making it crystal clear he intended no further discussion with Claire and Guy.

Trying to pursue conversation with Mr. Otto at that time was, needless to say, out of the question, so, instead, they walked over to the casket to pay full respects to Mrs. Otto.

"I only wish we could have helped you, Hillary," Claire said softly.

The service for Mrs. Otto began with the singing of a hymn. The sermon that followed was short and dispassionate.

"Guess we'll never know the full story on this one," Guy said to Claire on the drive back to their office.

"It wouldn't be the first time," Claire replied.

FOURTEEN DAYS passed. A man burst into the office of Caswell & Lombard, Private Investigation in the early afternoon. He wore a dark blue jogging suit, a baseball cap pulled low onto his forehead to obscure much of his face, and sunglasses. Upon entering, he closed the door firmly behind him.

"Mind if we lock this while I'm here?" he grunted in a low voice.

"The reason?" Claire asked.

"We need to talk. And to be safe."

"Certainly," Guy responded, getting up from his chair and walking toward the man. His gut instinct told him the man was okay and that bolting the door was an acceptable request.

"Please. Sit down, sir," Guy directed, indicating a specific chair.

Instead, the man walked over to the front windows and peered out through the Venetian blinds for some time. "Mind if we shut these, too? It may look as though the office is closed that way."

Claire and Guy darted quick glances in each other's direction.

"Go ahead," Guy said, a bit more uneasy than moments earlier, but still comfortable with the appeal.

The man walked over to the chair. He promptly pulled a gun from his pants pocket and aimed it wildly in the direction of both Guy and Claire. His eyes darted back and forth between the two investigators and he wore a look of hopeless desperation.

3

Justice, justice, we will undertake.
Make things right, make no mistake.
They can run, but they can't hide.
We will do our jobs with pride.

THE CHILLING STANZA, chanted in unison by the vigilantes, took on a tempo not unlike rap music. Low and somber in its tone, it was hair-raising in its tenor. Repeated two times in steady succession, the rhythmic rallying call could be heard only by those who muttered the ritual stanza. With his right hand, each man lifted his wine glass simultaneously, in perfect unison with the others, as if scripted. The goblets met over the center of the table and produced twelve sharp clinking sounds one after the other. The foursome then drank small mouthfuls of wine as they exchanged methodical glances, each pair of eyes connecting briefly with every other. The group members finalized the ceremony by nodding in silent understanding.

Whenever the unit came together for a meeting, the same strict rite occurred. Tonight was no exception. A dark situation had developed—one demanding serious planning and prompt execution. The supreme heaviness of the circumstances acted as a catalyst to help gear the men for the next mission. And, if one listened carefully, the sound of a distant rallying drumbeat could almost be heard in the surrounding aura of the ceremony. Or was it simply loud thumping of the four men's hearts?

College fraternity brothers, the quartet had bonded shortly after meeting at the University of Miami and became the closest of friends in no time at all. When graduation approached four years later, the young men had taken the powerful friendship a step further. Before each graduate had gone his separate way, the four had first entered into a solemn and literal blood pact. Standing outside one evening, late in the springtime of the year, amidst a cluster of nearby palm trees and under the light of the moon, the grave agreement had been solidified. Each of the foursome took a turn placing a cut in the palm of his own hand. Using the same pocketknife, swiped first with alcohol, as the wounds began to bleed each young man shook hands with every other, swapping an iota of blood all around. The union had been sacred and spiritual, and secured by an unbreakable covenant pursuant to mutual agreement.

And unlike the option of divorce in a bad marriage, this pact had no release or escape clause. It had been a somber promise made in the young men's salad days—a vow of honorable intent that two of the four would later live to regret.

Agreeing as a team to carry out important work, whenever duty mandated, not one of the members had ever reneged on his respective oath throughout the years that followed college. In fact, the total of the group's collective services had been performed on occasions that could be counted on two hands two times over with fingers remaining. And while any one of the members had the authority to summon a group reunion on an as-needed basis, this time, as always, Thomas Lastner had been the one to authoritatively and with urgency assemble the warriors.

He, alone, viewed himself as a kind of Robin Hood—a modern-day outlaw self-knighted to protect the downtrodden and equalize situations for members of society where the legal system had simply gone terribly awry. To give back what society had wrongfully taken. So, when the scales of justice held by Lady Justice tipped in a wholly and egregiously lopsided manner, one that could not be overlooked, at least in the eyes of Judge Thomas Lastner, he took it upon himself to level the scales, to mete out proper and necessary punishment, and to correct the societal wrong. This, of course, required the assistance of his enforcers.

THOMAS "TOM" Lastner, the self-appointed mastermind of the group since its inception, made all decisions on behalf of the team. A vote was never taken, straws were not drawn, and no discussion whatsoever took place regarding the designation. He simply assumed the position as a given, and none of the others questioned it.

Forever single, Lastner, the forty-year-old attorney-turned-judge member of the band, basked in his power. Much like the coach of a football team, Lastner devised every play and strategy for each mission—the only difference being that he also actively participated in the games.

After college, Tom Lastner had gone on to graduate from the University of Miami Law School, receiving his juris doctor degree. And while the practice of law seemed to fit him like a hand-tailored suit, after spending thirteen years practicing law in the private realm he had accepted an appointment to the bench as a state court judge—assigned to the Criminal Court Division in Miami–Dade County. This is when things went from bubbling to a boil. The position allowed him to see, firsthand, all the components of the criminal justice system: the good, the bad, the in-between, and the ridiculously ugly. Included in the last category were those occasions when he was forced to dismiss a case due to a mere technicality in the law or lack of admissible evidence.

And these reprehensible instances secretly made the honorable Judge Thomas Lastner's insides heave, causing his blood pressure to reach heights unknown to the medical world. In fact, he could specifically tie the atrocities he personally witnessed to the horrific migraine headaches that now took up a regular part of his life. The recurring, throbbing pains in his head—usually on the right side—always made him nauseated and usually distorted his vision, at times even making him feel he was going insane. Doctor-prescribed medications helped but a wee measure; the only thing that made the pain retreat completely appeared to be the righting of the judicial wrong that had triggered the occurrence in the first place.

Two months earlier, one such shocking matter had come to the attention of Judge Lastner, and after waiting the appropriate period of time to let the smoke clear he had telephoned the others to schedule a place for a meeting. Today, all members sat gathered in Miami, over dinner, in a dark and quiet restaurant on the Beach, strategically placed in a private, high-backed booth at the back of the eatery. Soon, the men would hear specific details of a new, impending undertaking. Anxiety hung in the air like mustiness in a root cellar as Tom Lastner cleared his throat and began to speak. Unbeknownst to the others, the right side of Lastner's head throbbed in a profound manner.

Labeled as "rebels" in college—always fighting for one cause or another—that classification had bonded the young men in an inexplicable way. Annoyed by grave injustices in the legal system the four witnessed during those formative years, wrongs doled out by an imperfect court system in an imperfect world, they had vowed to take matters into their own hands when circumstances dictated. And as fate would have it, years down the road, Tom Lastner had become an unsmiling and unbending judge, granted a front row seat to witness just such instances.

Thus, as situations presented in the years that followed college, and when it became possible to *correct* an injustice, together the group of four friends would set out to right a wrong—to help create a more equitable place for all. Lastner selected each undertaking with care, acutely aware that his team could not take on every serious inequality that crossed his path, but they were able to even the score in certain cases, and somehow that made a difference in the big picture.

Being a component of a group of citizens taking law enforcement into their own hands, clearly without the legal authority to do so, was a lifelong commitment that none of the college students entered into lightly—at least at the time. And once the first heroic deed stood behind them, the men had committed a crime that law enforcement could never condone. All eight hands had been marked with an invisible and permanent stain, and utmost silence concerning the actions of the vigilante squadron became the name of the game. Whenever the group carried out a societal correction, it was never to be discussed again, even within the perimeters of the group's private meetings. Like Lady Macbeth, each of the college friends learned that while bloodstained hands could be washed with soap and water, bloodstained minds could never fully be cleansed.

Over the span of years subsequent to graduation, the avenging squadron executed successfully each operation it took on. And while there had been a few close calls, when things did not go exactly as planned, where the men escaped the scene in the nick of time—just before law enforcement arrived, to date they had never been caught. So far, so good. Living on the edge, the fear of being apprehended dangling all around them, seemed to ignite the excitement to the nth degree for two of the team members. And, admittedly, society was a better place as a result of the group's hands-on approach to justice; at least that's what Thomas Lastner repeatedly told the others.

After receiving the call to rally on this occasion, the members as always made quick plans to attend this evening's dinner.

The four college friends may never have continued to be close in adulthood, as each man's life took a vastly different path thereafter. However, the blood pact bonded the group members like superglue, forever fastening the foursome into the interlocking clutches of unrestrained revenge.

KYLE TEDDY, "Reverend Kyle" to his parishioners, or simply "Teddy" to his friends, was the second member of the group and the only African American. He pastored a medium-sized Baptist church in Nashville, Tennessee, where he had made his home after obtaining a post-graduate doctor of divinity degree. Married at twenty-nine, he and his wife, Jayla, had four children in rapid succession—all girls. Jayla home-schooled the children and seemed to have an almost magical way with them. They obeyed her most every request and gave her little trouble to speak of. At forty, Kyle Teddy felt richly blessed by the peaceful and modest life that had unfolded before him. But there were those frequent, fitful nights when nightmares about the events he participated in with his college buddies overtook his sleep and awakened him in a frenzy of shaking and screaming. He would explain it away as reliving something he had seen on television, and his wife never said a word. In her alone times, however, she wondered.

Kyle Teddy tried, unsuccessfully, to justify to himself the foursome's forbidden functions as somehow being godly deeds of retributive justice (an eye for an eye). Yet the things he had done wreaked havoc on his very soul and allowed him little, if any, peace of mind. Some of the killings had been messy and had not gone exactly as planned. And Teddy had learned what it took to end the life of another human being—the psychological, physical, and spiritual determination and strength of it all. The very first time, it had split apart his foundation, and made him doubt and revisit his entire internal belief system, even raising the question of whether he had ever been pure enough for the ministry. He kept hearing a voice within him repeat, "Justice belongs to the Lord." The hidden dichotomy he lived with, day in and day out, had thrown him onto the mat of life, beginning a never-ending wrestling match, Kyle Teddy against Kyle Teddy.

His decision to be an equal quarter of the team was one made when he was a young, impressionable lad who had desired to fit in with his friends—to be accepted. Made in the heat of the moment, under inconceivable peer pressure, he now wished desperately he had never partaken in any of it and had simply walked away. Nevertheless, he had entered into the unthinkable blood oath, and there was no way out. Worse yet, he found himself forced to continue to engage in the gruesome deeds of the team as dictated by the oh-so-superior Judge Lastner. Teddy dared not discuss his reticence with anyone in the group, and he continued to drag around the unwanted psychological ball and chain of permanent membership wherever he went.

God alone knew of the internal struggle bending and distorting Teddy's innards. And while he continually prayed for forgiveness, he feared God would eventually turn a deaf ear; yet, even so, the reverend carried on, engaging in the behavior he knew was immoral, repenting each time, but never changing his actions. Depression set in and seemed to be an ever-present part of his make-up these days. He fought it continually, calling forth all the might within his core to defeat it, but he was losing the battle.

Along with the ever-persistent feelings of sadness and hopelessness, and of not being worthy to minister to his flock, Teddy had lost all interest in sex. He explained to his wife that he had been working too hard and was just plain exhausted. But in his heart of hearts he recognized the real culprit. He could not perform because guilt rode him perpetually, like a cowboy riding a bucking bronco in a rodeo with no end. Jayla did not push him, but in her quiet moments, she wondered. And she found herself pulling away from him emotionally.

Like a man under hypnosis, losing the power of voluntary action, when the recent call came in from Tom Lastner, Teddy dutifully obeyed the directive, explaining to his wife that he would be attending an impromptu reunion with his college buddies in Miami. She had smiled kindly and told him to have a good time. A trusting soul, she epitomized the perfect wife for a minister. He booked a flight, made arrangements with the associate pastor to temporarily take over his duties, and packed a light bag. Jayla watched him with interest as he folded his shirts. And she wondered.

SCOTT HARRIMAN, "Scotty," forty-one, a successful real estate broker in Phoenix, Arizona, was the third member of the ensemble. He was an alcoholic in denial. Raised in a staunch Irish-Catholic family (his mother being of Irish descent; his father of English-Irish descent), he, like so many of his relatives, fought the battle with the bottle. Three courses of treatment behind him, he continued to drink like a fish and refused to admit the inconvenient truth of his addiction. Thrice divorced, he had determined that marriage, while it may be good for some, was definitely not in the cards for him. He claimed he enjoyed his freedom with no ties and he liked being an incessant flirt. In actuality, however, his life had become a series of scattered, short-term relationships, and he spent the majority of his free time alone.

Harriman's career mandated ongoing travel all around the state of Arizona. He purchased land in his own name to re-sell for profit, and also represented others, both buyers and sellers, on high-end properties located throughout the pricey suburbs surrounding the Phoenix area—Mummy Mountain, Paradise Valley, Scottsdale, and Fountain Hills. A tough negotiator, he did exceedingly well monetarily and had built himself quite a nest egg over the years.

Although his clients adored him, as he could on demand act as if he had just walked out of charm school, behind his back, and unbeknownst to him, his associates in the world of real estate described him as a real dill pickle: vinegary, acidic, and sour—a wounded soul playing happy.

Being a part of the secret-society-of-four gave Scott Harriman enormous unspoken pride. No one could ever know about the acts in which he participated; yet, strangely, his membership in the band of vigilantes became his raison d'être—the one thing that really mattered. The loyalty he felt for the group went without saying, and it was his priority in life, hands down. Membership in the elite club bestowed feelings in him of importance and value, and somehow seemed to provide a deeper meaning to his otherwise rolling-stone-gathers-no-moss lifestyle.

When Tom Lastner phoned on this occasion, Scotty quickly agreed to the dinner meeting. He canceled all upcoming business appointments and made necessary flight and other travel arrangements at once. Thoughts of a new mission intrigued and exhilarated him. He poured himself a tall Scotch whiskey, downed it, and poured another, letting his imagination run wild as he packed his suitcase.

JACKSON MANNING, *Jack*, was the last to be called. At forty, the fourth member of the group was an unusually pleasant and good-natured kind of guy much of the time. The son of an English father and a Latina mother, he'd married his college sweetheart, Melissa, and together they now enjoyed a princely life in Fort Lauderdale, Florida. Having no children, the two spent most of their spare time together. After college, Jack had pursued his lifetime love of flying, first obtaining a single-engine and later a dual engine pilot's license. Excelling in the field of aviation, he'd also obtained his IFR rating and purchased a prized Twin Cessna aircraft.

A career of piloting charter flights throughout the state of Florida for wealthy clientele fell into place quite easily for him. It became a job that kept him away from home much more than he would have preferred in the perfect world, but it provided a comfortable income for Jack and Melissa Manning. Melissa pursued a career in creative writing for children and had been published several times over. They were in a relationship that worked. And they kept no secrets from one another. Well, except for the one Jack kept from Melissa—his ugly participation in the self-appointed group of enforcers.

When Tom Lastner called, Jack agreed to attend the dinner. But, in all truthfulness, he had come to hate these meetings, knowing all too well what would be expected of him soon thereafter. He was getting too old for this kind of energy-draining activity—vengeance, and all that—but he didn't have the guts to tell the others he wanted out. No longer the rebel of yesteryear, he yearned to be set free from the ill-considered lifetime obligation he'd naïvely entered into so long ago. But that not being an option, he did not dwell on the impossible.

Rather, he played his part when called upon to perform, and other times put it out of his mind completely. He was not proud of hiding his involvement in the secret society from his wife, but how could he share something of this dark magnitude with his beloved? Even if she promised never to repeat a word of it, he could not take the risk. How could she ever understand and accept the acts her husband had participated in if she knew the true and gory details? Ashamed of himself for his actions, Jack lived with an ever-present fear that Melissa would somehow discover the real Jackson Manning and leave him.

More and more these days anxiety plagued him, to the point of becoming a neurotic fixation. Infrequent heart palpitations and shortness of breath reminded him in a profound way that the secret part of his life was alive, well and kicking, and slowly gnawing away at his innards.

Why oh why did the hideous actions of the group not seem to bother any of the others? He didn't understand. How could the spirit of the pact be broken? Was there a way?

TOM LASTNER, the conductor of the vigilante orchestra, scratched his chin. Had he detected a bit of lackluster in the voices of Kyle Teddy and Jackson Manning when he'd called to invite them to the upcoming meeting? He hoped not. For that simply would not be permitted.

4

"DON'T DO ANYTHING rash," Guy pleaded. "If you do, you'll regret it." He rose slowly from his desk to a standing position and cautiously inched his way toward the gun-wielding man.

"Stop! Don't come any closer!" the man yelled, leveling his pistol directly at Guy. "I mean it! I *said*, don't come any closer!" His entire body quivered.

Claire gave the man a considered look and thought she saw a tear rolling down his cheek. Or was it simply a bead of sweat? She couldn't be sure. What motive did this man have for holding the investigators at gunpoint? She seized the opportunity.

"You don't want to harm anyone, sir," Claire said compassionately. "You're hurting and confused. Please, let us help you. You came to us for a reason."

Like a miniscule pinprick in an overly inflated balloon, the unmistakable kindness in her voice and eyes began to defuse the frenzied man.

Moments of jittery silence followed as the man's edginess slowed and seemed to melt away before the investigators' eyes. Then, unexpectedly, the man dropped into the chair and placed the gun onto his lap. He started to weep. "I'm sorry. So sorry," he said. "Forgive me. Nothing matters anymore. I have nothing left. My rage is not toward you. I do need help … I do need help. Help me. Please help me," he pleaded with a broken voice.

Claire was the first to respond. "Of course, we'll help you, sir. Now, sit back, relax, and tell us what you need. Would you like a glass of water?" She threw a glance of relief in Guy's direction.

The man's sobbing eased, and he released a prolonged breath. He grabbed the pistol with his right hand, bent down low, and placed it on the floor between his feet. He removed his cap and sunglasses.

"It isn't loaded, anyway," he bleated, cupping his face in his hands.

Three days later
Approaching Athens, Greece

MINUTES BEFORE landing, Claire and Guy stretched their necks to take in the limited view of the city afforded them by the small windows of the giant 747 aircraft. Who would have imagined days ago they would be flying to Greece, of all places, and then on to the island of Crete, just south of Greece, in an attempt to locate the man responsible for blowing up the plastics factory owned by Mr. Chadwick Warren Otto?

The two sleuths had been so surprised when the gun-toting man in their office had revealed himself to be none other than the grief-stricken Chadwick Otto. Straddling the line between sanity and insanity, anguish had pushed the man beyond the limits most humans could endure. He had acted out hysterically—temporarily not responsible for his actions. Alive, yet dead in his wounds, he wanted revenge.

Even more startling, once he had regained a semblance of composure, Mr. Otto had handed Claire two pairs of round-trip airline tickets between Miami and Crete (via Athens, Greece), together with a handful of other papers. He had begged the famed sleuths to hunt down and bring back the man responsible for reducing his life to shambles. And he had warned the two that the Cretan police would be of no help to them in this matter; that the lawbreaker had always boasted that in Crete he was untouchable—immune from the arms of the law.

Chadwick Otto was a desperate man taking desperate measures.

Life had squeezed Mr. Otto to a pulp. It had pureed, mashed, pressed, creamed, and minced the poor man. Now, with whatever remained left of him, one thing and only one thing mattered—to see the excuse for a human being responsible for destroying his life pay … and pay dearly. In fact, Mr. Otto would not rest until he saw this evildoer convicted of the heinous crimes he had committed and sentenced to a life in prison without parole, locked up in a cage like the animal he had become. Retribution became Mr. Otto's reason for being, igniting a powerful force within him that grew stronger with each passing day. He would not give up until justice pounded its gavel in a profound way.

Other business owners in the neighborhood where the plastics factory once stood lived in irreconcilable fearfulness of the man responsible for the explosion of the plastics factory. They knew all too well the name and the face of the predator who kept them in constant psychological torment. Mr. Otto, single-handedly, had dared to refuse to pay the extorter's ongoing fees to protect his business in the neighborhood. Mr. Otto, alone, had taken a stand against the brute. Mr. Otto, with help from no one else, had refused to be bullied any longer—something no other business owner dared to do. And, in return, Mr. Otto, singularly, had suffered death-dealing consequences.

Now, Mr. Otto no longer feared the barbarian in the same way. For there was nothing left for him to take, other than the life of Mr. Otto, and he cared little about that at this point. He would spend the total sum of money his relatives had sent him to get back on his feet to accomplish one goal and one goal only—to ruin the criminal still walking free, to force the courts to deal with this seemingly unable-to-be-convicted felon once and for all. Retaliation at any cost made Mr. Otto a dangerous man.

When he'd visited the police after burying his wife to demand the arrest and prosecution of the perpetrator, Sergeant Massey had referred him to Caswell & Lombard, Private Investigation—to "the finest investigative team I've ever worked with"—to locate the sociopath, because word on the street was that he had fled the country immediately after the explosion. Sergeant Massey had explained that he lacked the jurisdiction to go after the bastard and return him to the U.S. for trial, but Claire Caswell and Guy Lombard were not so limited.

"Bring the good-for-nothing sonofabitch to me, along with some hard evidence against him, and rest assured I'll make damned sure he rots in prison for the rest of his natural days," the sergeant had told the fractured man. This promise made to Chadwick Otto on that day in Sergeant Massey's office became food for the starving man.

Reliable sources in the neighborhood could be overheard on every street corner, discussing the wicked perpetrator who had fled to his homeland—the island of Crete, where he was holed up, escaping the future behind bars he so deserved. And that buzz made its way to the ears of Chadwick Otto.

In the midst of his delirium, he had walked into the office of Caswell & Lombard, Private Investigation waving his weapon, trying to coerce the well-known investigators to go after the elusive madman. He had never meant Claire Caswell or Guy Lombard any harm, but he had to convince them he meant business. In hindsight, he bitterly regretted the approach he'd used on the famous sleuths; yet, his technique had worked. They had taken the case, accepted the challenge, and that was all that mattered.

Although it was a difficult, if not impossible, order to fill, Claire Caswell and Gaston Lombard had accepted the man's desperate plea, but not without a great amount of apprehension. After much vacillation and discussion, Claire, in the end, decided to nudge justice in the right direction for the sake of the late Mrs. Otto, taking on Mr. Otto as a client of the firm. It was the least they could do, she thought.

Athens, Greece

ONCE THE plane set down in Athens, Greece, Claire and Guy found themselves amidst a horde of travelers in the bustling airport. Signage they could neither read nor understand seemed to be posted everywhere. Greek, a language with the longest words either had ever seen, baffled the two investigators.

Each had packed in a single, wheeled suitcase, and once they retrieved the luggage from the moving carousel, the two followed the throngs of people seemingly heading toward the terminal's front exit doors. When in doubt, follow the movement of the people who appear to know where they're going, Claire told herself. It always worked.

Trailing feet behind the flow, the two investigators glanced around in all directions, taking in everything as they walked, looking at each new sign they passed to see if they could possibly understand any one of them—but no such luck. Once outside, they observed the taxi stand and walked over to take a place in the line of others waiting to hire transportation.

Out of sheer habit, Guy reached into his pants pocket to touch his cell phone. It wasn't there. He grimaced. "Shit!" he said loudly. "I think we forgot our cell phones in their chargers when we left in such a hurry to catch our plane."

Claire checked her purse and winced. "How could we have done this? *How*?" She looked annoyed. "Let's hope we don't need them."

Fifteen minutes passed before the next cab belonged to them. The driver loaded both cases into the trunk, and Claire and Guy jumped into the back seat, happy to be on the way. Claire handed the driver a piece of paper noting the name and address of their hotel in Greek. (Thankfully, Mr. Otto had taken care of all such details of the trip beforehand.) As he accepted the note, the driver turned slightly around in his seat and looked his passengers over. He smiled broadly, revealing a mouth filled with very few teeth. When he faced the wheel again, Claire noticed him continuing to peer at the two Americans through the rearview mirror. She stared back at him, wondering just what was on his mind. He mumbled something incomprehensible and sped off.

Claire's quick research on the Internet prior to leaving the U.S. had familiarized her with the euro. She had learned the approximate cost of a cab ride anywhere in Athens, including tip, and felt prepared to handle the situation even if language became a barrier.

When they reached their destination, the driver pulled up curbside at the side entrance to the hotel, and turned to face the pair of more-than-obvious tourists. Once again, he displayed his toothless grin. He demanded a fare approximately ten times greater than Claire expected.

"*How much?*" she asked. A look of disbelief owned her face.

He repeated the amount in a matter-of-fact voice tone, again smiling from ear to ear.

"That's outrageous! You'll get the *regular* fare from us and nothing more!" Claire retorted. Ire mounted rapidly within her as she realized the smiling cabbie was nothing more than a rip-off artist.

His jovial expression at once turned forbidding, and he began to shout words that neither Claire nor Guy could understand, although they got the gist of his communication with no problem whatsoever. At that moment, both sleuths realized how fortunate they were not to understand the Greek language. Claire grabbed the correct fare from her purse and threw it over the seatback in front of her, onto the front passenger seat.

"Come on, Guy, let's get out of here!" She nudged him, and the two quickly exited the cab.

The driver continued to scream at the investigators as he leaped from the car and walked to the rear of the taxi. He pointed to the trunk and shook his head from side to side. It was obvious he planned to hold the luggage hostage until the riders paid him more money. He held a hand open. "More," he stated in a gruff manner, in English. "More."

Now Guy had had enough. He faced the driver head on, and in an icy and authoritative tone, he spoke calmly. "You're nothing but a *gonif*! [Thief]. Maybe you'd like us to call the *police* and get them involved!"

The man seemed to immediately understand the word "police." He opened the trunk, pulled out the bags, and slammed them to the ground. Then, in a few short, quick steps he was back in the driver's seat. He bolted off, leaving a trail of smoke behind. This all happened in record time and certainly before Guy had to repeat his threat a second time. The word *police* had served its purpose.

"I hate it when that happens," Guy said as they walked into the hotel.

"I agree. Very stressful," Claire said.

They checked in and explained to the English-speaking desk clerk what had just transpired. He chuckled knowingly.

"You look like *Americans*," he said. "We don't see many Americans in Greece, so, unfortunately, you stand out in a crowd. If people think you do not understand our money system and language, the unscrupulous ones may try to take advantage of you. I apologize for that dreadful experience. Most of us here are nice, honest folk. Quite nice and quite honest, actually."

As he spoke he ogled Claire, giving her a lascivious wink and making her feel wholly uncomfortable. "If you have any questions about anything, young lady, you come see me. I will personally take care of you."

His gaze penetrated through her bones and made her skin crawl. She looked away.

Guy was busy picking up tourist brochures and maps on the counter in front of him and did not notice the clerk's demeanor.

"Always insist the cab drivers drop you at the *front* entrance of the hotel, where hotel employees and doormen mill around," the clerk continued. "Never be dropped off at the *side* of the building again. Drivers will not attempt a stunt like that if hotel staff are present." He spoke directly to Claire. "It is for your safety, Miss. You are a foreigner here. You must be vigilant," he warned. He ignored Guy completely, as well as the fact the two guests were obviously a couple. "I am most concerned for your safety," he said.

"Well, thank you so much," Guy piped in, at last cognizant of the unwanted attention being hurled at Claire. "Your information is most helpful, sir. Now, about our room. . . ."

The clerk handed a key to each of them and pointed toward the elevator. "Need help with your luggage?" He looked directly at Claire as he spoke. Again, she looked away.

"No, we're fine. Thank you," Guy said. His protective instincts had kicked into high gear. Enough was enough.

"Very well then," the desk clerk replied. "Please be aware that all taxi service from the hotel is to be arranged at the front door with the doorman on duty. That way, we keep the cabbies straight and honest." He again winked at Claire, and then confirmed what the normal cab fare should be traveling around the city.

On the way to their room, Claire looked over at Guy. "Actually, I think we managed that taxi situation just fine. And, by the way, thanks for noticing and handling that desk clerk the way you did. He's a bit of a creep."

"Yes, my dear. Always happy to be at your service. Think of me as your gladiator . . . your knight in shinning armor . . . your protector. And, by the way, it's my absolute pleasure to defend a damsel in distress." He grinned at her.

She raised her eyebrows. "What *would* I do without you?"

The room was clean, but unremarkable, and offered an interesting view of the bright lights of the city. Claire picked up the phone and ordered room service, delighted to see that the menu was in English as well as Greek. The employee taking the order on the other end of the line spoke broken, but understandable, English. The meal arrived shortly and satisfied their hunger. Tomorrow was another day, and they were booked on an early flight to Crete.

The firm of Caswell & Lombard, Private Investigation had taken on a different type of work in this case: the serious business of locating a missing person; that is, a person missing from the United States—a dangerous criminal, actually—and arranging to have the criminal returned to the U.S. to stand trial. Claire Caswell and Guy Lombard wanted, and needed, to be at their best to tackle the task ahead. Cool and prepared minds at all times must prevail. Before going to sleep, Claire pulled out the information Mr. Otto had provided regarding the subject of the search. After both she and Guy reviewed all information thoroughly, they skimmed over it one additional time, memorizing the data.

The focus of the pursuit was forty-nine years old. In the United States he went by the name of George Zeppano, but in this part of the world he would use his family surname—*Zenonakis.* Of this, Mr. Otto had been quite certain. Five-foot-ten, George Zenonakis had a thick, muscular build. He had dark hair, dark eyes, bushy dark brows, and thin lips. By that description alone, he could have been just about any man Claire and Guy had seen at the Athens airport earlier in the day. But they also had a photograph, or more correctly, a mug shot of the man. It was a snapshot that Sergeant Massey, Miami–Dade Police Department, had provided Claire upon request, one taken at an earlier time in an arrest that had led nowhere.

And although appearances could change, either naturally or intentionally, the two sleuths felt incredibly thankful to have a photo of the lawbreaker they sought. A picture is worth so much more than a mere description, Claire thought.

Her mind quickly drifted to past notable criminal cases where perpetrators had used disguises to alter their appearance—wigs and hairpieces, dyed hair, false mustaches and beards, fake tattoos, hats pulled down low, mirrored sunglasses, colored contact lenses, non-prescription eyeglasses, and clever applications of makeup. Some had even inserted dummy teeth or a mouthpiece to transform a jaw line, utilized voice-changing devices, or deployed clever changes in speech patterns or in manners of walking.

Certain features and characteristics, however, could not readily be made to look different without reconstructive plastic surgery—like the shape of one's eyes or nose. And, of course, while weight could be gained or lost, height remained a constant unless employing shoe lifts.

The two seasoned investigators would rely heavily on their combined expertise to ferret out this monster. Working on their side was the probable assumption on the part of George Zenonakis that no one would travel from the United States to Crete to come after him. They were counting on his letting his guard down while in his homeland, believing he had reached a safe harbor. That fact alone might be the only secret strength they had working on their side.

Guy kissed Claire goodnight. "We need to use extreme caution in this matter," he said. "The man we seek is dangerous and has a lot to lose. Not a good combination. We can take no unnecessary chances. We need to stay together at all times."

"I understand fully."

"Sweet dreams, my love."

"Sweet dreams back to you."

Nestling closely together, sleep came quickly.

THE TWO awoke early, showered, and readied for the day. An hour later, they walked into a coffee shop located on the hotel's main floor to order a quick breakfast. The hostess seated them and dropped menus on the table. Just as Claire started to sit down, a patron dashed past her in an overly clumsy manner, pushing into her so roughly that her chair teetered from side to side before finally righting itself. The man continued on his way.

Guy said loudly, "Hey, watch what you're doing, pal!"

The unresponsive stranger looked down and ran from the room.

"What an ass!" Guy said. "Are you all right, Claire?"

"Yeah, I'm fine. But that was weird! How strange that he didn't even apologize."

"Well, there are a lot of contemptible assholes in this world. Excuse my vernacular. Talk about a total lack of couth."

"It's odd," Claire said. "It's like he didn't want me to see his face."

5

AS JACK MANNING let his mind wander, he recalled vividly the recent meeting with his college buddies. Tom Lastner had taken the floor after dinner.

"Another criminal has escaped just punishment," Tom Lastner began. "As watchmen of our society, we must undertake to correct the situation immediately. Like surgeons, we will strategically remove the poison that is alive and well and operates within our community."

His eyes glazed and even appeared crazed. With his right hand, as inconspicuously as possible, he applied pressure to the right side of his forehead. Overwhelming feelings of nausea gripped him, but he tried his best to ignore them. He hesitated. The other group members would never be the wiser, he told himself. Continuing to speak softly, he battled the pain within his head, determined it would not get the upper hand. He needed to lie down in a dark room, to rest his head, not to move an inch, but that option was not on the table. He persevered, as he so often did in life, a true commander-in-chief at all times.

Teddy, Harriman, and Manning looked on curiously, wondering what seemed to be happening to the always-in-control Judge Lastner. Something did not seem quite right. The three leaned forward in an attempt to catch every word he uttered, but the noise level in the eatery seemed to soar with each passing minute, and despite earnest efforts of the three to take it all in, they could not.

"Speak louder, Tom," Harriman said. "Having trouble hearing you."

"Me, too," Manning said.

"Me, three," Teddy said. He chuckled. No one else did.

"Not long ago, an explosion lit up and leveled a plastics factory here in Miami," Tom Lastner told the boys. "It occurred in the wee hours of the morning, taking the life of the owner's only child who worked tirelessly on the company books the day the factory was blown up. The Otto family had owned and operated the business for several decades."

The three comrades listened on with keen interest.

"Rumor has it old man Otto had been threatened by a local thug who commandeered the neighborhood and demanded that each and every business owner pay up or suffer the consequences. Otto was the only holdout, open and vocal about his refusal to bend to the pressure. He shouted from the rooftops his utter abhorrence with this so-called protector who attempted to extort from him his hard-earned money.

"Otto flatly ignored each threat made to him by this thug, including his promises that unpleasant situations awaited the Otto family, and that Otto would regret bitterly his decision not to comply. But old man Otto stuck to his guns, nevertheless, proud to be combating the extorter and never paying one red cent to the hooligan.

"And although Otto was warned not to go to the police, he did exactly that. He told the local police everything and agreed to testify against the brute at trial. But then, after the violent explosion, the thug disappeared into thin air. Left the country. Without the defendant, there was no arrest, no case, no prosecution, no trial, and no conviction sending the perpetrator to prison. Police have no doubts on the identity of the culprit. None whatsoever. Fits his past modus operandi in all respects. His signature is all over it.

"Seems that when it comes to this particular perpetrator, witnesses tend to forget what they know—to stay alive, of course. So, for similar past crimes known to have been orchestrated by this same man, he has skated every time. He's done it before; he did it this time, and he'll do it again if he is not stopped. That's where we come in."

Lastner paused and looked deeply into the eyes of each man. He did not blink.

"Hold on. Things get worse here. Although the Ottos' *only* child, Billy, was presumably killed in the explosion and resulting incineration that morning, his body was never recovered. Mr. Otto's wife had a nervous breakdown soon after the tragedy and never recovered fully. Heavy sedation at all times kept her functioning at some basic level, and then recently she passed away at age sixty-two. Cause of death cited? *Natural causes.* Natural causes, my ass. Word is her heart just stopped beating—with no family or personal history of heart disease. Extended family members say she literally died of a broken heart.

"The Ottos lost their entire savings in the fire. Not trusting banks, Mr. Otto kept all the family money in a safe—located in the upper level of the business. The strongbox was designed to protect against theft and fire, but could not withstand plastic explosives. A heap of smoldering concrete and debris was all that remained of the factory in the light of morning."

"What about insurance?" Harriman asked.

"Good question, Scotty. Insurance has refused to pay on Otto's claim, stating foul play cannot be overlooked. The matter is under investigation. So, as you can see, this man has lost everything there is to lose. How much can one human take? I wonder."

"He must be on the edge," Kyle Teddy chimed in. "Poor soul."

"I would say *over* the edge," Lastner said. "Otto became vocal about seeking justice against the man who had destroyed him. Listen on. The justice arena also knows exactly who is behind this horrendous and despicable act of cowardice. He is a man said to be of Greek-Cretan heritage, a man who has engaged in this type of extortion and madness for far too long. A man able to evade conviction by hiring the most flamboyant and unscrupulous defense attorneys money can buy—those who use clever legal manipulations of the system to get the charges dropped whenever it appears that a case may stick; those lining their pockets with money as they throw their code of ethics to the wind.

"There will always be defense attorneys who keep a step ahead of the play-by-the-book prosecutors. Always have been. Always will be. I see them in my courtroom all too often. Those dirty lawyers will win at any cost.

"Conveniently, this Greek criminal has not been seen since the explosion, and word on the street is that he absconded immediately after the blast to his birthplace of Crete, where he hides in the open, protected by family.

"Our job is to find this mobster. You know the rest. We must put a permanent end to his dastardly deeds. I don't want to see him return to the U.S. when the heat is off, only to watch him walk, as usual, through the cracks in the legal system." Lastner paused. "Questions?"

At first, no one said a word, taking time to absorb all they had heard. After a few moments, a voice broke the silence.

"How much time are we talking about—to be in Crete, that is?" Kyle Teddy asked, a look of consternation on his engaging face. He was never eager to leave his family, or his church without a senior minister, for any length of time, and this would be no exception.

"Good question, Teddy," Lastner said. "Once we fly there, we will first have to locate this guy—a task *guaranteed* not to be a walk in the park. We have to assume his family will shield him at any cost. We'll need to find a way around this safeguarding. Nothing we haven't accomplished before, mind you, but this time we will have our work cut out for us. Being in a foreign country, a high-speed exit will be imperative after the hit, before the strike is discovered. Momentum is our ticket of escape. We must act as decisively as we ever have, perform flawlessly, and vanish before we are even placed on a list of possible suspects."

Lastner glowered. It was a look that always repulsed Kyle Teddy. He looked away and swallowed hard.

"As usual," Lastner said, "we will rid the world of one more scumbag. So, in answer to your question, Teddy, we will be there just as long as it takes ... and not a moment longer."

"When do we leave?" Scott Harriman asked, unable to hide his obvious jubilation.

"As soon as possible," Tom Lastner responded, stroking his chin with his thumb and forefinger. "We need to get this done."

"I'm game. Count me in," Scott chimed in.

"Yeah. I'm in, too," Jack Manning muttered without gusto.

"Me, too," the reluctant Kyle Teddy said. "As if we have a choice," he added under his breath.

"*What*, Teddy?" Tom Lastner asked. "Do you have something else to add?"

"No, I do not," Teddy responded. He lacked the courage to take on the rage of the mighty Tom Lastner.

"Good," Lastner said. "Then I'll make travel arrangements at once and call each of you tomorrow with the specifics. Make sure your passport is in order and pack a bag. Any other questions?"

No one had any.

"Then, *yassou*—that's how you say hello or good-bye in Crete. Start getting used to the language. Cretans will warm to you if you at least know that word."

The opening chant recited in a low pitch, the wine glasses clinking together simultaneously, the obligatory exchange of nods, the dinner of rare Porterhouse steaks and a pricey Cabernet, and the meaningless, light conversation were nothing more than the warm-up acts. The main event, orated by Judge Lastner, informed the men of the upcoming mission they would soon face.

The meeting ended, and the out-of-towners headed back to their hotel rooms. The following morning each would return to his home and prepare to leave at a moment's notice.

Jack Manning continued to let his mind wander, recalling what had happened after the dinner.

He had entered his hotel room, turned on the television, and flipped through the channels until he'd located CNN. He had listened for a time to dialogue concerning the terrorism that had crept across the world scene. So unexpectedly, the world as he knew it had changed forever. His very foundation had been shaken to the core by the unprecedented attacks on the United States on September 11, 2001. A deep sadness and feelings of great apprehension had overtaken him. Staring blankly at the screen, he had let his mind drift.

Another assignment from Tom Lastner had been dumped onto the group. Would there be no end to these escapades? It was just what he didn't want or need to be involved in. Each time he had wished it the last. He had more important things on his mind, and this would only mean spending more time away from Melissa … and, of course, more dishonesty. He yearned to be liberated from this revolting commitment; yet, how could he be the only one to back out? He knew it could never happen. If you're drowning in quicksand, with seemingly no means of help around you, how do you free yourself from the horrific force pulling you under? He longed for the answer.

He had picked up the phone and dialed a number.

"Hello?" came the sweet sound of her voice.

"My dear Melissa. I miss you. How is everything at home?"

"I'm fine, Jack, but the house seems empty without you. Is everything okay? Are you enjoying the reunion?"

"Having a great time," he lied. "I'll be home later tomorrow. Can't wait to see you."

"Get here safely. Remember, I love you."

"Always know that I love you, too."

He had ended the call and experienced an inward shiver of repugnance. He couldn't move. He hated being duplicitous with his wife; yet, this blasted college pact forced him to be exactly that. He loathed the fact that the great Tom Lastner never considered that maybe, just maybe, he, Jack Manning, no longer liked playing the role of avenger extraordinaire.

He had looked out of his hotel window into the dark evening sky and wished upon a star. Show me a way out of this damned blood pact, he had pleaded aloud. But in his heart of hearts, he realized it was an unrealizable dream. He remembered so fondly being a young child and believing that wishing on a star would make whatever he wished for come true. If only…

Jack Manning did not know the reaction of the others after the dinner meeting.

KYLE TEDDY had walked into his suite, dropped onto his bed, face down, and wept. How could he get out of this horrible obligation? He wanted exoneration in the worst way, yet the possibility seemed impossible. This overwhelming feeling of hopelessness indwelled him each and every time he left a business meeting with the others. Something had to give. He wanted out. But he was in too deep, drowning in the quagmire of the dark side he had so willingly but not wisely stepped into as a young man. He dropped to his knees on the floor and prayed for forgiveness.

"I am your servant, oh Lord," he had begun. "Forgive me, for I have sinned. I have devoted my life to serving You. Please know that my heart is in the right place and provide me a means of escape from this unpardonable mess I am involved in. Show me a way out."

He had climbed back onto the bed and fallen fast asleep.

SCOTT HARRIMAN had walked directly to the mini-bar in his quarters and poured himself a double Scotch whiskey. "To settling the score," he had toasted himself, aloud, before downing the libation in a single gulp. He'd refilled his glass and did the same thing a second time. Four belts of whiskey later, on top of the wine he had consumed with dinner, he had crashed on the hotel room mattress, snoring loudly throughout the night, waking from time to time after temporary cessations of his breathing.

Drinking alcohol—Scotch whiskey, in particular—numbed the nagging, ever-present feelings of loneliness now incorporated deep into his being. In his dreams that night, as every night, he had donned a mask, cape, and tights, and soared through the atmosphere, circumventing the globe, righting wrongs, and helping others in dire need. People admired him, clapped when they saw him coming, and made him feel significant and valued. Scott looked forward to this imaginary world, a place where he could be a hero.

TOM LASTNER had driven to his home that night, carefully crawled into his plush, king-sized bed, making certain to hold his throbbing head as still as possible, and planned the trip for the foursome in his mind as he slept, a look of determination on his serious face.

JUDGE LASTNER in essence directed the actions of Reverend Kyle Teddy, Scotty Harriman, and Jack Manning when it came to carrying out each covert mission. As puppeteer, Lastner pulled the strings of his minions to manipulate each show and produce the end results he desired. A loner since college graduation, he always seemed a bit agitated about things in general not working the way he thought they should. He would control the world if handed the reins, and thoroughly enjoy each minute of the ride.

The judge was the quintessential example of the quote: "Power tends to corrupt, and absolute power corrupts absolutely. Great men are almost always bad men" (attributed to Lord Acton, moralist and historian). A superior judge, initially, the freedom given him to preside over and command the lives of others had quite simply gone to his head. A supersized ego destroyed a formerly decent man.

Teddy, Harriman, and Manning were never permitted to question Tom Lastner's authority. It was not acceptable. All three men actually feared the judge… to varying degrees, for each had witnessed the inappropriate hint of pleasure and gratification gleaming in the eyes of Judge Lastner immediately after one hit or another. Finding delight in destruction seemed a bizarre reaction, and it had not gone unnoticed.

Tom spent his early years in one foster home after another. His ultimate adoptive parents—the Lastners—came on the scene when he had reached the age of eight. Welcomed into an upscale home and lifestyle, he had been treated as royalty and virtually handed anything and everything he desired. Materially, that is. However, the feelings of emptiness, deep down inside, those emanating from belonging to no one as a young boy, the persistent feelings in his formative years of everything everywhere around him seeming to be out of control, these deep-seated scars stayed with him, much like toting around a Siamese twin for life. Controlling whatever was within his power to control remained the only thing that brought any center to his life. And he did that whenever possible.

Highly intelligent, and without question the most handsome of the fearless four, the judge's smarts had a way of turning off every member of the opposite sex within minutes of contact. Analyzing, re-analyzing, and then analyzing again every subject or topic that came up for discussion became quickly tiresome for anyone on the receiving end. And his know-it-all attitude made women run in the opposite direction as soon as they caught wind of it.

His life to date had been a series of manipulations of everyone around him, both men and women alike, until, in the end, no person would have anything to do with him, by choice. Going through people like popcorn, his only semblance of closeness remained with the group of college musketeers. With them, he felt a sense of camaraderie, believing they admired him and his accomplishments, and assuming each one could not wait to engage in yet another of his capers for justice.

In reality, however, only Scotty Harriman looked forward to new and exciting James Bond-like escapades planned by the die-hard Tom Lastner. Scotty was the only true and loyal follower of what had become Tom Lastner's avenging obsession. Reverend Teddy and Jack Manning remained mere movable strings-of-convenience of the master, both feeling trapped like a squirrel in a cage, silently disenfranchised with the whole business of retribution, yet unable to shed the now unthinkable skin of a forever obligation. And neither Teddy nor Manning knew of each other's similar thoughts.

So, for now, it was *show time* once again.

6

The island of Crete
City of Hania (Chania)

THE FLIGHT SOUTH from Athens to Hania took about an hour. The short hop delivered the two sleuths to the Hania International Airport (Daskalogiannis Airport) in the outskirts of the city. Hania, the second largest city on the island and a major tourist destination situated on the western end of the island's northerly coastline, seemed like the logical place to start the search for George Zenonakis.

After collecting their luggage, Claire Caswell and Guy Lombard took a twenty-minute taxi ride to the villa-styled hotel that Mr.

Otto had reserved for their stay. The day was early, and they had time to kill.

The hotel manager spoke several languages and appeared to be an immediate source of good information. He suggested a grand tour of the city to help them get their bearings and recommended the tour company most popular with other tourists. Not surprisingly, he sold the tickets needed for the two-hour excursion right there at the desk. The earliest bus left at 9:00 a.m. and departed from a point approximately one and a half blocks away.

The manager informed Claire and Guy that Hania had an Old City—Old Town—on the waterfront (the Venetian Harbour), as well as a new city. He explained that the old waterfront harbor contained most of the trendy cafés, bars, and restaurants, and also many unique shops offering jewelry, antiques, clothing, and a variety of other goods. And he mentioned that the shop hours varied with every day of the week. Mondays, Wednesdays, and Saturdays most shops stayed open from morning until about two in the afternoon. Tuesdays, Thursdays, and Fridays most all stores opened in the morning and closed around 1:30 in the afternoon, re-opening for a few hours in late afternoon and evening. He also added that if a store was crowded with tourists, it might stay open all afternoon. The afternoon hours when the shops closed were for *siesta* or resting.

The villa, located on one of the back cobbled walking streets leading to the Old Town waterfront, was welcoming in its ambience. Venetian in appearance, the open-air atmosphere overflowed with romance and charm. Sporadically placed good-sized clay pots sat filled to the top with bright flowering shrubs, adding spots of color to the grand courtyard of the inn. The Old World architectural designs of the connected buildings brought an almost storybook quality to the setting. Claire felt drawn in at once.

Glancing around, Guy observed patrons eating a casual breakfast outside on the veranda, only steps away from where they stood. During check-in, the manager informed the guests that they would receive a breakfast each morning consisting of thick, Greek-style yogurt, accompanied by a side of Cretan honey, as well as fresh fruit and coffee. And they had a choice of room service or dining outside on the "exquisitely peaceful and inviting patio." They were to indicate their choice by checking the card left in the room and hanging it on the outside doorknob before 2:00 a.m.

An employee of the hotel escorted the two investigators to a more than spacious multi-level room one floor up and handed them two keys. Guy tipped the man, the two unpacked in record time, and they left to run to the location of the tour bus. The manager called out to Claire and Guy as they hustled through the lobby.

"While you're here, you should see the White Mountains. Just take the road to Omalos."

"The road to *Omalos*?" Claire called back. "Where is it?"

"You'll see signs everywhere. Just follow the 'To Omalos' signs. You can't miss them. The snow-capped mountains are a must-see for all visitors to this place. Make sure you take the unforgettable drive."

"Thanks for your advice, Sir," Guy hollered back.

"Don't miss Omalos. Fit it into your schedule," the man persisted. "If you don't, you'll regret it. Just follow the signs." His voice trailed off as he walked in another direction to take care of other waiting guests.

Claire made a mental note to take the drive if time allowed.

"We'd better get going or we'll miss the tour, Claire," Guy said. "Come on."

They sprinted the short distance to their destination, arriving at exactly five to nine. The bus doors were just closing, but the driver opened them to let the last two customers board. After handing the driver the tickets, Claire and Guy scurried to an empty bench seat and quickly sat down. Seventeen other tourists were already in place, and both the driver and emcee for the excursion seemed anxious to get started.

An announcement was made in English, followed by the same announcement in Greek, that sites along the way would be noted in both languages. The bus began to roll.

"By boarding our tour bus, you will return with wonderful memories," the emcee said. He smiled as if cued.

The two sleuths hoped the guided tour would help orient them to the unfamiliar territory in fairly short order, enabling them to move around more quickly in their search for George Zenonakis.

As the bus started along its pre-determined path, Claire shared with Guy what she remembered reading about the healthy Mediterranean diet of the Cretans. "They eat lots of fruits and vegetables, consume serious amounts of olive oil, and drink some wine—a glass or two a day with meals," she said. She told him of a study she had read that indicated the Cretans are some of the least likely people in the world to develop heart disease.

"Go on," Guy said.

"Well, at the time the study was done, a typical Cretan lived a lifestyle amazingly different from the majority of Americans. They walked to work every day, ate fresh vegetables, bread dipped in olive oil, lamb or chicken once a week, and fresh fish a couple of times a week. And after the main dish, they ate salad, or dates, fruit, and nuts."

"Interesting," Guy said. "And terribly healthy. Sometimes I think Americans just don't get it. But, maybe that's starting to turn around some."

"Apparently, though, the near-vegetarian Cretan lifestyle has begun to change. You know … it's evolved with the passing of time.

The people here now consume more meat, cheese, and fish than ever before in their history, and physical activity has also decreased."

The voice of the tour guide could be heard loud and clear over a built-in system.

"We are at the beginning of our tour," he said in English; then, as promised he repeated the sentence in Greek.

As the motor vehicle continued on its prescribed route, Claire and Guy casually gazed out of the windows, back and forth from left to right and right to left, as the guide pointed out sites of significance on both sides of the road. He interspersed the history of Crete in an interesting way as he referred to one prominent feature or landmark after another.

"Crete is an island where the gods lived among men. It is an island with a history forever intertwined with Greek mythology," he said. "For example: Cretans believe the god Zeus has lived here for thousands of years as the never-at-rest guardian of our vibrant island and its history. In fact, the very first known European civilization was born on this very island. And, as a tourist to our lovely land, you can even walk amongst the ruins and view them for yourself." The emcee broke to gulp some bottled water.

"You will feel the heart and soul of the Cretan people as you inhale and savor the flavor of this island—the vibrant flowers, tropical palm trees, ancient rock, towering mountains, and some of the most beautiful beaches, I'm sure you'll agree, in all the world." He grinned widely as he scanned the faces of the bus tour participants. "Our love of life is evident in our music, song, dance, and spirit. Cretans are filled with energy and excitement just about being alive. Generosity of heart is our widely known trademark, and we are a proud and independent people."

While his speech was definitely scripted, and one he'd repeated many times before, Claire and Guy absorbed every word he uttered like dry sponges, eager to learn anything and everything they could about this faraway place they knew so little about.

"For generation after generation, Cretans have continued the legacy of their ancestors by feasting on great food and wine and dancing their hearts out," the emcee said with twinkling eyes.

"Is this the largest of the Greek islands?" an excited passenger asked the tour guide.

"Yes, it is. And it's the fifth largest island in all of the Mediterranean, next to Sicily, Sardinia, Cyprus, and Corsica. And as a point of reference, an island called Gavdos, located off the southern shore of Crete, is actually the *southernmost point* in all of the European continent."

"Interesting, isn't it?" Guy whispered to Claire. "I'm fascinated by the history of this place. I only wish we were here on a pleasure trip so we had more time to see these sites up close and personal."

"Me, too."

The guide continued on, spewing forth a wealth of information about the "land of mystique." He pointed out the many orange, lemon, and olive groves, picturesque beaches, distant mountains, caves, and gorges, and the captivating plants and flowers of many varieties.

"Look at the poppies and daisies," Claire commented softly to Guy. "And jonquils and tulips. They grow wild here."

The guide started up again. "The Cretan climate is temperate. We have a good amount of sunshine and one of the healthiest climates in all of Europe. Our rain comes mainly in the spring and autumn seasons, and sometimes we have strong winds blowing our way from the continent of Africa. But, mostly, it's just … a Mediterranean paradise."

Claire focused and fixated on the mountains in the far off distance. The taller peaks appeared to be covered with snow. She was reminded of the words of the hotel manager, "You must take the road to Omalos." He had seemed almost pushy. She knew once the tour ended the real purpose of their trip would kick into high gear. The sole purpose in visiting the island was to locate a man and return him to the Unites States to stand trial. The seriousness of the mission hit her squarely between the eyes, and her daydreaming about snow-covered mountains came to a screeching halt.

She glanced broodingly in Guy's direction. Learning about Crete had seduced him. Claire refocused and listened to the guide.

"I will give you a brief background on our history. It is a history so long and so full that it is impossible to cover it all, but I will touch on some important parts of it. The Republic of Venice captured Hania in the early to mid-1200s and remained under its sovereignty until 1669, except for a short period of time from 1260 to 1290 when the Genoese took control. So, for around four-hundred years, give or take a few, Hania enjoyed the reputation of being the Venice of the East under Venetian Occupation. And, as you can see, the Old City of Hania still bears a striking resemblance to Venice to this very day. Please note that historical accounts vary on some of the dates.

"From around 1669 to 1898, the Ottoman Empire fought the Republic of Venice and her allies for the Venetian possession of Crete, and won. The Turks who took control of this island were a cruel bunch, and many native Cretans fled up into the hills to escape the invaders during the Turkish Occupation. The Cretans formed *villages*, much like what we today call *communes*, where they dwelled as one large family, taking care of one another … living peacefully, away from their subjugators. Later, the villagers armed themselves with pistols and other weapons, and no one, other than family and friends, was allowed anywhere near the villages. It was the way they survived … and the way they held on to their heritage. Today, many families still live in the communities in the hills, living the *old* way."

He stopped briefly and took several sips of water.

"When the Turks left in 1898, it was because the Great Powers ... France, England, Russia, and Italy ... interceded and declared Crete to be an independent Cretan state (The Autonomous Cretan Republic), with Prince George serving as its high commissioner. In 1913, the final union of Crete with Greece took place. It was at that time that the Greek flag was installed in Crete.

"With that change came an international makeup ... culturally, socially, and economically. Neoclassical architecture based on western European prototypes began to appear and dominate the style of houses and villas. We became a glorious melting pot of Orthodox native Cretans, Turkish-Cretans, Bedouins, Jews, and Europeans—together creating the cosmopolitan cache of ethnicity you observe today while walking through our beautiful, once-ancient city."

While he had not touched upon all of Crete's history, he had covered some important aspects of it, and just as he finished speaking, the bus returned to the tour station. Perfect timing.

As they disembarked from the bus, the guide handed out materials suggesting other points of interest to visit in and around Hania, including museums, the City Market, shopping areas, and restaurants. Also, he distributed a handout recommending several driving excursions, including a venture part way across the northern coastline, along the beautiful blue waters of the Mediterranean Sea, to Heraklion, a city comprised of the *old city* located within the Venetian walls remaining from the days of Venetian control, and the thriving metropolis *new city*, situated all around it, a layout not dissimilar from the city of Hania. A walk through the archaeological site of the Palace of Knossos (located on Heraklion's southeast side), the largest of the Minoan civilization palaces and the earliest European civilization known, dating back approximately five-thousand- to seven-thousand years, was highlighted as a *do not miss.*

After tipping the driver and narrator and thanking them both for an enjoyable and memorable morning, Claire and Guy walked back to their villa at a steady pace. They ordered lunch on the mosaic-decorated veranda. It was time to devise an attack strategy. Locating George Zenonakis on this island would not be an easy task.

7

THE SUN, SHINING in all its glory, illuminated the vibrant blue sky of Hania. Not a cloud kept it company. The second largest city on the island of Crete, and its former capital, Hania was known as the most romantic city of Crete. After lunch, the two investigators strolled a couple of blocks along the narrow and picturesque medieval cobblestone walkways, designed for pedestrian use only. It felt good to walk. They passed a mother cat and her kittens hovering in a doorway, and an occasional youngster playing along the path.

Before they knew it, the expanse of the old city waterfront faced them. They strolled to the sun-drenched water's edge and peered in to see their reflections clearly floating on the calm surface. Scanning the area, the two took in the splendor and beauty of the old Venetian pier. Sounds of hearty laughter, vigorous chatter, dishes clanging, birds chirping wildly, and minstrels singing cheerfully to musical accompaniments, filled the lively atmosphere. An inviting promenade snaked its way along the circular waterfront. Cafes, restaurants, and tavernas, overflowing with white tablecloth-covered outdoor tables, completely filled the space adjacent to the walking path. Also, small hotels and bars appeared in the mélange. Behind the restaurants, architecturally diverse, pastel colored, two- and three-story Venetian-style buildings competed for space in a limited, concentrated area. Many appeared to be the open air remains of old structures.

A sixteenth-century landmark lighthouse, one of the oldest in the Mediterranean, stood stately at the end of the pier in the old harbor, and the remains of the ancient fortress of Firka could be seen in the harbor entrance. Small fishing boats of various kinds and coloration moored in the shallow cove, painting a floating collage of sorts atop the water's surface. A breakwater of huge stones protected the Venetian haven.

White horse-drawn carriages taking tourists from spot to spot, bicycles, and numerous walkers whirled past them as they stood in awe taking in the charming, picture-perfect setting of old Hania.

Looking out over the water into the distance, Guy noted that the intense blue color of the water seemed to be a nearly perfect match for the strong blue hue of the sky, making it difficult to distinguish a line of demarcation.

Standing next to Guy, her hand engulfed in his, Claire allowed her mind to flash back to the time they had first met. When she had looked into his eyes, there had been a feeling of familiarity, of being reacquainted with someone she had always known. It's always in the eyes, she reminded herself again. In no time at all, their relationship had grown into a strong friendship and then progressed into a powerful and amorous love affair. Despite her nagging reservations about marriage, she knew if she ever did decide to take the step, it would be with Gaston Lombard. Life together was grand. Radical honesty, the cement that bonded the union, made him irresistible to her.

The sleuths had browsed through the tourist literature the villa provided and decided to spend the afternoon walking around the Old Town and the New Town of Hania. Behind the enchanting Old Town encircling the Venetian harbor, the area brimmed with narrow, winding alleyways of local shops, all connected in a maze-like layout. Roaming in no particular direction seemed a better plan than following a map. The Old Town hummed with the sounds of life. Reminders of the past seemed everywhere present, with leftover influences from the Venetians, Turks, and other decades of foreign domination visible in the surrounding building designs, many with deteriorating stonework.

The goal of the day was twofold: to ask questions, whenever appropriate, hopefully obtaining answers to help narrow the search for George Zenonakis, and to get the walking layout of Hania down to their satisfaction. They wanted to stay in Crete only as long as it took to accomplish the goal before them. Mr. Otto had agreed to pay all basic expenses for the investigators. There was not much time to enjoy the captivating country, other than what was necessary as a part of the mission.

Claire and Guy meandered along the streets of shops, passing through many of the stores and boutiques on a random basis, posing as tourists and potential customers, listening to the languages of Greek, English, and German being spoken by patrons and salespersons, alike. They engaged every English-speaking clerk and shopper, whenever possible, in friendly conversation that almost always led to the Zenonakis family. Means of obtaining helpful information were limited, as they could not simply ask local law enforcement officials for assistance; thus, soliciting information from individuals seemed to be the best source to find out what they needed to know. But each time the infamous family name came up, mouths closed tightly. People refused to talk any longer, and walked away, or quite rudely returned to what they had been doing before the conversation began.

Claire spotted a small, intriguing gift store and strolled in with Guy. The owner greeted them warmly, in English. As they perused her elegantly handcrafted merchandise, attractively arranged in glass display cases, Claire spotted an unusual pair of rectangular-shaped silver earrings, topped with clear, square, royal blue stones.

"May I try them on?" she queried, pointing to the specific pair she liked.

"Of course, my dear. Try on anything that catches your eye."

Clipping them into place, Claire looked into a small, stand-up mirror and admired them. "Quite lovely," she said.

"They look good on you, missy. You visiting from Europe?" she questioned.

"No, actually we're from the U.S.," Claire said.

"Oh, long way from home." She chuckled.

"We are." Claire smiled. By the way, do you personally craft these incredible pieces of jewelry?"

"Well, thank you, kindly. I do," she replied. "May I offer the two of you some *raki*?"

"*Raki*?" Guy chimed in.

"Yes. *Raki*. We all drink it here. It's the Cretan spirit … the national drink of Crete. Similar to ouzo. Many claim it's what keeps us so healthy. That, along with lots of olive oil, of course." She sniggered again as she pulled out a bottle of clear liquid and three small, disposable plastic cups from underneath the counter. She filled each cup to the rim.

"Drink up," she said, downing hers in a single gulp.

Guy followed suit and emptied his cup.

Claire took a sip. Immediately her eyes began to water and she coughed vigorously. "Strong stuff," she said politely, thinking to herself that paint thinner or nail polish remover would probably be easier to swallow. She couldn't finish it.

The woman laughed heartily.

"I kind of like it," Guy said. "It tastes a bit like strong gin, or vodka."

"You like?" the owner asked.

Before he could answer, she had filled his cup again.

"Go ahead," she said to Guy. "Enjoy." She downed her second. "It's made from the must-residue of the grape press—the waste of stems, seeds, and grape skins. It's what is leftover in the grape press after wine is produced. Potent, isn't it? If you drink good *raki*, you will never have a headache the next day, despite the fact that it's forty percent alcohol." She smiled broadly.

"Forty percent alcohol? That'll knock your socks off," Guy said. He downed the second cup.

"I don't know about your socks, mister," the lady said, "but it will eventually cause a spin in your head." She noticed Claire holding her burning throat. "You okay, little lady?"

"It took me by surprise, that's all," Claire admitted. "But I certainly appreciate your generosity in letting me try it."

"It's part of our culture, missy. You come to Crete … you drink *raki*," the woman said, refilling Guy's cup a third time.

"Well, thank you for breaking us in," Claire said, with a chortle. "I'd like to buy these earrings, by the way." She removed them from her ears, handed them to the owner, and set the appropriate amount of euros on the counter.

"Not so fast," the woman eyed Guy. "You have a full cup of *raki* sitting in front of you. Drink up! In our country it is impolite to refuse a cup of *raki* if someone offers it to you. If you do not want to drink any more *raki*, it is wise not to empty your cup. Otherwise, your host will continue to refill it each time."

After a moment of careful consideration, Guy drank a portion of the *raki* before him, leaving a small amount in the bottom of the cup. "That's it for me," he said. "It was delightful. Thank you."

"Now, where were we?" the owner asked. She collected the cups from the countertop and put the bottle out of sight. "You'll love the earrings, missy," she said, turning her full attention to Claire. After wrapping the purchase and entering the sale in the cash register, the owner handed Claire the correct amount of change and the parcel.

"And for you, sir, I am throwing in some worry beads. Gratis. We call them *komboloi*. They are a good way to vent all your daily stress. The men in Greece and Crete let them dangle from a middle finger. Watch when they walk past you and observe how they flip them continually until each bead, one at a time, rests in the palm of the hand before being released."

Guy thanked her for the kind gesture.

Claire seized the opportunity to ask some questions. "Have you lived here in Crete all your life?" she asked the owner.

"Yes. I've lived several places around the island, but this is home to me and I could never leave."

"It seems like a beautiful place, I must say. Lovely people." Claire continued to look into the nearby display cases. "Oh, I'd love to ask you, do you know the Zenonakis family?" she asked. "We've heard so much about them." She did her best to look wholly disinterested. "They seem to have quite a reputation in these parts." She looked at the woman and chuckled.

The owner stared at Claire and an uncomfortable silence followed. Finally, the woman spoke. "Asking about one of them in particular?" Her eyes narrowed to slits, and all signs of friendliness melted away like ice cream on a hot day.

"Well, we're actually interested in *George* Zenonakis," Claire said. "Talk is he's a real-life mobster. What do *you* think?" Claire made a silly face and snickered, as if affected by the *raki*.

It seemed a daring move on Claire's part, but they needed answers.

Guy stood silent.

"*George* Zenonakis? Why on earth would two polite, enjoyable tourists from the United States want to talk about that despicable man—a man even our police will not go near?"

The woman darted her eyes elsewhere and acted as if she did not understand the reason for the question. She mumbled words under her breath in Greek. Her gaze then went to the floor and stayed there. The clear and noticeable chill in the air got colder.

"Thank you, kindly," the owner said stiffly, refusing to look at either of them, as if the shared *raki* and playful conversation of minutes before had never taken place. "I'd be careful if I were you. I'd watch my step," she whispered.

"Careful?" Claire asked. "Of what?" She laughed.

"Good day, now," the woman said. She turned and walked into the back room.

Once outside, Guy faced Claire. "I don't like this," he said. "Hearing the name George Zenonakis transformed that woman into a different person before our eyes. It's like nothing I've seen before."

"She's afraid," Claire said. "I could see it in her eyes."

"Well, this isn't working," Guy said. "The questioning. It's just not working."

"Hang in there. We've only just started, and it's the only tool we have at our disposal right now." She looked up and noticed the look of exasperation on Guy's handsome face. "If we look hard enough, we will find something. Always do."

The two inquisitors spent the remainder of the afternoon and evening questioning people wherever they found them, trying desperately to glean information about the whereabouts of the elusive George Zenonakis. Prying information out of a mime, however, would have been easier.

"Remember, Guy, we can't tip our hand to anyone we question," Claire said. "No one can know the real reason for our visit to this island. If they find out, you can rest assured George Zenonakis will know about it immediately, and then our lives will be in danger. I know I came close with that storeowner earlier today, but I think we're okay. She probably thinks the *raki* made me giddy and that's why I asked strange questions." As a pensive look overtook Claire's face, she stared straight ahead. "We need to find someone we can trust ... a native Cretan who will talk straight with us ... perhaps someone who detests George Zenonakis."

8

THREE DAYS FOLLOWING the dinner meeting, the four comrades reassembled at the Miami International Airport and boarded a late afternoon 767 aircraft bound for Athens, Greece. The nearly fourteen-hour flight landed at the Eleftherios Venizelos Airport early in the afternoon the following day. Two hours later, Tom Lastner and his men embarked on one of the frequent ferryboats leaving the port of Pireaus, in Athens, to continue the journey southward to the island of Crete, to the city of Hania, another six or more hours of travel time.

Despite sleeping on the overseas flight and nodding off on the boat ride, all of the men suffered from fatigue due to the time change when at last they arrived at their destination.

The group of four checked into a moderately priced hotel, Tom Lastner taking the lead. He signed the registration card using the alias *Bradley Rentsal* and presented a forged passport in that name. He booked two rooms and paid cash, up front, for one night. Each morning they wished to stay another night, he agreed with the desk clerk to the same payment scenario. He refused daily housekeeping services for the two rooms, as he did not want anyone snooping around and seeing anything that would give their mission away and cause them trouble down the road.

As was the now well-established pattern, the group would leave no evidence of their identities behind. Tom Lastner took it upon himself to purchase euros at a currency exchange kiosk at the Miami International Airport prior to take-off, making certain he collected each man's proportionate share of the expenditure soon after boarding.

As the men ascended the stairway to reach the rooms, Jack Manning mentioned that he was starving.

"Teddy, you're sharing a room with me," Lastner said authoritatively, at first ignoring Jack's comment. "And Harriman and Manning, you're sharing the other room. We'll get settled in and meet downstairs in half an hour to walk somewhere for dinner." He glanced at his wristwatch, "Make it 10:30 sharp. I'm sure we'll find a restaurant open late … they all are here." He chuckled. "We'll have no trouble finding a good meal."

So much for discussion, Kyle Teddy thought to himself. He would have preferred sharing a room with Jack Manning, but he did not dare make the suggestion.

Minutes later, the men met, walked outside, and traveled on foot along the narrow, winding cobbled stone walkways situated in the maze-like formation surrounding the hotel. The passageway took them between and around the most extraordinary pale-colored Venetian-style buildings, plainly visible in the nighttime lighting of the quaint city. Not unlike following the yellow brick road in *The Wizard of Oz*, the men trekked along in search of a restaurant. Minutes later, the foursome ended up at a flight of easy, wide, stone inlay steps and followed them down. All of a sudden, outdoor cafes appeared everywhere, one after another, in a long line in either direction. It looked like an endless café community. They had discovered the Old Harbour waterfront in Old Town Hania. In full swing, and packed to the gills with what appeared to be locals and tourists alike, the hoards of people seemed to be having a great time. Much chatter could be heard coming from all directions, and great laughter from patrons enjoying the ambience of the moment. Lastner pointed to one of the establishments and led the way to the hostess stand. Minutes later, the four sat down at an empty table in the cozy, outdoor setting.

Greek salads, made with local vegetables, feta cheese, and Kalamata black olives, were ordered all around, together with fresh grilled fish—both prepared with extra virgin olive oil—and to drink, Cretan wine. Boiled greens and fried potatoes accompanied the entrées, and for dessert Lastner ordered a tray filled with an assortment of mouth-watering cookies, confections, and cakes, all made with large quantities of honey, fruits, creams, and nuts. The superb food was just what the men needed to sate growling stomachs. It had been a long two days of travel, and a substantial meal was exactly what the four men craved. Tonight, sleep would come easy; that is, if they could find their way back to the hotel by way of the complex myriad of paths.

While eating the savory food and drinking the ambrosial wine, the foursome quickly forgot about feeling tired and lost all track of time. Before they realized it, the midnight hour had long passed. There was something about that wine that seemed to lull them into oblivion. The way back to the hotel turned out to be as confusing and bewildering as they feared and took twice as long as it should have. Through trial and error, and after walking in several wrong directions, they finally spotted the familiar sign above the door to their hotel.

Lastner quickly collected a handful of tourist brochures containing maps of the area from several neat piles sitting atop the check-in desk. He handed the stack to Harriman, the experienced real estate member of the group who excelled at navigating his way around unknown territories.

"Take a look at these, Scotty, my friend. Familiarize yourself with each map. I want to start out fresh in the morning and waste no time getting around. Learn the area and learn it well," Lastner commanded.

"Roger that, commander," Harriman replied, slurring his words like a true tippler as he saluted Lastner. Now, bedtime would not come soon for Harriman, and, unfortunately, sleep was what he needed most.

"We'll meet in the lobby at precisely 8:00 a.m.—ready to start the day. Sleep well," Lastner said.

He then called Scott over to him and whispered something in his ear.

AFTER AN early breakfast the following morning, the quartet started out on their mission. They spent much of the day touring the city of Hania. The island was new territory for each of them, and getting their collective feet wet—accessing the surroundings with clarity—was the number-one imperative. This would enable quick movement, when necessary. Between them, they collected every brochure and handout available to tourists and digested the information in all of them.

In short order, it became readily apparent that the vast majority of the population of Crete lived on the northern half of the landmass—and mostly along its northerly border—the southern portion being quite mountainous.

Yet, George Zeppano, or Zenonakis, could be anywhere on the large island, a fact each of the four knew only too well. If George wished to maintain a low profile, he may have opted for the anonymity of living amongst large groups of people, in a city or town. Or, maybe, he had selected the obscurity of the hills or mountains where he would be extremely difficult if not impossible to pinpoint. There was also the possibility that he was holed up somewhere in-between. In reality, he could be hiding anywhere. It was the task of the vigilantes to pick up his scent and follow it to conclusion.

The bet seemed safe that George Zenonakis had not announced his return to the island to many people and that he was living as discreetly as possible. The fewer folk that knew about his presence, the easier it would be to keep it a secret. After all, living inconspicuously was always the safest way to remain out of sight—in case, just in case, this one time someone really did come looking for him. The group agreed to split up for a time—each checking out a different surrounding area—and, afterward, rendezvous for lunch to discuss discovered findings.

The four men would sniff out the trail, locate the target, and promptly move in for the kill. If executed correctly, Zenonakis would never know what hit him.

PERCHED HIGH on the side of a steep cliff, strategically positioned to be nearly inaccessible to humans, the spectacular white stone mansion sat proudly in its elevated position on the mountain. The custom design of the magnificent villa provided nearly a 360-degree vista of the sea, with breathtaking and unforgettable panoramic views. On a clear Cretan day, its inhabitants could see for miles in all directions. The luxury, gated estate had served as the Zenonakis family residence and hideaway for many generations.

In addition to the highly lucrative shipping industry owned and operated by the family for countless decades, acres upon acres of olive trees had also provided an abundance of income for the Zenonakis clan. Throughout the years, the family earned the well-deserved reputation of being exceptionally shrewd and even malicious in business dealings, often stepping on but not over legal boundaries.

High walls of stone surrounded the estate's courtyard and protected it from cold temperatures, winds, and unwanted visitors. A table and chairs sat within an attached covered portico, surrounded by manicured green lawns and meticulously kept gardens.

Inside walls had the appearance of distressed gold Venetian plaster. Large Turkish rugs decorated the polished dark wood floors. And the beds, nestled between massive headboards and footboards, sat neatly dressed in the purest of white cotton linens topped with regal red coverlets. Carefully chosen furniture was monastic in flavor, and original works of art hung on the walls.

The ambiance of the dwelling sent at once a serene and foreboding message.

Grandfather Nikos Zenonakis asked his grandson to sit down with him and talk. The two walked outside and sat down on oversized chairs in the open-air portico. Face to face, in the shade, Nikos stared deeply into the eyes of his son's offspring, George. Nikos had seen a lot in his ninety plus years of life, and the look he observed in his grandson's eyes troubled him deeply.

For he had watched George grow up as a youngster, always fighting with other children, depressed, angry, and mean-spirited—a genuine *bad seed*, and in his teens and young adult years, he seemed to get even angrier, if possible. People, including relatives, began to steer clear of him, having no desire whatsoever to step into his war zone. Nothing and no one seemed to be able to get through to him.

And Nikos had watched his own son, Spiro, gain one hundred and fifty pounds of excess weight over a relatively short few months, and die unexpectedly in his mid-forties from cirrhosis of the liver. Nikos recalled looking on helplessly as Spiro's abdomen and legs swelled grossly out of proportion, when his walk had become markedly unsteady, and as he had developed speech problems, before the end came. Unable to establish with certainty what had caused the disease in Spiro, the team of specialist doctors had thrown their hands up in the air, totally stumped, as Spiro rarely drank alcohol, and it was not known then that one does not have to consume large amounts of alcohol for the disease to occur.

Well, things had gone from bad to worse to beyond retrieval for George after the death of his father. He felt hurt and crushed that his father had *abandoned* him—this, after his mother had first left him at so young an age—and, like gasoline on a fire, his new orphan status fueled his untamable behavior even more so.

Beside himself with the daunting task of raising the troubled child on his own, Nikos called on help from extended family members. However, whenever a pair of George's aunts and uncles took a crack at raising him, even for a short stint, they returned him prematurely to the mansion, finding the wild child to be intolerable. And so it went. Nikos did the best he could, on his own, with the difficult situation passed along to him.

In school, George became known as the class bully, picking fights on a daily basis, often sending other classmates home with a black eye or a torn shirt. Because of his incorrigible behavior, the principal's office became his class away from class, where he learned by watching and listening to staff members fast at work performing various functions to make the school run like a well-oiled machine. And when no one was watching, he'd grab several of the toasted almond shortbread cookies that a certain female employee baked each night and set out on the coffee cart every morning, gulping them down in short order, making certain all crumbs falling onto his school clothes were brushed away in a flash.

In fact, George's big challenge of the day became how many cookies he could grab and inhale before an employee looked over at him—the only evidence he'd eaten the mouth-watering morsels occasionally being a trace of confectioner's sugar left behind on his lips. And on those days when the baker of the cookies glimpsed the white powder remnants on George's mouth, she would always smile and wink. She seemed to enjoy knowing he was eating her cookies as much as she enjoyed making them.

Sitting in the office became George's favorite place to wile away the hours waiting for the school bell to ring signaling the end of another day. And George, unbeknownst to all, absorbed all the business transactions he was privy to, thereby educating himself in the ways of the adult world.

As a teenager, and later as a young man and adult, George acted glib, manipulating everyone in his path, eventually becoming a pathological liar. He was a man who engaged in ruthless and contemptuous behavior and exhibited no remorse whatsoever for his loathsome activities—a man incapable of showing or accepting love or being on an intimate basis with another human being. He engaged in criminal activities, lesser violations at first—like petty theft, later stealing automobiles or anything else he saw and wanted just for the challenge. He continued to engage in physical altercations with anyone who disagreed with him, swore a blue streak at police officers daring to question him in connection with local crimes, and pulled his pistol on individuals who asked him to leave the premises because of his insufferable behavior.

And, sadly, he got away with all of it—every bit. He was never called to task for his outrageous or illegal behavior because he was a member of the Zenonakis family, and that status made him untouchable. He moved on to greater criminal activity.

Grandfather Nikos continued to look deeply into George's eyes, remembering how he'd watched his grandson change from impulsive to irresponsible to unreasonable to irascible to paranoid—suspicious and obsessively anxious. Where had they, and later he alone, gone so wrong in his grandson's upbringing? They had tried to love him unconditionally, at least Nikos had, despite his continually unacceptable behavior.

George's mother, Lia, not married to Spiro at the time of George's birth, had been ordered away by Spiro and instructed never to return or have any contact with the child. Spiro had paid her a handsome sum of money to disappear—to live her life elsewhere and not return. This had been a command and not an option. They never saw her again. George would be raised at the Zenonakis estate without the influence of his birth mother or her ne'er-do-well family. No mention of George's mother was ever to be made, as the union producing this child had been a terrible mistake between young people of two feuding families, and Spiro wanted no reminder of the woman after the birth of his son—only the boy to raise as his heir, the sole heir to the Zenonakis family fortune. When George inquired about his mother at age four, he was told that she had died in childbirth and that had been the end of the discussion.

Raised without any mother figure in his life, childhood had been both difficult and unhappy. George cried a lot. He'd never felt the soft, comforting arms of a mother cradling him and telling him how much he was loved; he'd never had a mother to pamper and adore him. He never had a mother to read him childhood stories at bedtime, and he never experienced a mother tucking him in at night and kissing him gently on the forehead, bidding him sweet dreams. He had not had a mother to anxiously welcome him home from school each day, or care to look at his drawings or writings, or make fresh honey puffs or donuts like he'd heard other kids talk about. And he had not had a mother as he matured, to be in his corner, to love and support him without condition.

Rather, George had been raised initially by a father wholly disinterested in him as a person, and later by an elderly man who was no match for a growing, hurting, needy child. And despite the occasional warmth exhibited by his grandfather, George acted and felt like a feral child—out of control.

He grew up being angry with everyone, including society as a whole. As a young adult, he had left to travel to America—to make his own way, to rid himself of Crete and all of his ugly childhood memories. To start anew.

Grandfather Nikos had heard very little from or about his grandson after the departure, and that had been fine with him. Quite frankly, he had welcomed the break. About two years passed when he heard through the grapevine that George remained a veritable *monster* in the United States—leaving a wide trail of destruction behind him on his walk through life—engaging in shameful extortion and most other illegal activities, muscling his way around as he had in his youth, and always narrowly escaping justice, but escaping it nonetheless, only to continue on his fuming rampage.

And now, after a good twenty plus years of not hearing a word from his grandson, George suddenly, without warning, appeared on the doorstep of the Zenonakis mansion, acting strangely, obviously in trouble—and this time Grandfather Nikos knew it was *big* trouble.

A grave expression overtook the face of Grandfather Nikos and he spoke slowly. “It’s time for a serious talk, Georgy,” he said, speaking Cretan Greek and using the name he had called George in his formative years. “You have brought great shame to our family.”

9

HOURS AFTER CLAIRE Caswell and Guy Lombard had arrived in Hania, on the very next scheduled flight into the city from Athens that day, a passenger dressed in brown had landed at the Hania International Airport. The traveler had collected a single piece of hard-sided luggage from the circulating carousel and hurriedly walked off to find a taxi. There was work to be done. The stay would be brief.

THE TWO investigators had learned much about Crete and the city of Hania in a relatively short period of time. The bus tour had provided information on the island and its history, as well as highlighting different landmarks and areas within the city of Hania; they had read and digested every bit of information in every brochure they could get their hands on regarding Crete, its topography, and the city; and they had learned much about the area from conversing with countless numbers of people since the moment they arrived. The only thing they had no information on was the whereabouts of George Zenonakis. That information seemed to be highly secretive and protected.

But the morning was young and the sleuths had renewed energy and hope that this day would be more productive. They spent hours walking the streets of Hania, venturing in and out of some of the other shops and businesses clustered near and around the old city. Again, they initiated conversations with many employees and clerks along the way, and patrons, hoping to steer the informal exchanges toward a discussion of the Zenonakis family at some point. Each and every time they got close to broaching the subject that morning, however, something or another got in the way and put a halt to it. The morning was not proving to be productive.

Lunchtime arrived and both Claire and Guy were hungry. They selected an outdoor café, sat down, and ordered Greek salads and mineral waters. While they ate, the two discussed further plans of action for locating the elusive George Zenonakis. The family had police protection on its side—at least Claire and Guy understood that to be the case. The two investigators were left to their own devices. People on the island of Crete knew the family all too well; yet, no one would speak about them.

"Someone will help us. We just haven't found that person yet," Claire said optimistically. "We have to keep trying."

Refreshed, they started out anew, repeating the morning exercise until the shops closed in the late afternoon. Together, they engaged a variety of clerks in typical tourist talk that eventually led to questions about either George Zenonakis or the Zenonakis family in general. Things went quite well in each instance until the conversation turned to the dreaded subject of the infamous family. And then, one by one, the dialogue suddenly crashed and burned. It seemed as if the entire city had been instructed not to discuss George Zenonakis or his family with Claire Caswell or Guy Lombard—the Americans. They were getting nowhere fast.

Next stop was the Municipal Market located in the heart of Hania. The impressive and immense building had a glassed-in section within its upper story, providing a source of light for the vendors and shoppers alike. Opened in 1913, the structure was constructed in the shape of a cross, with four entrances—one on each arm. Home to more than seventy-five shops, the market floor appeared full to overflowing with cartloads of local produce and merchandise, making it a true sight to behold.

The Mediterranean certainly seemed to be the perfect climate for growing fruits and vegetables, as evidenced by their mere size. It seemed as if all produce, without exception, had eaten the side of the mushroom that made the eater grow bigger, right out of *Alice in Wonderland.* Cabbages rivaled basketballs in size, radishes resembled large red softballs, and oranges and lemons looked overdosed on steroids. Each and every large display cart brimmed to overflowing with amazingly colorful produce.

To top it off, the displays sat artistically arranged in neat and attractive order, as if a famous artist had placed the contents of each exhibition just so in order to paint a still life. Some of the open four-wheel carts offered whole fresh fish ensconced on masses of crushed ice—red snapper and others with fins and tails. Also shrimp, lobsters, and even octopuses were available for purchase. A wide variety of meats and cheeses, all types of vegetables and fruits, bags of pistachios and cashews, Cretan herbs, honey, olive oil, soaps, and so many other local foods and products appeared on the various carts, together with arts and crafts of all kinds. And there were stations selling nothing but local, handmade leather goods.

Throngs of people made their way up and down each aisle, looking over the innumerable items the marketplace had to offer, skillfully maneuvering in and around the other shoppers, buying fresh goods for dinner, and picking up other items along the way. The flow of the crowd took on a momentum of its own, with participants caught up in the movement of the masses, chattering away in Greek, and clearly enjoying the day's adventure. The combination of sights, sounds, smells, and shoppers overwhelmed the sleuths and provided few chances to question anyone.

Finally, Claire and Guy stumbled upon a more tranquil section of the marketplace. It was there that they walked into a booth filled with a miscellany of purses, perfectly placed on standing racks and upon shelves along the sidewalls.

"Looking for anything special?" a saleslady asked Claire. "Please let me know if I can assist you in any way." She spoke perfect English.

"Just browsing," Claire responded, picking up a sleek black leather bag and looking at it with interest. "This is beautiful."

"It is. You have good taste, madam. That's a nice one," the young salesperson said. "It's handmade here on the island." Her eyes lit up.

Claire asked the price and quickly drew the salesclerk into light conversation. Guy stood at Claire's side, silently watching the born sleuth at work. He never ceased to be amazed at her ability to elicit information from people who never realized they were doling it out. She didn't look like the stereotypical investigator, and that always seemed to work to her advantage.

"I think I will take this," Claire said, handing the purse to the clerk. "Have you always lived in Crete?" she asked pleasantly, taking extra time to dig through her purse purportedly to find the exact amount of money to cover the purchase.

While the woman wrote up the receipt, wrapped the bag, and

collected the payment, she conversed with Claire. "Oh, yes, except for the year I spent abroad, in the United States, during college. While that was a great experience for me, I truly love living here. This is my home, and I would never leave it permanently. I travel to Greece and Italy, on occasion, but I always come back to Crete."

"I suppose you know many people on the island, then."

"Yes, pretty much." She grinned at Claire and Guy, obviously proud of her ability to converse in English and happy to find Americans to visit with. "I know lots of Cretans—if not by their first name, certainly by their family name. We all know the common Cretan family names."

"I've heard of the *Zenonakis* family," Claire said. "Is that a well-known family on the island?" Her face pleaded ignorance.

The saleswoman's smile went flat, and her eyes instantly drained of their warmth. "Will there be anything else for you today, madam?"

Claire looked at her quizzically. "No, thank you." She smiled kindly. "I enjoyed our talk. Have a good evening." She collected her package.

"Thank you for your patronage. Use it in good health," the young woman said. Immediately, she busied herself by straightening the bags already sitting in perfect alignment on the shelves within the booth.

The coolness in the air made Claire wish she had a sweater to throw over her shoulders.

Claire and Guy strolled the remainder of the aisles within the city market, strangely intrigued at how, without exception, the mere mention of the name Zenonakis garnered the reaction that it did. Guy wondered if they had taken on something over their heads, and the better part of him thought seriously about packing up and flying home. After all, they were going after a dangerous man, in a foreign country, and they were unarmed and operating without the assistance of the local police. Probably not very smart.

Once outside, Claire took in a deep breath, held it, and expelled the air slowly. "Aah. Better," she said.

"This isn't going to be easy," Guy said. "I hope you realize that."

"We'll have to figure out another way to track down George Zenonakis," Claire said, undeterred by the latest reaction to the family name.

The two had walked about two long blocks when out of the blue someone rammed Claire from behind. It happened so quickly and with such force that the impact hurled her to the ground and sent her package flying through the air. The woman responsible for the collision fell directly on top of the stunned investigator.

"I'm so sorry," the lady said, speaking very loudly to Claire. "I was in a hurry, I was running, and I looked the other way for just an instant. I apologize for my clumsiness. Are you hurt?"

The woman pulled herself up, and she and Guy each extended a hand to help Claire to her feet. Without hesitating, the lady walked a few steps to retrieve Claire's package, handed it to the still-stunned sleuth, and hurried off. Claire turned on her heels and followed the woman with her eyes. She never looked back, and the scarf that covered most of her face hid her identity.

"Are you all right?" Guy asked. "People have died for less."

"I think so, but she almost knocked the wind out of me." Claire breathed slowly to catch her breath. "I got a glimpse of her eyes and I'm not sure ... but I think that was the woman I bought the purse from. It's always in the eyes, Guy."

"What? Why would she ..."

"Not sure."

Back at the villa, Claire lifted the bag from its wrapper, anxious to look at her newly acquired purchase. When she did, a small folded piece of paper fell out onto the floor. She picked it up, opened it and read it aloud.

"Sorry for the surprise bump. I had to make it look good. The man you are searching for will not be easy to find. I would suggest you travel to Heraklion and seek out *the old woman who feeds the birds*. She will most surely assist you. Do not come and see me again. And please burn this note after reading it."

Claire and Guy exchanged quick glances, stunned by the revelation.

"Looks like we're traveling to Heraklion tomorrow," Claire said.

"Heraklion it is," Guy said.

Claire lit a match over the toilet and disposed of the writing.

GRANDFATHER NIKOS grabbed both of George's hands, and looked directly into his dark eyes, penetrating deeply into the windows of his soul. "Why are you here, Georgy? What brings you to Crete?" The somber tone in Nikos's voice made George Zenonakis swallow hard. His grandfather spoke no English and hearing him speak in Cretan Greek brought a flood of childhood memories rushing through George's head.

"Papou," George said, trying to play on his grandfather's sympathies. *Papou* was the name George had called his grandfather since George was a small lad. It had always made his grandfather smile, but not today.

"This is a sad time for me, Georgy," Nikos said. "A *very* sad time."

George replied, "Why do you question me? I came to visit you. Do you need more of an explanation than that?"

"Georgy. Georgy. An ignoramus could see that you do not speak the truth. Do not lie to me. What do you hide? What brings you here, now, for a visit after such a long time away? What kind of trouble follows you?"

"I tell you. I am fine. I have no problems." He pulled his hands away from his grandfather's. "This is my house, too, is it not? Can I not visit my home whenever I choose? Am I not the sole heir to the Zenonakis fortune?" George asked boldly.

"You've never been *fine*, Georgy," his grandfather fired back determinedly. "And you have never had *no problems*. You have been a hostile soul since you first came into this world." He sighed. "Trouble seems to follow you; or rather, you seem to follow trouble, wherever you go. And I fear this time you've gone too far. Tell me I am wrong." He scratched his head pensively, his eyes riveted on his grandson. "I see it with my heart, Georgy. You are in trouble. And the trouble is profound."

"Papou. Relax. I do nothing I cannot handle. I have money. I have power. And I do whatever I want to do. Get it? Now, back off and give me some peace. And by the way, it's good to see you, too."

"We have all done things we are not proud of, Georgy. But you, you keep repeating your mistakes time and time again. You do not seem to learn from your mistakes like other people. I have never understood..."

"No, you haven't. No one has *ever* understood me," George interrupted. "My soul is restless. That is all you need to know."

"I will not help you this time," Grandfather Nikos said, keeping his eyes burrowed straight into George's. "I will not."

"So what *else* is new?" George retorted. He seemed to hold little regard for what his grandfather had to say.

"This is it, Georgy. Your day of reckoning awaits you. I feel it in my decrepit, aching bones. And I will not bail you out this time. You are on your own."

George stood, took a step toward his grandfather, and kissed him—first on his right cheek, then on his left, and then on his right again. "I do not *want* nor *require* your help, old man. Old, old man!"

He turned abruptly and walked away.

Nikos went after him, following George back into the house. He stepped in front of his grandson, blocking his path. "I have not finished talking to you," Nikos said, pointing an index finger in George's face. "And I will not allow you to speak to me with such disrespect. Not while you are in my home."

"Papou. How quickly you forget. Soon, quite soon, this will all be mine. Look around you. *All* of this will be mine. Now, fuck off!"

That was it. Grandfather Nikos raised an open hand in the air and brought it down hard across George's face. "This is what you needed a long time ago," Nikos said. "A little discipline. Maybe if your father and I had used some on you when you were young you would not have turned out the way you did. Now, I would like an apology from you, young man."

"First of all, don't bring my father into this discussion. Second of all, I am not a *young* man. And last but not least, you'll wait a long time to get an apology out of me. Longer than the days you have left to be alive. Now, move aside! Get out of my way!"

Nikos refused to budge an inch, and George grabbed him by the arm and pushed him away using unnecessary force. Grandfather Nikos fell to the floor and moaned.

Refusing to help him to his feet, George whistled as he walked toward the doorway, leaving Nikos in a collapsed position and in obvious pain. "I'm the kingpin now, old man. Don't you forget it," George said, stepping from the room.

Grandfather Nikos did not respond. Steeped in thought, he remained on the floor in a crumpled position for a long fifteen minutes before struggling to get up. He muttered soft words for his ears only. "You have sealed your fate, George Zenonakis. You have sealed your fate."

Hania, Crete

THE SQUADRON-OF-FOUR DECIDED to spend the day attempting to elicit information from Cretans to zero in on the whereabouts of the elusive George Zenonakis.

Tom Lastner and Scott Harriman could not hide their intense enjoyment at the prospect of searching out their mark, taking aim, and ending a life for a life taken. It was the single solution that made any sense in their collective worlds.

Kyle Teddy, on the other hand, struggled in an internal ethics and morals match, rivaling none to date. With every cell in his being, he did not want to participate in this hit—no matter how Tom Lastner justified the action to the group, and he wanted to be unleashed from the never-ending, despicable, and shameful commitment that knew no bounds.

He no longer thought like the rest of them and desperately needed to restore the synchronization of his inner soul. Feeling off-kilter to the depths of his being for some time now, the pull to line up those things that made Kyle Teddy "Kyle Teddy" overtook his thoughts day and night. He wanted to return to the real Kyle Teddy—the man of the cloth. The phrase "Vengeance is mine; I will repay, saith the Lord" haunted his thoughts until he could stand it no longer. He had even preached a recent sermon telling his congregation, "God did not say vengeance is ours to exact. Rather, it belongs to God alone." He felt like a king-sized hypocrite.

Just last night, he had silently vowed to God that this was the last time—that he would no longer succumb to the pressures of Tom Lastner and the group, that he would not back down from this promise under any circumstances. He pledged to play along until the timing was right and then make his move to extricate himself, completely, once and for all.

Jack Manning, likewise, felt troubled, but for moral not religious reasons. He fantasized and dreamed of a life with Melissa free from the hideous pledge-without-end that dragged him into the mire, time after time. He thought if only one other in the group shared his feelings, maybe then, just maybe, with two of the four wanting out, the pact could be dissolved, forgotten and buried so deep that it would never again be restored. And each of the four college friends could walk away and get on with his life, no longer hovering beneath the dark shadows of the group's activities.

Manning knew Tom Lastner and Scott Harriman were committed lifers, but he was not so sure about the reverend. Therefore, watching Kyle Teddy more closely and broaching the subject with him when the two were alone—and when the timing seemed right—became a strong desire for Jack Manning. It was a risky proposition, however, and if Kyle Teddy was not on the same page, the results could be devastating.

Deep down, Manning felt great fear of retaliation from the group should they ever discover his true state of mind regarding the violent and vicious deeds that had resulted from the blood pact. And while they had rid the world of some cruel and wicked felons, the *corrections* had not been theirs to undertake—not legally, at least, and certainly not morally. After all, criminal courts existed specifically to handle just such persons. And if a few criminals slipped through the cracks, here and there, then so be it. For the most part, the system worked pretty damn well, he reasoned. But he did fear for his own life, should he attempt to back out.

Earlier that morning, Jack Manning had phoned Melissa to tell her he loved her, and she had asked how the diving trip was going in Crete. He had been dishonest with her another time, telling her the dives were remarkable. As always, one lie snowballed into more. And he knew Kyle Teddy had also used the diving trip story with his wife. On the spot, Manning decided that one day soon the lies would stop; the day would come when he would face the blood-oath creature head on, tangle with it, and the better of the two would prevail. This thought helped him breathe easier. Now, he needed a plan … a window of escape.

The four college friends walked back to the Old City waterfront, selected an outdoor café, and sat down at a round table to order breakfast. The plentiful number of eateries, all overflowing with tables and chairs, and diners, aroused the curiosity in the men, and they glanced around in all directions to absorb the essence of the culture.

Small groups of elderly Greek men, engaging in long and friendly conversations with one another, enjoyed the day over strong coffee and unfiltered cigarettes. Bright-colored bougainvillea grew freely and without control, hanging ubiquitously from most of the upper stories of the mix of Venetian and Turkish-styled buildings. And pots of hydrangeas could be seen in many a windowsill.

The natural slow pace of life—the laid-back attitude in Crete was readily apparent. The people lived primarily off the land, growing a wide variety of fruits and vegetables, producing olive oil, and harvesting honey. The Cretan diet was fresh and tasty, sensible and well balanced.

A young waitress approached.

"English-speaking?" she asked, looking from person to person.

"Yes," they answered in unison.

"Okay. What can I get you for today?"

Before they ordered, Tom began to pepper the young lady with questions—including where she was from, how long she'd been in the area, if she knew most of the people who lived nearby, and on and on. Initially, the server answered his questions with straightforwardness, in broken English, but she quickly tired of his persistent hammering and intrusiveness and became oblique in her responses, looking in another direction as he spoke.

"Too bad I don't have you on the witness stand, missy," Lastner said. "Then, I would force you to answer my questions." He laughed, but it was not funny.

She was definitely put off by his attitude and gave a fleeting thought to walking away and letting another of the wait staff tend to the difficult table. But she refused to let this impertinent man get the best of her.

"You placing breakfast order this morning, or not?" she retorted.

Fresh-squeezed orange juice and Greek coffee was ordered all around, as well as substantial amounts of food. The Mediterranean air seemed to make the men hungrier than usual.

Kyle Teddy apologized to the server for his friend's lack of tact. She immediately took a liking to the man whose eyes exuded kindness and warmth, and when talking was required from that point on, she spoke only to him. Tension catapulted to a palpable state between Lastner and Teddy, and the men exchanged no words while inhaling the edibles.

"We'll get nowhere fast doing something like that again," Kyle Teddy said to Tom Lastner, breaking the silence as the group walked away from the restaurant. "You catch more bears with honey."

"What did you say to me, Teddy?" Lastner said loudly, stopping dead in his tracks.

Kyle Teddy repeated himself.

Suddenly and unexpectedly, Tom Lastner grabbed Teddy and slammed him up against the nearest building, pinning him there against his will. Lastner spoke an inch or two from Teddy's face and in a tone so low that only he could hear the barely audible but threatening words.

"If you *ever* chastise me in front of the group again, or for that matter in public or in private—*ever* again—you'll regret it."

"Oh, so you're *threatening* me?" Teddy asked loudly and boldly so all could hear.

"This is between the two of us, for now," Lastner whispered. "But heed my warning, Teddy. Heed my warning."

"Okay, Mr. Counselor, or should I say, Mr. *Dictator.*"

This confident and courageous side of Kyle Teddy surprised Tom Lastner, but he refused to let it show. Instead, he released Kyle Teddy with a sudden jerk of his hands and walked away.

Jack Manning watched the scene with great curiosity. Maybe things were not so rosy in all the land after all; perhaps the breaking point for Teddy soon approached. Manning would silently, but diligently, observe the situation. At once, the whispering between Lastner and Harriman last evening at the hotel made sense. Lastner had intentionally roomed with Teddy to watch him closely and keep an eye and ear on him. Could it be that Lastner suspected a potential defector? And did that also mean he had advised Harriman in the covert conversation to observe him—Jack Manning? He suddenly felt more uncomfortable. Was the arrangement the foursome had shared for so long beginning to bulge at the seams?

Scott Harriman, too, looked on as Lastner castigated Teddy, but, unexpectedly, he did not jump in to support the group's ringleader. Both Kyle Teddy and Jack Manning thought it odd. Maybe it was nothing more than the fact that Harriman realized Lastner could handle the job without his help. Time would tell. But, if truth were told, a head-on collision between Lastner and Teddy seemed inevitable.

The group walked for ten additional minutes before the ire dissipated. Then, the men decided to split up for a period of time to scour the area closest to the waterfront, looking for any individual who could shed some light on the whereabouts of George Zenonakis. They started out in different directions, but this did not last for long.

Kyle Teddy caught up with Jack Manning. "Mind if I tag along with you, Jack? We can look together."

"I'd like that," Jack Manning said. He smiled.

Likewise, Scott Harriman ran up to partner with Tom Lastner.

"We've got trouble," Lastner said to Harriman, looking straight ahead.

"Yeah," Scott replied.

"Me thinks he wants out," Tom said.

"Me agrees."

"Sorry, *amigo*. That will never happen."

GEORGE ZENONAKIS walked outside and sat down on a chair in the portico. Gazing outwardly onto the nearly surreal setting of majestic mountains and deep valleys that spread before him like butter on bread, he realized why so many fine artists had vividly captured the magnificent scene on canvas. There was nothing like it in the entire world, at least in his opinion. He took a sip of hot coffee and inhaled the clear and fresh Cretan air.

Speaking Cretan Greek gave him great pleasure. It was the only language permitted in the Zenonakis mansion when conversing with Papou, the bodyguards, or any visitors. George enjoyed being bilingual and having the chance to use his childhood language on the island.

He loved this land, as much as he was capable of loving anything. And he had some childhood memories of living there, none of them good, but he had childhood memories nonetheless that were his alone. In fact, he would classify nothing in his life as ever being *good.* For some reason, he never fit in, and he'd been angry since birth. Maybe he had lived several lifetimes before and didn't want to come back this time for another round? And his father's dying so young hadn't helped matters one bit. He exhaled deeply. Life certainly had dealt him a bad hand: a deceased mother, a deceased father, no siblings, no partner, and no children. He was an orphan walking the walk of life, and most of the time it felt lonely. Papou remained the only living relative in his realm that would have anything to do with him; yet, George had directed his internal rage at the poor old man. It was something George himself did not understand. One day soon Papou would die, and there would be no one left that gave a rat's ass whether George lived or died. Could it be that he blamed his father for the plight he lived called life? And Papou just happened to be the only one left to heave his anger upon?

His grandfather walked from the house at that moment and sat down on an adjacent white rattan chair. He settled into its high back and placed his forearms onto the large armrests the seat provided. His bones felt cradled, and the comfortable seating provided rest for his weary and sore body. The anger between the two remained.

"Morning, Georgy. Quite a view, isn't it?"

"Morning back to you, Papou."

"What occupies your mind on this divine day, Georgy?" Nikos asked.

"I'm just reminiscing. About my childhood. . . ."

"What kind of memories do you have, Georgy?" His tone did not exhibit warmth.

Since the incident, Papou, the only human being that George had ever received a modicum of sympathy or understanding from, now seemed less vigorous in his attempt to act kindly toward his grandson. It was as though something had broken in an unfixable kind of way.

"A few of my father, none of my mother, and two handfuls of you," George responded.

"Do you remember how we tried so hard to make you happy? Do you recall any of that?"

"I do not. Nothing ever made me *happy*, and nothing ever could. I was angry when I was born and remain in a temper to this very day. I cannot explain it."

"Sad. To go through life that way." Papou shook his head.

"Yeah? Well, guess what? That's how it is. You should try it next time around." George's face displayed a mocking smile, and his eyes gleamed with evil. "I care about two things and two things only: control—*ultimate* control—and hard cash. But the second one is a given, isn't it? The love of money runs in my bloodline." He continued to stare at his grandfather, torn between loving him and hating him. "And I'll do anything I have to in order to get what I want. Understand, Grandfather? I'll destroy anything that gets in my way. *Anything*, and *anyone*."

"You need help, Georgy. Professional help. A man with no conscience is a barbarian. He will meet with no good end."

With eyes narrowed to slits, George stood and faced him. "I enjoyed our conversation tremendously, Papou. We'll have to do it again some year." George lowered and raised his head slightly, a single time, indicating an unexpected nod of respect toward his grandfather, then walked to the doorway and disappeared into the house, foaming at the mouth, as usual.

Papou remained seated on the veranda chair, pondering the ongoing dilemma in his mind. Alas, the responsibility to make things right fell squarely on his shoulders.

GEORGE SQUEEZED his hands together tightly. What was wrong with him? He could not stop his hands from shaking. Thoughts of his impending demise clutched ferociously at his psyche. Why was he feeling this way? Never in his life had such horrifically morbid premonitions plagued him; yet here they were again, and he could not seem to shake them. Death was near. His death. He yearned to discuss this with Papou, but he could not. It was clear his grandfather would never understand any of it.

Suddenly, George felt the urgent need to pee. But, when he tried, only a trickle oozed out. He ran to the sink and coughed up blood. He hated being controlled by the haunting feeling of certain doom. It was eating him alive.

11

Heraklion (Iraklion)

THE MORNING IN its infancy seemed peaceful and full of promise. Claire and Guy took turns driving the compact, red rental car eastwardly along the northern coastline, as together they navigated the road to Heraklion—the largest city on the island, and its capital. Solidly aware that the two-and-a-half hour drive from Hania could prove to be nothing more than a wild goose chase, they nevertheless had a clue to follow, and it was their first real lead since stepping foot on the intriguing Greek island of Crete.

And, after all, the saleslady had no apparent motive to be anything but truthful—at least none that they knew of. Why would she send them down a dead-end road when she had seemingly gone to great lengths to pass the note to Claire? So all investigator instincts told them both to heed the call and go forward in search of *the old woman who feeds the birds.*

The motorway—*coastal highway*—to Heraklion allowed for a top speed of sixty kilometers per hour. The slow drive provided Claire and Guy an unbroken view of the splendor of the island's northerly shoreline, and in no time they found themselves captivated by the experience.

The investigators passed a U.S. Naval Base, positioned not far outside the city of Hania. Guy noticed a sign posted adjacent to the facility's entrance warning in several languages that photographs were strictly forbidden. Impressive young American military personnel, some who had been stationed on the elongated island for a six-month stint, stood near the building's grounds, ready, willing, and able to answer any and all questions posed by tourists and passersby.

Tooling along through sporadically more populated areas, they observed the glorious and noteworthy turquoise and teal waters of the Aegean Sea—part of the spectacular nearly landlocked Mediterranean Sea. Guy studied the map of the area as Claire drove. It showed the lineup of countries that shared the stunning body of salt water sandwiched in between southern Europe, southwestern Asia, and the northern coast of Africa.

"Claire, listen to the list of countries that sit on the Mediterranean Sea," Guy said. "Spain, France, Monaco, Italy, Slovenia, Croatia, Bosnia and Herzegovina, Montenegro, Albania, Greece, Turkey, Cyprus, Syria, Lebanon, Israel, Egypt, Libya, Malta, Tunisia, Algeria, and Morocco. Amazing. I never realized. . . ." He paused briefly, continuing to consider the map. "And the Mediterranean Sea is connected to the Atlantic Ocean at the Strait of Gibraltar, to the Red

Sea and Indian Ocean by the Suez Canal, and to the Black Sea at the Dardanelles and Sea of Marmara."

"You can see why the area has always been an important part of history. Whoever controlled it controlled the water transportation trading between all of those countries," Claire said. "That's why it became known as the cradle of civilization—the highway of commerce."

Guy looked over at her.

"Many rival civilizations competed to dominate the Mediterranean Sea throughout history," she continued. "Control of the area was important during both World Wars and remains strategically important today to the U.S. and Europe."

"Okay. I'm impressed," Guy said. "And here I thought I was the history buff."

"You are." Claire laughed. "I did some internet research before we flew here because I wanted to learn more about the area."

"Okay then, Miss Smarty Pants. Answer this one. What are the four main subdivisions of the Mediterranean Sea?"

"Well, one is the Adriatic."

"Correct."

"Another is the Aegean."

"Go on."

Claire paused. "I'm afraid I can't remember the other two. What are they?"

"What is the answer worth to you, my beauty?"

She thought for a short time. "How about two kisses the next time we stop to switch drivers?" She looked over and smiled.

"Deal. The other two subdivisions are the Ionian and the Tyrrhenian seas."

"Ah, yes. Now I recall."

"Okay, final question, my love," Guy said. "What is the quality of the Mediterranean Sea water? Is it clear or polluted?"

"That one's easy," Claire said. "Sadly, it's very polluted."

"How right you are. And that's the end of the quiz for today."

"Whew! I thought it would never end." She chuckled.

A half hour passed, and Claire pulled over to let Guy take a turn behind the wheel. As they crossed paths behind the car, Claire stopped, pulled him close, and kissed him gently on the lips two times.

"To be continued later," Guy said, grinning widely.

Long stretches of deserted, sheltered, white-pink sand beaches and picturesque bays presented on the left-hand side of the roadway, occasionally interrupted by groups of sunbathers basking in the ever-present sun that seemed to splash over the Mediterranean coastline from every angle of the sky.

Recreational, fishing, and shrimp boats speckled the deeply colored waters.

The map indicating their route promised to take them past a copious miscellany of lodgings and resorts, mills, churches, monasteries, ancient sites, caves, monuments, lighthouses, and other points of interest.

Claire took special note of the more remote sections of the island's coastline that offered national parks, camping sites, and mountaineering refuges. Good places for one to hide out, she thought.

Driving farther and onward along the highway, the sleuths passed through a city called Rethymno, and also observed occasional red clay soil banks and an old stone fortress, again on the left-hand side of the road. On the right side, Guy pointed to a grape vinery and numerous olive tree groves that seemed to be carefully designed and planted along the hillsides.

Volvo tour buses traveling in both directions caught the attention of Claire. And they passed a series of hotels, including massive, white, Mediterranean-style beach hotels, and the Eliros Hotel. Several new construction sites—apparently stopped mid-stream, as evidenced by the steel reinforcing bars protruding from the roofs—also appeared from time to time along the journey.

The majestic castle-like Palladion Hotel, the color of milk, and other great-in-number apartment complexes drew comment from Claire. Colossal aloe vera plants and patches of petite yellow flowers brightened the drive, and showy ivory longhaired black-faced sheep peppered the hillsides. Several taverns provided interest along the scenic drive, and a massive valley filled with olive trees also grabbed the attention of the two investigators.

Gray, snow-capped mountains filled up the misty distance, and longhaired sheep appeared again and again scattering the nearby steep rock inclines as they continued the trek. Many types of lush trees and shrubs, all native to the island, grew in abundance on both sides of the asphalt road.

Claire observed additional new home construction sites—many with a distinctive Mediterranean flair—as they traveled along the roadway, and residential communities developed or under development quite close to the road's edge, together with other flat-roofed houses white as the driven snow.

Sections of the highway had been forged through steep hills of rock and led them up, down, and along curvy, sometimes nearly vertical, passages. Onward they traveled, eager to reach their destination and search for *the old woman who feeds the birds*, fascinated by what they saw and taking it all in. They passed diminutive all-white churches, identified only by a single cross attached to each rooftop, and signs announcing the Gerani Bridge and Cave, and an industrial area.

As Guy manned the wheel, he pointed to an elderly Cretan man walking slowly alongside the edge of the roadway, making his way in the same direction they headed. He was wearing a plaid shirt and dark suspenders, and sported a long and pointy white beard.

"Guy, stop! Maybe he would like a ride," Claire said. "Pull over."

Guy glided to a stop on the shoulder, twenty feet or so ahead of the man.

Claire jumped out and waited for the man to near the car. She closed her eyes and felt the sun on her face and the cool, subtle breeze blowing her hair. For a brief moment, she let herself forget the pressure she felt related to finding George Zenonakis and delivering him back to the United States to stand trial. The old man approached.

"Hello, sir, may we offer you a ride?" She pointed to him and then to the back seat of the rental car and smiled.

The tiny dark eyes of the Cretan sparkled with kindness, and his skin glistened with perspiration. He returned the smile. Many deep-set wrinkles depicted his age, and the coating of dust on his beard indicated he had been walking for some time.

He touched his chest twice with his hands in rapid succession, and then immediately touched his upper legs two more times in a similar manner. He shook his head from side to side and uttered the word "*Efharisto*" before stepping around her and continuing on his way. She understood that he wanted to walk, and would later learn he had uttered the words, "Thank you."

All other individuals they passed that day were in vehicles—Nissans, Fiats, BMWs, Mercedeses, and others. Intermittent roadside stands offered fresh tangerines, oranges, tomatoes, and cucumbers for sale and tempted Claire to stop, but she did not. They were on a mission. There might be time for that later.

The time to switch drivers approached, and Claire took her turn behind the wheel. Shortly thereafter, she spotted a sign indicating eighty-three kilometers to Heraklion. The absorbing, low-speed drive had eaten up time like Pac-Man gobbling up pac-dots in the ever-popular arcade game. But soon now, they would reach their destination.

The cramped rental car rolled on, leaving behind another stone fortress, concentrated miles of white brick Mediterranean-style housing on the beach side, seemingly ever-present pink, yellow, and peach-colored buildings, petrol stations, more beach hotels, solar-paneled structures, remnants of a once-under-construction small stone house, hillside villages, a vista of foothills, additional scenic mountains in the far distance, many valleys, and other sections of the road that had been forged through steep red rock.

Claire and Guy munched on pistachios and shared a carton of no sugar-added, preservative free, peach-apple-orange-pineapple-grapefruit-passion fruit-mango-kiwi juice—goodies they'd bought when last filling up the rental car with petrol. The highway zigged and zagged and took them up, down, and around the curves of the coastal road.

Guy noticed Claire glancing periodically into the side-view mirror, at seemingly regular intervals, since she last took over the driving. Initially, he assumed she was merely exhibiting cautious behavior while driving in a foreign country, but now he wasn't so sure.

"Hey, what's so darn fascinating back there?" he asked.

"A lemon-colored Volkswagen Beetle, that's what," Claire said. "Three cars back, right-hand lane."

"And? What's so alluring about a yellow VW?"

"It's been on our tail for awhile, Guy, maybe all the way. Not sure. I noticed it a few miles back. It may be nothing, but it never passes us, and seems to stay just the same distance behind us. I've watched it speed up and slow down to maintain that exact position—three cars back, right-hand lane. Seems a bit strange, don't you think?

Looks like a single occupant in there."

"You should have said something, Claire," Guy said. He pulled down the visor in front of him, unhooked it, and maneuvered it just so, enabling him to observe the car in question through the mirror.

"I didn't want to send out a false alarm. I'm still not certain if the person's following us."

They agreed to stay alert and watch the yellow car behind them.

The next stretch of highway was scattered with numerous roadside umbrella-covered stands, mainly manned by elderly Cretan women, offering for sale netted bags filled with fresh oranges. They passed a milk truck and spotted several Marlboro and other American cigarette advertisement billboards and signage. Guy commented that cigarette smoking seemed to be strangely ubiquitous on an island so well known for its *healthy* inhabitants.

The drive continued to be hilly and curvy, and Claire was starting to feel fatigue set in, but she refused Guy's offer to take over the driving as they were close to arriving at their destination. "Attention: Danger" signs now appeared from time to time, when falling rock was a certain possibility, grabbing Claire's attention and snapping her back to alert status.

The lemon-colored Beetle remained behind them—three cars back, right-hand lane.

Claire rounded a bend on the motorway and all of a sudden slammed her foot on the brake pedal, swerving to avoid hitting a brown goat crossing the road directly in front of them. The animal was in no particular hurry that morning and gave no indication it noticed the near miss.

"That was close," she said, sighing with relief.

More terraced groves of olive trees dotted the hillsides and vivid purple azalea bushes colored the landscape like strokes from an artist's brush.

Crete, tucked amidst the three Old World continents of mainland Europe, Asia Minor, and Africa, drew many vacationers from Scandinavia, Germany, the Netherlands, and other European countries, but was an uncommon destination for Americans due to its great distance away.

They passed Lygaria Beach, and a white BMW shot past them in the opposite direction. Claire looked into the rearview mirror, as she had periodically continued to do, and, sure enough, the yellow VW was still a close distance behind them—third car back, right-hand lane. The car is consistent, she thought.

At last, they approached the city limits of Heraklion—a large city about the size of Athens, settled along the waterfront. A power plant appeared in their upcoming left-hand view and more new home construction became visible. Suddenly, cars began to speed past them, one after another, eager to be arriving at their destination. However, the lemon-colored Beetle did not race past their rental car like the others. Rather, it remained the exact same distance behind them.

Driving into the city, Claire and Guy searched for a hotel and found one that looked suitable in a good location on a main street. When the two investigators checked in, they informed the desk clerk they did not know specifically how long they would be staying in the beautiful city of Heraklion.

"This is not a problem for us," the clerk informed. "Just let us know each morning if you'll be staying the night."

"Could you pick a nice spot and make a dinner reservation for us for this evening?" Guy asked the hotel employee.

"Certainly, *Kyrie*. Time preference?"

Guy and Claire talked briefly and agreed on eight p.m.

"Around eight would be nice," Guy answered.

The clerk began to chuckle.

"Is something funny?" Claire asked.

"In this fair city, madam, we *never* eat before nine. Actually, between nine and eleven is typical."

They were stunned at his words but did not show it.

"Okay, then. Could we stretch it to eight-thirty?" Guy asked.

"Very well *Kyrie*, I'll see what I can do. But, please understand, you'll be the only two dining in the place at that early hour. It will be lonely."

They thanked him and went off to find their room, each pulling along a suitcase.

"When in Rome . . ." Claire started.

"When in Rome . . ." Guy repeated.

"Do as the Romans do," she completed their sentence.

As they walked across the lobby, the two investigators failed to notice a man sitting in that area observing their every move.

12

CLAIRE AND GUY entered the elevator and pressed the button for their floor, and the doors closed tightly in front of them. Without delay, the stranger in the lobby walked over to the check-in desk and registered as a hotel guest.

"My rental car. Where do I park it?" He spoke to the clerk in a dismissive and rude manner.

"Either on the street or in our underground lot, *Kyrie*."

"I'd prefer the lot,"

"Very well. Then I must register your car. Type?"

"Volkswagen."

"Model?"

"Beetle."

"Color?"

"Yellow. Do you believe it?" The man grunted. "They gave me a *bright yellow* car. Only one they had left, supposedly. Might as well be *flashing neon*!"

"Yes, *Kyrie*. Year?"

"It's a *rental*," he snapped. "How would I know what year it is?"

"No problem. License plate number?"

"I didn't memorize it," he retorted sarcastically. "And I left the paperwork inside the glove box."

"Okay. No problem, *Kyrie*. You can get that information to me later. You're all set then." The clerk smiled and handed the testy guest a temporary parking sticker, together with a diagram showing where to place the decal on the car's front windshield. "This will allow you free access to and from our lot at any hour through an automated gate."

The man grabbed the sticker and instructions from the desk clerk's hand.

"Length of stay, *Kyrie*?"

"I don't know that either. I'm here on business and I don't know how long it will take. I'll keep you posted. How about that?"

"Not a problem. How will you be paying for your room?"

"Cash. Cash each morning that I'll be staying the night. Fair enough?"

"Fair enough. Not a problem."

"I wouldn't think it would be." The man made a low, short guttural sound. He paid the hotel employee for a night's stay.

"Do you need assistance with your luggage?"

"Did I ask you for assistance? It's in my car and I'm quite capable of bringing it in when I so decide."

"Excuse me, but we always offer our assistance." *Rude American*, the desk clerk thought. He maintained a forced, insincere smile and handed the guest his room key. "It was my absolute pleasure to assist you, *Kyrie*."

The guest uttered a gruff noise that did not resemble a thank you. He picked up a complimentary newspaper from the counter and returned to his chair in the lobby. Once seated, he held a section of the paper in front of his face, purportedly reading.

THE SLEUTHS wasted no time unpacking. Both were anxious to begin searching for *the old woman who feeds the birds.* Minutes after entering their room, they left it. They rode the elevator down to the main floor and made their way across the expanse of the lobby, heading toward the hotel's front entrance. Before exiting, Guy stopped to ask questions of the concierge who sat behind the desk strategically placed near the main doors. The employee seemed eager to be helpful. He placed a city map in front of Guy and picked up a red pencil. Claire stepped closer to observe and listen.

"We are here," the concierge said. He drew a circle around the location of the hotel. He then proceeded to place Xs at interesting points of interest, recommended restaurants, and shopping areas, all within walking distance of the hotel.

"Thank you, kindly. This will be of great help to us," Guy said. Shaking the hand of the concierge, Guy passed the man a generous tip. Knowing full well he could be of great help to the sleuths down the road, he thought it was best to start things off on the right foot.

The man sitting in the lobby peered over the top of the newspaper, eyeing Claire and Guy with riveting interest. As the two investigators exited through the front doors, the stranger set his reading down and followed them out. He lagged an easy distance to the rear, appearing to be like any other tourist out to enjoy the city. He scratched his face, digging his nails in deeply. The fake facial hair itched like crazy. He was sure the adhesive he used to attach the pieces caused the irritation, and in the worst way he yearned to yank the beard and mustache off. But they served a purpose, and he had to put up with the discomfort associated with the disguise for the time being. After all, the price was small for being led directly to his quarry.

Guy grabbed Claire by the hand, and together they walked the few blocks to the Old City waterfront and harbor. At one point along the way, a densely packed crowd of people stood gathered on the street attracting the attention of all passersby. As the two approached the swarm of onlookers to take a closer look, they noticed a parked van amidst the throng. Its rear doors had been propped wide open and the driver stood next to the vehicle's open back. He held a properly dressed pig by its feet, offering the prepared and cleaned animal, ready to be cooked, to the highest bidder.

"I could have lived a long, happy life without seeing *that*," Claire said, walking quickly away from the scene.

"Ditto that," Guy said. "Not a pretty sight."

Cars, buses, taxis, local dogs and cats, pedestrians, motor scooters, dirt bikes, and motorcycles crammed the streets. Drivers did not signal turns; traffic lights did not exist to control the flow, and an abundance of horn honking filled the air. Strolling in and around the neighborhood, the sleuths saw a myriad of interesting retail shops, historic landmarks, an old lighthouse, and the remnants of a fortress wall that centuries ago protected Heraklion from its enemies. A large number of both locals and tourists scurried in and out of the retail shops, while others stood or sat outside in the open air, simply enjoying the day or viewing historic sights located within the area of the Old City waterfront.

Birds hopped, flew, and perched everywhere, chattering endlessly. Children and adults threw crumbs to the flamboyant feathered residents of the city, giggling at how quickly every morsel disappeared as soon as it hit the ground. As hard as Claire and Guy looked, they did not see a single woman who qualified as an *old* woman feeding the birds.

"Let's buy some bird food and sit over there on the bench," Claire suggested. "We can feed some of these creatures and keep our eyes peeled." She pointed to the only empty bench visible in the immediate area.

"We can do that," Guy said, clearly not thrilled at the prospect.

They made a purchase and sat down. Every few seconds, Claire tossed a handful of birdseed mix out into the air in front of them. As fast as she could fling the morsels, they vanished from the ground. Before long, more and more birds appeared, seemingly out of nowhere, and soon the flying vertebrates surrounded them. Like starving people, the creatures fought with one another and pounced on the limited mouthfuls of food.

"They're insatiable," Guy said. "And aggressive."

"Almost scary," Claire said. "Reminds me of Alfred Hitchcock's movie *The Birds*." She shuddered. "I still get the willies every time I think about that film."

"I remember it well," Guy said. He thought for a moment. "I know a man who has an abnormal and irrational fear of birds. Ornithophobia, I believe is the term for the condition. He can't be near them as they send him into a frenzied state. One flew into his villa years ago, and he locked himself in a room for hours, until someone came to his home, captured, and removed the poor thing. These phobias are no laughing matter."

Yards away, the man following the two investigators leaned up against a fence. He deeply inhaled the last drag of his cigarette, and tossed what was left of the thin cylinder of tobacco to the ground where it joined an ever-growing pile of others. Immediately, he lit up another, tapping his left foot on the ground in a constant motion. Patience was not his strong suit.

"I don't see an old woman feeding birds," Claire said.

"Nor do I. And I have been looking."

"Me too. She may not even come to this particular area. Who knows? We will find her, though. I know we will."

"I hope you're right," Guy said. "It was a long shot, and it didn't pan out. We may want to talk to some people in the stores and see what they know about her."

"My thoughts exactly. Let's go."

Claire dumped the remainder of the mix on the ground near the bench and leaped backward, out of the way, just as a mass of birds swept in with the speed of lightning to attack the pile.

"Now I remember vividly why *The Birds* gave me the utter creeps," she said.

They quickly walked away from the ferociously feeding fowls.

"Eerie. Just plain eerie," Claire said.

Guy grinned his famous grin. "Honey, it was *only* a movie. Remember that."

She drew in a deep breath and exhaled.

Just then, a hand grabbed her from behind and locked on tightly around her waist.

Claire jumped involuntarily, screamed, and spun around to see who gripped her.

A local boy with enormous dark eyes stood behind her. Taking notice of her uneasiness around the birds, he had thought it would be entertaining to get the attention of the pretty reddish blonde-haired tourist lady and to show her one of the innocent feathered beings up close. He let go of her arm and pointed to the bird he held in his other hand. He stroked its feathers to indicate the bird would not harm her. Several friends of the lad stood off in the distance, giggling.

Claire exhaled a sigh of relief. "You really startled me!" she said to the boy.

The lad gave her a quizzical look that indicated he did not understand her language. He released the bird and immediately pulled a miniature red accordion from his belt. He began to play the portable instrument. The melody he struck using the keys and buttons needed serious work, but she appreciated his effort nonetheless.

She clapped and smiled sweetly at the child. Reaching into her pocket, she brought out a handful of coins and extended them to the young performer. His face lit up like a Christmas tree, and he grabbed the money and ran off. Claire watched as he made his way over to a street vendor and purchased an ice cream treat.

"Let's get out of here," she said to Guy. "Away from the birds." *These birds,* she thought. *These birds*!

The two walked one long block.

"What a beautiful child," Claire said pensively. "Did you notice that amazing head of black curls? And those eyes? I'll never forget his face."

Ambling down several quaint stone streets, they absorbed the history of the ancient city like eager students. There were literally blocks of stores all around the Cathedral, and the investigators ended up walking in and out of many, searching for someone to talk with—someone who spoke English and might be able to shed some light on the whereabouts of the old woman. But conversations that day seemed short and unproductive.

They strolled farther. Passing a corner jewelry store, Claire stopped to glance into its elegant window displays. Designer pieces of jewelry, each bedecked with diamonds, emeralds, rubies, or sapphires filled the cases. This high-end jewelry store intrigued her.

"I think we should go inside," she suggested. All instincts within her screamed out in agreement.

Guy nodded.

They walked in and a friendly man greeted them using faultless English. "Come in, friends," he said. "I'm one of the owners. You are Americans?"

"Yes, we are," Claire said. She knew at once this man would be helpful to them. "Actually, we'd just like to browse, if that would be okay."

"Of course, my lady. Be my guest," the owner said. "Where in America do you come from?"

"Florida," Guy replied. "Miami."

The man's face illuminated. "I've been there several times on business. In fact, I've attended jewelry conventions all over the United States. I love America!" He smiled warmly. "May I please offer the two of you a taste of *tsikoudia . . . raki*?"

Oh, no, Claire thought. *Here we go again. More raki*!

"Why, that would be very nice," Guy said.

The owner poured three small glasses of the potent locally made liquor, filling each to the brim.

The strong odor made Claire twist her face into an ugly expression.

"You must down this in a single gulp," the man said. "It's tradition here in Crete."

Guy and the owner emptied the libation with one swallow, as Claire struggled to down a tiny sip. It burned like fire traveling down her esophagus. She coughed as tears came to her eyes.

The owner studied her. "You do not like, little lady?" His face and tone exuded a great love of life, and his eyes twinkled with amusement; yet his look was one of disbelief.

"Not much of a drinker," she said. "But many thanks just the same. I appreciate your generosity with us so very much. I'm sure Guy will be happy to finish mine, won't you, Guy?" She looked directly at him and passed her glass his way.

He drank it down. The jeweler refilled all three glasses and pushed two in Guy's direction. Thankfully, he knew not to empty the two or they would be refilled once again without delay, and he would be expected to down them both. Guy consumed part of one and stopped.

The jeweler chuckled. "It takes a bit of getting used to. But wait. Before you leave Crete, you'll be drinking several shots at a time, and develop a craving for it." He winked at Guy.

"We would love to know more about your amazing island," Claire said. She looked at the owner and turned the corners of her mouth up, exposing her front teeth.

Outside the store, off to one side, stood the stranger. He pretended to gaze at the many superb items portrayed so exquisitely in the window cases, but, in actuality, the jewelry did not interest him in the least. He narrowed his eyes as he looked past the elegant displays and into the store, watching the two investigators with hawk-eyed vision.

13

Still in Hania

PAIRED OFF TO cover more ground, each two-man vigilante team set out to discover the information the group needed to get on with their mission. They all wanted to get the job done and travel home as soon as possible. Tom Lastner, partnered with Scott Harriman, headed in one direction, and Kyle Teddy, partnered with Jack Manning, walked off in the opposite direction.

LASTNER AND Harriman made their way into a men's clothier, feigning interest in purchasing new clothing. In-between trying on suits, slacks, and shirts, Scott Harriman took the lead in interrogating the salesman so subtly that he never knew an agenda was in play. But as Harriman's attempts to obtain useful information failed, Judge Lastner broke in and took over the questioning. With the grace of a sledgehammer, he peppered the unassuming young man with questions, demanding answers. And when the intimidated salesperson hesitated with his responses, Lastner became overtly irritated. Before long, the unwitting store employee stopped talking altogether and refused to speak another word.

As the men exited the shop, they were no closer to pinning down their target than when they had entered. Without purchasing a single item, and after the heavy interrogation, all the two had managed to accomplish was offending the modest store clerk.

Thankfully, many retail establishments and most restaurants had English-speaking personnel, and language rarely presented itself as a barrier.

The two strolled down the street purposefully and entered another clothing store, immediately striking up a conversation with the proprietor and capturing him in the net of friendly banter. After minutes of necessary small talk, Tom Lastner got to the meat of the chitchat.

"Ever heard of the Zenonakis clan?" he asked the unsuspecting man.

"Who hasn't?" the owner responded.

"Know any of them personally?" Lastner continued.

"Who wants to know?"

"We do. That's who." He forced a disingenuous grin.

The man looked at Tom Lastner for a long minute and then turned away. He began re-folding shirts on a front display table. "Can't say that I do," he replied, feeling Lastner's eyes drilling into his back.

"Oh, really?" Lastner kept on him.

"Told you. I don't know any of them."

"Not even *George*?"

"Especially not George. Now, if there is nothing further … I have some boxes in the back that require my attention. If you will excuse me."

Another dead end had just confronted the inquisitive duo. Judge Lastner certainly did possess the magic to turn people off. Continuing on down the street, Scott looked over at his comrade.

"Next time, Tom, let me handle all of the questioning, will you buddy? I work with people all the time—buyers and sellers alike who need to be coddled and babied like newborns. Let me try my hand with the next person, will you? I'm very good at what I do. So don't rush me. It may take a little more time than what you expect, but I'll get us to our destination in one piece."

Tom eyed him with cautious distrust. "You're not criticizing me, are you Harriman?"

"Certainly not," he replied. "But let me have a go at it next time, will you? Don't break in and take over, even if you're tempted."

"Agreed, Harriman. The next dupe is all yours. Let's see how you do."

Tom Lastner was a narcissist, pure and simple. He held a grandiose opinion of himself. Shallow and haughty, he viewed himself to be the best of the best. Truthfully, however, he was not intellectually the brightest of all bulbs, and he had to work harder than his peers to graduate from law school. His gift of manipulation, though, was genius. He yearned for power and truly cared for no one but himself. Lacking conscience, due to his early chaotic childhood, he would do anything to get his way. And he needed the adulation of Scotty Harriman, so he didn't want to push the man too far. Therefore, he remained quiet, allowing Harriman to fail at his quest.

Then, Lastner reasoned, Harriman would beg the judge to take over.

The pair entered a third retailer on the same street—a lady who created and manufactured custom pieces of jewelry. She looked up and smiled somewhat when they entered her establishment.

"May I offer the two of you some *raki*?"

She placed three undersized paper cups on the countertop and slowly filled each with the clear liquid.

"Drink up!" she demanded, grabbing one herself. "You must drink in one gulp."

They accepted graciously, each downing the libation without delay. Even though it was not yet noon, the liquid went down smoothly, burning all the way.

"You like?" she asked.

"We like," they said in unison.

She refilled all three cups, and seconds later those also sat empty.

"Strong stuff," Tom Lastner said. He rocked from side to side.

"It tortures my innards in such a good way," Scott Harriman said.

All three laughed aloud as she refilled the cups a third time. Again, all of them downed the libation.

The woman kept refilling the cups until even Harriman felt the effects of the powerful drink.

Scott started in with the now-routine series of meaningless questions, followed by the serious ones that mattered.

"You know the Zenonakis family?" Scott asked the woman. His words were slightly slurred.

Her gaze turned to a venomous glare. "Who's asking? And *why*?" she hissed.

"We're looking for George Zenonakis. Can you kindly point us in the right direction?" He wore the foolish grin of a sot.

"What is this all about?" she asked. It seemed the *raki* had not affected her in the slightest. "You're asking me for information about a man our local police fear greatly? A man our own law enforcement will not go near?" She bit her bottom lip. "A whole group of you in town all looking for the same man? What are you up to?"

"I don't understand," Scott said. "Please tell us what you mean."

"Well, there were two others of you in here a day or two ago."

All Harriman really took in was that two others asked her the same questions before he did. He looked over at his partner. Tom Lastner did his best to stand up straight, but finally gave in to the urge and leaned his upper body over onto the counter, drunk from the *raki*. He braced himself up on an elbow.

"Huh? Today?" Harriman stared at the woman. He wavered on his feet. He assumed Kyle Teddy and Jack Manning had made their way to the same shop earlier that day.

"No. I said, *yesterday*," she asserted, standing firm, "or the day before. I can't recall which day it was."

"Two men, you said?" Harriman asked.

"No, I did not say that. One was a man, one was a woman."

"Really? I wonder …" He grabbed the edge of the counter to balance himself. He liked this *raki* drink. "Americans, you say?"

"Yes. Attractive couple, they were. But they also asked too many questions, just like you," she snapped. "You're all on my nerves."

"What'd they look like?" Scott asked, persisting in his questioning. "This American couple?"

Tom stood by, obediently silent, now laying his head on the counter and closing his eyes.

She stared at them both and did not answer right away. Scott gave her a decidedly quirky grin, and Tom tried to open his eyes but to no avail.

"What's in that alkohaul?" Tom managed to get out without opening his eyes.

"Who are you people, anyway, and what's in it for me?" the

woman asked, defiantly.

"Let's just say, we're the *good* guys in the *white* hats," Scott Harriman said. He placed the equivalent of twenty dollars in euros on the counter.

She turned her head. "Not interested."

"Still not talking?" Tom Lastner asked. His eyes opened narrowly. He reached into his pocket for euros and set a wad of the paper money in front of the owner. "That's all we're good for. Now, talk. Please."

She grabbed the money and counted it silently. Together, it totaled just over the equivalent of one hundred U.S. dollars. She slipped the money under the counter. "Double it and we're in business," she said.

Reluctantly, Tom complied with her request. Still crunched over the counter from his waist up, he reached for his wallet. He glanced over at Harriman. "Buddy, pull out another hundred worth of euros for the nice lady, will you?" What choice did they have? They needed this information in the worst way. And, as usual, money did the talking.

"She was pretty," the lady said. "Real pretty. Fair-colored hair. In her thirties, I'm guessing. The man was not bad to look at, either. Graying hair, husky build, maybe in his forties. Decent people, real decent . . . but exceedingly nosy."

"What did you tell them? What can you tell *us* about the Zenonakis family? Where can we find them?" Scott asked.

The lady leered at them.

"I would say you got your money's worth out of me today," she said. "And the information I gave you is all you will ever get out of me. Don't know why you all want to know about that family anyway. No good, they are. No good."

She poured herself another cup of the intoxicating liquor, drank it down, and turned away from them.

"That's it? That's what two hundred freaking dollars in euros buys us?" Lastner grumbled.

"That's it," the woman said.

Scott thanked the lady for the information and the *raki*—but not in that order. He felt a great buzz. He grabbed Lastner by an arm, and together they stumbled from the store.

"Who the hell do you think the American couple is?" Harriman asked Lastner.

"Anybody's guess," Lastner said. "But there is one thing we know for certain. Other Americans are here searching for that nogoodnik, sonofabitch, George Zenonakis. We need to find him first. And the American couple can't know that the four of us are here. If the two of them get in our way, you know what needs to happen."

Scott Harriman nodded. He walked Lastner to an outdoor café and helped him into a chair at an empty table. As soon as Scott sat down, a server approached.

"Bring my friend a strong pot of Greek coffee, will you please?" Scott asked.

"And for you, *Kyrie*?" the waiter asked.

"Nothing for me. I'm just fine," Harriman replied. He was enjoying his drunken state too much to diminish it.

KYLE TEDDY and Jack Manning approached Kotzabazi Square. In front of its gated entrance stood a mulberry tree, *a cursed tree*. They read the information posted at the sight and learned that the Turks, when in control, hung Cretan freedom fighters from its branches as an example of what would happen to insurgents. It was a historic time filled with violence.

On they went to the square of the new shops, passing sporadic busts of freedom fighters as they walked. A mosaic showing an erotic episode between Poseidon (the ancient Greek god of the sea—believed to have the power to cause earthquakes) and the nymph, Amymoni, dating from the Hellenistic Period, caught the eye of Manning and Teddy. For minutes, the two stood gazing at its seductive charm.

That morning the two questioned individuals in many boutiques and shops, trying desperately to learn the location of the Zenonakis family so they could move in, make the hit, and board a plane to travel home. But all efforts proved fruitless. Like Lastner and Harriman, they also found that whenever they raised the question of the whereabouts of one George Zenonakis, mouths closed tightly. It had become the patently predictable pattern.

Manning pulled out his cell phone and called Lastner to check in. When Tom answered, he told Manning to come with Teddy to the café. Lastner passed the phone to Harriman who gave Manning the address. Harriman then described the location, explaining to the best of his ability the path he and Lastner had taken to get there.

OVER LUNCH, the foursome discussed the lack of useful information gleaned by either team that morning. Lastner had sobered up to the point that neither Teddy nor Manning suspected his earlier condition.

"We found out one thing," Tom Lastner informed Teddy and Manning. "We've got trouble. There are more sharks circling in the water . . . and they're hungry."

14

GEORGE ZENONAKIS COULD not rest or relax. His demeanor was that of a fidgety, agitated man, shrouded by mental uneasiness. He sensed trouble coming his way and his instinct toward self-preservation had kicked into high gear. Armed and dangerous, he possessed a mindset of kill or be killed. His hands shook, a little at first, and then wildly. He held them together and exerted pressure to stop them from trembling. Yet when he let up, the rapid side-to-side movements resumed in a forceful manner. He interlocked his fingers and gripped tightly.

Crete was his birthplace and homeland, and he knew the island blindfolded, including most all of the back trails leading to the most remote places on the island. The Cretans were his people—his family—and regardless of the criminal activities he partook in elsewhere in the world, he believed he could always return home and convince his relatives that he was in the right. At least, he relied on this supposition. His relatives would protect him at any cost, and see things his way, as in the past. He was sure of it. So sure.

The Zenonakis family wielded both money and power. No one had ever objected to anything the family had done—be it right or wrong, legal or bordering on the illegal. The family had been a mighty force within Cretan society, contributing large sums of money to beautify the island through the creation of parks, playgrounds, and museums, and also through the building of schools and historical monuments. And with the generosity came privileges. The family asked for and received insulation from the local police. As a result, Cretan police officers and other law enforcement officials refused to cite any member of the infamous family with as much as a traffic ticket.

For the first time, however, things seemed a bit different here in Crete. Grandfather Papou had changed. Always and forever in George's corner in the past, Nikos no longer seemed to be there. And although George refused to verbalize it, that fact bothered him immensely.

Strange thoughts had possessed George's mind since he had returned to his homeland, and unpleasant sensations had racked his body with previously unfelt physical pain. He could not seem to shake the feeling of impending doom creeping up on him from all directions. Were things really closing in on him, or was he just imagining it? Was his time running out? Did he suffer from the same ailment that took his father's life?

Upon walking into the great room, he thought he heard the creak of a floorboard behind him. Jerking his head to one side, he looked back over his shoulder, convinced beyond a doubt that someone had entered the room behind him. "Who is it?" he roared. "Who's there?"

Silence clanged in the empty room.

George moved unsteadily, walking carefully so as not to fall. He made his way to a large sofa and dropped into it. He fell into a fitful sleep.

Two hours later, he awoke with a start. He sauntered into the den and fell into the massive black leather chair sitting behind the colossal desk. His mood was pensive, prompting deep, reflective thought. He lit up an unfiltered Camel cigarette and smoked it to the end, savoring every puff. Sweating profusely, he reached under the desk and pushed a red button. Seconds later, two bodyguards appeared, dressed in black from head to toe.

"At your service, *Kyrie*," they uttered in unison.

"Sit. Please," George said.

Obediently, the duo walked to the chairs in front of the desk and took a seat. Like Dobermans awaiting the next command, both men stared unblinkingly at their master. George spoke in Greek to the guards.

A large fabric chair, facing the only window in the rear of the room, quietly concealed the silhouette of a gaunt, elderly man. Hiding in plain sight, Nikos absorbed the ensuing conversation.

"Without giving you specifics, I order you today to be on highest alert at all times," George Zenonakis began. His voice was cold and deadly. "Be on the lookout twenty-four seven. Something is about to play itself out, and although I cannot predict exactly what will happen, I want you to watch my back every second, every minute, and every hour of the day, round the clock, in my waking moments and when I sleep." He paused and took in another deep breath. "I fear for my life." His eyes gushed fury. "Executioners are coming to get me. I can smell them. They lie in wait to kill me." He paused again. "I can feel them closing in." He eyed the guards carefully. "I'm doubling your salary. Keep me alive!" he boomed. "Use any means you have at your disposal to accomplish this goal—any means and any weapons. Blow them away when they get within range." His brown eyes turned black and burned into them. The message rang loud and clear.

Like assembly-line automatons, both protectors nodded in unison.

"I will stay secluded here until this thing blows over," George said. "I'll expect one of you to go for supplies on an as-needed basis, while the other stands guard. I am never, at any time, to be left alone. Is that understood? Never!"

Again, robotically, the men bobbed their heads in synchronized agreement.

THE FOLLOWING morning, George Zenonakis picked up the phone and made a call. An hour later, one of the bodyguards announced to George that a gentleman named Ambrose had arrived to see him.

"Yes. Yes. I am expecting him. Send him in. Send him in," George commanded.

The visitor, toting a sleek, black, Zero Halliburton carbon fiber attaché case, was led to the study where George sat in the large and heavy leather chair behind the desk. When Ambrose entered the room, George stood and extended his hand, greeting the man cordially and warmly.

"Close the door behind you on your way out," George instructed the bodyguard. "Please, Ambrose, take a seat." George motioned to the chair strategically placed across from him on the opposite side of the desk.

"I haven't seen you in many, many years, Mr. George. What brings you back to Crete?" Ambrose asked. A look of extraordinary curiosity owned his face.

"Business, Ambrose. Business."

"What is it that I can do for you this time?" the visitor queried.

George passed him a small packet.

"Look for yourself."

The man carefully opened the packaging and poured its contents into the palm of his left hand. "Ooh. Nice. Quite remarkable, I would say." He examined the contents carefully.

"I want top dollar. Do you understand?" George asked. "*Top dollar.*"

"Of course. You should expect nothing less. Haven't I always treated you right, Mr. George?"

"That's why I continue to do business with you, Ambrose. If you ever cross me, it will be your first and last time."

A wave of wickedness wafted across the face of George Zenonakis, sending an upsurge of queasiness through Ambrose. He squirmed uncomfortably in his seat, trying desperately to get through the meeting.

"I want this transaction taken care of as quickly as possible," George said.

"Of course, Mr. George. Of course."

Ambrose returned the contents to its original packaging and with caution placed it inside a zippered compartment in his elegant briefcase.

The two stood. The meeting concluded with another solid handshake. When Ambrose attempted to pull his hand away, George held on tightly, forcing his visitor to look him squarely in the eyes.

"Don't disappoint me, Ambrose. It would not be a wise thing to do."

Ambrose shuddered internally, repulsed by the obvious threat. "I will contact you as soon as I've secured a deal, Mr. George."

"Make it soon, Ambrose. Make it happen."

George buzzed for a bodyguard, and his visitor was escorted from the room.

GRANDFATHER NIKOS had heard it all. Comfortably seated on the other side of the wall behind the desk chair, he sat in a secret passageway listening curiously to the entire conversation between George and Ambrose. During the construction of the mansion, generations earlier, Nikos's own grandfather had incorporated the hidden corridors into the blueprints. Now known only to Nikos, the existence of the mysterious narrow corridors and their concealed entrances had never been divulged to George. Simple in nature, and originally created to be a hiding place from invading enemies, the passageways enabled Nikos to travel anywhere he wanted throughout the entire three-story dwelling without being seen, heard, or detected. And his ability to make himself invisible had come in handy on many occasions—today being one of them.

The private hideaway was stockpiled with weapons, ammunition, water, and foodstuffs, and provided him the luxury and safety of remaining out of sight for short or long periods of time, as situations dictated. The absence of a sufficient air supply was the only thing that could present a problem on long stints inside the hidden area, but square holes to the outside could be accessed by pulling out plugs, when necessary, to create cross-ventilation. Nikos's grandfather had thought of everything.

Nikos scanned his secret arsenal of pistols and revolvers, a stash highly enviable to any handgun aficionado. Adding to the collection over the many years, he now owned enough weaponry to take on the destruction of an army or a city single-handedly, if so inclined. But he was not. Guns offered him nothing more than a feeling of security—protection from a world gone mad ... and from a grandson with a fragile mental state. Nikos had never planned to use any of his weapons to maim, kill, or destroy, unless in self-defense. Not until now.

A wide variety of handguns made up his hidden cache of arms—9mm semiautomatic Glocks, Smith & Wesson K-frames, .38 caliber revolvers, Nighthawk custom .45 caliber 1911-style pistols, and Wilson Combat .45 caliber handguns—all made to his specifications and smuggled in from the United States or other countries. Further, he had collected Italian-made .40 caliber Beretta PX4 Storm Type F pistols and Israeli manufactured Desert Eagle handguns, both .44 and .357 Magnum varieties, and even one .45 caliber Israeli Barak pistol, a newly designed metal and polymer high-performance weapon.

Nikos had also obtained an endless supply of ammunition for each weapon, enough to last a lifetime, presumably. He practiced shooting each type of firearm monthly; at least he had until George so unexpectedly showed up on his doorstep. One thing Nikos knew for certain: Under no circumstances did he want his grandson to discover the concealed passageways or his arms collection.

One by one, Nikos carefully disassembled each firearm. He cleaned, lightly oiled, and reassembled every piece using practiced fingers. The task took several hours. These were his babies, and he pampered the lot.

ANOTHER DAY passed and George Zenonakis continued to be plagued by repeated and nagging thoughts portending his imminent demise. He dropped his head to the desk and grabbed it with both hands, pushing hard on the temple areas, attempting to stop the sudden onslaught of the mental pictures of his grandfather peering down at George's dead body neatly tucked inside an open casket.

He was certain the prescription the doctor had given him for anxiety was responsible for these wild images. Grabbing his medicine, he hurled it violently into a wall. The container burst open and pills flew everywhere. Never again would he swallow one.

George wanted to crawl out of his body to escape the torment so vividly depicted in his nighttime dreams, and now in his daydreams, as well. Never had he felt so utterly vulnerable. Whether awake or asleep, he found no relief, and he couldn't handle it much longer.

15

APPROACHING A LEATHER goods store, the potential purchaser sauntered in and looked around, scanning the merchandise quickly. Spotting a showcase that displayed a wide variety of knives and leather, wooden, and other ornate sheaths, the customer walked over to it and leaned in to take a closer look. Upon scrutinizing the multiplicity of choices with obvious interest, an English-speaking clerk approached to offer assistance.

The shopper pointed to three different models.

"Would you like to see them up close?" the salesclerk asked. "Our knives are known for their pleasing-to-the-eye decorations. Each one is quite durable and made from a single piece of steel. Many of our knife covers are made of authentic animal horn."

The consumer nodded and again pointed to the three specific pieces.

"Ah, exquisite taste. You must be a connoisseur, or a collector, I would guess?"

The shopper quietly grunted.

"Please, take your time. Do you own a collection of these special and beautiful pieces?" the salesman persisted.

Another low and guttural sound emanated from the consumer's mouth. Interested only in examining each piece and making a decision on which one to purchase, the customer clearly found the small talk of the clerk an annoyance.

"Do you own others of this quality?" the salesman asked, unable to be put off.

"Enough talk!" The voice was hoarse and irritable.

"Very well then." The clerk set the three knives down on the countertop. "Let me know when and if I can be of help in any way." The inflections in his voice sent the unmistakable message that he was insulted by the extremely ill manners flung toward him. Taking four steps away, the clerk turned and looked back. It was then that he noticed the hands examining the knives. Certain of the fingers were bent and twisted in a way he had never seen before. The sight froze in his mind, and he would not soon forget it.

Holding each knife, one at a time, in misshapen hands, the buyer assessed the weight of every blade and also determined the comfort level of each grip. Finally, a selection could be made. Slapping cash on the counter, the customer pointed to the carefully chosen knife. The salesman wrapped it in tissue and placed it in a bag. The purchaser tucked the parcel under one arm and walked out.

The flat, wide, seven-inch metal blade would do the job nicely. Meandering down the street, the buyer imagined the act in great detail. The tables would soon turn, and the poison of the conscienceless criminal would at last be detoxified.

16

AFTER SPENDING THE remainder of the day unsuccessfully pursuing information on their target, the two-man vigilante teams met up in the lobby of the hotel. Harriman suggested they discuss their failed strategy over a cocktail, and the others agreed. The foursome walked into the lobby lounge and spent quality time commiserating about the unproductiveness of the day. Despite all the efforts of the quartet, not a single solid clue had surfaced to help them pinpoint the whereabouts of the infamous George Zenonakis. Rather, they had been confronted with very bad news. Other Americans were on the island searching out their mark.

Tom Lastner's mind wandered.

What had the other Americans learned? Who were they? How long had they been in Crete? What were they doing on the island? These questions without answers tormented Lastner the most.

Other people searching for the man they hunted could only result in serious problems. Who would reach him first? He knew that the couple had already questioned one Cretan that he and Harriman had paid to obtain information. Had they also previously questioned others that his team had interrogated? Was this the very reason he and his men met with one brick wall after another? This situation was not acceptable. Lastner was not about to let this American couple nix the plan of the vigilantes for retribution. Nothing was going to stop what George Zenonakis had coming to him. If the team could locate the meddlesome couple, they would have to meet with an unforeseen tragedy of some kind. It was as simple as that. In the meantime, Lastner had to come up with a quick plan to ensure that he and his men would locate George Zenonakis first. Lastner downed his drink hastily and shared his concerns with the others. After he'd finished, he made a suggestion.

"We should go have a nice dinner this evening. Tomorrow, we will need to hit it harder," Judge Lastner said. "I don't want to drag this thing out longer than we have to. We need to get it done." His eyes connected with Teddy, Manning, and Harriman, in that order. "Tomorrow's the day, men. Whatever we have to do, it happens tomorrow. *Comprendez*?"

"That may be wishful thinking," Teddy said.

Manning and Harriman nodded in agreement.

"The negative thinking stops now, comrades!" Tom boomed. "When I say it will happen *tomorrow*, I mean just that. No more jabberwocky."

Scott Harriman proposed a toast. "To tomorrow, then."

"To tomorrow," Manning chimed in.

"Tomorrow," Teddy added, lacking vigor.

"Tomorrow, it is," Lastner repeated.

They clinked glasses all around.

Harriman downed his and ordered a refill.

Lastner got up and walked to the front desk. He asked the clerk on duty for a suggestion for dinner. The employee recommended a popular Greek restaurant, two blocks away. "It's an easy walk," he said. "I'll phone ahead and let them know the four of you are on the way."

The men ambled along the cobbled streets to the eating establishment, and the hostess seated them at an outdoor table. They ate delicious food, drank sweet Cretan wine, and had a merry time. After all, tomorrow was another day.

GEORGE ZENONAKIS shook his head several times in rapid succession, trying desperately to clear the fogginess that had moved into the space between his ears. Why was his thinking so cloudy? He felt in discomfort and bloated, and his face looked puffy when he passed a mirror and looked at his reflection. Concentrating on anything seemed a difficult task. Usually strong and bullish, he now felt physically weak and worthless. Why did he suddenly seem so thoroughly disoriented? So uncertain? What was happening? He shook his head again, forcefully. The confusion in his head needed to find another place to reside.

A knock at the bedroom door startled him.

"Yes? Who is it?" George called out.

It was one of his bodyguards announcing that Ambrose had returned to see him.

"Bring him to the study," George commanded. "I will meet him there momentarily."

George walked unsteadily toward the meeting room, gripping the hall walls when necessary for balance, and sat down in the immense chair behind the desk. I am in control, he told himself. I am in control.

One minute later, the bodyguard appeared with Ambrose and announced him.

"Thank you," George said. "Please close the door on your way out." He nodded to the guard.

The door clicked closed, and George shot a hurried but penetrating glance in the direction of Ambrose. Curiosity had the best of George, and he needed answers.

"Sit down, Ambrose."

"Thank you, Mr. George." He sat in the chair across the desk from George.

"Well?" George asked. "You have kept me in great suspense, Ambrose."

"You'll be pleased, Mr. George." Ambrose smiled.

"Tell me, Ambrose. Do not delay."

"A magnificent ruby is uncommonly rare; they are so few and far between, in fact, that scarcely any buyers, or jewelers for that matter, have ever come across one," Ambrose began. He paused to make sure he had the full attention of George.

"Go on," George commanded. "Do not keep me on edge."

"Fluorescence is the explanation."

"*Fluorescence*?" George asked.

"Yes. The unforgettable red color in a ruby is attributable to trace amounts of chromium—an *impurity* that causes a ruby to *fluoresce*, or glow brightly, when exposed to sunlight or ultraviolet light. And that fluorescence is what makes *Burmese* rubies, in particular—meaning those found in Burma—shine with such an amazing red brilliance. Fact is, Burmese rubies contain more chromium than most rubies found anywhere else on earth. They simply have more fluorescence."

"Your *point*?" George demanded. "That is, if you *have* one." He slammed his fist down on the desk.

"Indeed I do," Ambrose said, maintaining his composure. "Burmese rubies seem to have an extraordinary appeal to buyers, despite—or maybe because of—the limited quantity of them in existence. There is an almost total reliance on smuggling of such stones to get them to the outside world. And buyers, especially collectors, always want what is not easy to find. It boils down to a game, I guess, of who can take possession of the world's rarest gems the most quickly, if you understand my drift. . . ."

"I get it. Now, about . . ."

"Mr. George," Ambrose broke in. "You need to hear me out and understand what I'm telling you. Please bear with me."

"Never interrupt me when I'm speaking!" George raged. The chilling iciness in his voice shot a shiver down his visitor's spine. "I will remind you of this only once." He leveled his eyes on the now shaking man. "Go on."

Ambrose swallowed with difficulty. "Very well, Mr. George. When two rubies of comparable size and quality are presented to a potential buyer, it's almost a guarantee that the ruby from Burma will bring twice the price of the other."

"My ruby is in the Burmese category," George declared. "I am well aware of that. You're telling me nothing I do not already know."

Ambrose waited for George to finish. "Yes, Mr. George, it is of the Burmese ilk. But I doubt if you know the particular history of your stone."

"I know what it cost me. A small fortune."

"I can only guess what you paid for it, Mr. George. You see, rubies are usually considered the most expensive of all gemstones—the *crème de la crème,* so to speak. And gemstones are difficult to trace. Therefore, buying and selling them on the black market is common."

"And? And? And?" George pounded his fist onto the desk a

second time. "Ambrose, what did you do for me? Get to the damned point before I lose my fucking mind."

Trying not to show his extreme anxiety with the situation, Ambrose inconspicuously sat on his trembling hands. His poker face refused to reveal his unease to George, and the perspiration soaking the underarms of his shirt stayed hidden by his black suit jacket. Whenever he found himself in leathery situations, he had learned never to let his trepidation show—at least not on the surface.

"Mr. George, your ruby is close to a 16-carat *Mogok* beauty. Mogok rubies come from a specific area in northern Burma and are the most sought after rubies in the world. And the color of your precious stone—*Pigeon's Blood Red*—is also *highly* favorable.

"As the story goes, a safe deposit box in New York held this very gem for over twenty years. Then, surprisingly, it showed up at an auction years ago, when its sales price created quite a hullabaloo." He stopped and cleared his throat. "You see, it sold for *$3,600,000*—making its over-a-quarter-million-dollars-per-carat price the highest price per carat *ever* paid for a ruby."

George looked on with an absence of emotion.

"After the purchase, rumor had it the prized stone was set in a ring, in England, yet the exact location of the ring was kept a secret. Until now, that is. I do not know how you came upon it, Mr. George, and I do not want to know."

"How much, Ambrose? Talk money to me," George said, brusquely. If he was moved in the least by the astounding information Ambrose had just proffered, he did not show it. "How much? What's the bottom line? What price did you get for me? Impress me, dammit!"

"I have been offered a flat *five million dollars* for your extraordinary gem. To be wired to an account of your choosing, once you provide the wiring instructions and account number," Ambrose said without flinching. He appeared quite proud of himself for obtaining such a lucrative offer. "The offer stands open for one day and one day only. If you fail to respond within twenty-four hours, the offer will be withdrawn."

"Five million big ones, eh?" George asked. A look of selfish desire became visible on his face as he studied Ambrose and contemplated the information he had just relayed.

Out of the blue, George thought he heard a noise, a squeak of some kind, coming from behind the desk chair, actually from behind the wall behind his desk chair, where he sat. He swung around, madly, and found himself staring at a bare wall. He shook his head to clear it. Then he turned back to face Ambrose. "Make the deal. Do it!" He jotted down transfer instructions.

"Anything wrong, Mr. George?" Ambrose asked.

"Ghosts, Ambrose. Just ghosts. Make the deal," he ordered.

They shook on it, and George summoned a bodyguard to escort Ambrose to the mansion's front doors.

INSIDE THE office wall, secreted away in his special hiding place, Grandfather Nikos also shook his head—but for a different reason. He had heard the entire conversation between George and Ambrose through the thin wall. At last he knew what George had been hiding from him, or at least a good part of it. And now he better understood the earlier conversation his grandson had had with the bodyguards. The best evidence of wrongdoing is a guilty man's fear of being caught, Nikos thought. And George seemed terrified of that possibility. The cards were stacking up against his grandson every day, and the only available remedy seemed more and more clear.

GEORGE DAYDREAMED. He thought of himself as rather clever. After all, look what he'd accomplished this time with little or no effort. To him, gems equaled portable, concentrated wealth. Paper—like stocks, bonds, and money, and even real estate for that matter, could lose its value or even become totally worthless. But never superior gems.

He smiled a sly smile. Could anyone do things better than he?

He had entered the plastics factory before the explosion that night, with a simple plan to first blast open the vault and, with the help of his goons, grab the money before detonating the explosives. But a problem had surfaced. He'd walked in on a man working late into the early morning hours, and he'd had to take care of the unfortunate obstacle that had surfaced. With leather-gloved hands, he'd pulled a high-carbon steel piano wire from his pants pocket and silently snuck up behind the unsuspecting worker, catching him totally unaware. The silly man had fought valiantly for his life as he struggled to rid the strangulation wire from his throat, but George had finished him off with ease. After all, George had always had superhuman strength, and that night the job had been easily achieved.

George had not planned on the murder, but the unforeseen problem had called for an immediate resolution. Would he have opted for that complication? Certainly not. But how could he have changed what he had to do? To let the poor man go, to leave an eyewitness to the crime, in all probability would have resulted in a lengthy prison term for George. The matter was behind him now; it was time to dismiss thoughts of the murder from his mind.

Transportation of the money taken from the safe—four million dollars—had actually been the bigger problem he had encountered that night. A million in single dollar bills amounted to almost one ton of money, and took up approximately forty-two cubic feet of space. Thankfully, the vault had been loaded with hundred dollar bills. Yet it had still taken time and effort to load it all up. He had seen to it that his men trucked away the bundles of cash before he'd detonated the explosives.

Afterward, George had been left with the dilemma of coming up with a way to condense the pickings—to be able to travel home to Crete with the ill-gotten gains, and, brilliantly, he'd devised a plan to buy gems with all of it. His associate in the States had then come up with this incredible *Mogok* ruby, a 15.97-carat stone, available at the purchase price of four million dollars, a single piece weighing in at a mere eighth of an ounce, just slightly more than the weight of one copper penny. It was ingenious!

George had jumped at the opportunity. And now? Now he'd make another cool million dollars to boot on the re-sale of the handsome red stone. Could life get any better? Without warning, his mind and eyesight clouded again. He could no longer focus on his euphoric daydream. His head fell back on his chair, and he closed his eyes. A vision of a man struggling for his life, a piano wire being pulled tightly around his neck, cutting into his windpipe, replayed one time after another in George's mind. But in his vision, the victim was not the young Mr. Otto. It was George himself.

The murder he had committed would torment him to his death.

17

CLAIRE CASWELL AND Gaston Lombard shared instant rapport with Kostas Michaelakis, the owner of the exquisite jewelry store located in the Plaka—the center of the grand shopping area in Heraklion. After the three exchanged quick introductions, Kostas explained that ancestors in his father's lineage had established the jewelry business over one hundred years earlier.

Just then, a man walked onto the showroom floor from a back office. Kostas introduced him as Panos, his brother and business partner. While Kostas spoke fluent English as a second language, Panos spoke only Greek, but understood a limited amount of English. Nevertheless, he stood and listened to the ongoing conversation between Kostas and the friendly American couple. And although he could not join in without Kostas acting as interpreter, he did a lot of nodding, indicating he understood the gist of the informal exchange of words between those speaking English.

Kostas showed interest in anything and everything about the United States of America. Many thought-provoking questions poured out of him regarding the country he found so fascinating, and Claire or Guy answered every one.

In a short time, it became evident by the frequent grins on the faces of the brothers that they genuinely enjoyed visiting with Claire and Guy. No other customers were shopping in the store at that time, and the sleuths hoped for an opening to question the owners about the decidedly slippery George Zenonakis. However, the timing did not prove to be right. It was too early in the relationship, and inquisitive probing at this point would have put a stopper in the spigot. They knew that scenario all too well.

Kostas moved to refill the cups of *raki,* and Claire put her hand over hers. She smiled kindly and shook her head from side to side. Kostas uttered something to Panos in Greek, and the two men laughed wholeheartedly. Claire was certain Kostas had probably called her a wimp or a lightweight, but it made no difference to her. Jovial stories were exchanged over the next hour, and a friendship began to blossom.

Guy's eyes wandered to a nearby glass showcase displaying several styles of handcrafted money clips, and zeroed in on one in particular.

"Can you make that one in *rose* gold?" he inquired. He pointed to a yellow gold piece.

"This one here?" Kostas asked. He pulled it from the case and examined it closely. "In *pink* gold?"

"Yes. May I take a closer look?" Guy asked.

"Of course," Kostas said. He handed the clip to Guy. "Take your time."

It took Guy about ten seconds to make up his mind. "I like it. Is it possible for you to make one just like this in rose gold?" he repeated.

Kostas conversed with Panos in Greek. Panos was the goldsmith of the two, and he would be the one to answer the question. Excitement appeared in the eyes of both brothers.

"We've not done that before, but, yes, I think we can make it for you," Kostas said. "And personally, I think it will look rather nice in pink gold."

They bartered over price until a compromise was reached, and Kostas informed Guy it would be ready around five p.m. the following day. Guy paid him the agreed upon amount in euros.

Lively conversation continued, and Kostas seemed totally intrigued by the two visitors from the U.S. Additional cups of *raki* were poured and enjoyed by everyone except Claire.

"Can we bring you a Coca-Cola, little lady?" Kostas asked Claire.

"No, thank you. But if you have a *Diet* Coke or a Coke *Lite*, I would love that!"

Kostas burst into hysterical laughter and shared what she had just said with Panos. He, too, laughed robustly. Kostas disappeared into the back room and reappeared a few moments later, a Coke Lite and a glass of ice in hand.

Claire smiled and gladly accepted the cold beverage.

"If you could come back around six p.m. today, I would like to show you both around my village—the place where I grew up. I will drive you there," Kostas offered.

Claire and Guy looked at each other and then back at Kostas.

"Are you sure it would not be an imposition?" Claire asked.

"An *imposition*? Not at all. It would be an absolute pleasure. Say six o'clock, then?"

"It's a date," Guy said. "We'll see you back here at six o'clock sharp. And thank you."

"Again, the pleasure is mine alone, I assure you," Kostas

answered back.

Handshakes were exchanged, and Claire and Guy left the shop.

The figure lurking outside the store had keenly observed every move the investigators had made. Now, the individual ducked behind a car to hide as the couple exited the jewelry store and walked down the street. Once the two had covered approximately fifty feet or so, the follower again took to strolling behind the sleuths, close enough to keep them in his line of vision.

Claire and Guy visited several other shops and local businesses, going in and coming out of each in rather short order, always stopping long enough to nonchalantly chat with any English-speaking individual in each setting; but every time they got around to casually fitting something into the conversation about the Zenonakis family, men and women alike virtually closed down, refusing to utter another word. It reminded them of a bad movie with scenes that were all too predictable.

Knowing their best bet would be with Kostas later that day, they breathed somewhat easier. Kostas liked them, and they liked him. If anyone could help them in the short term, it would be Kostas Michaelakis. The two were excited to see his village and observe how the Cretan villagers lived; yet, more importantly, they were itching to learn the whereabouts of George Zenonakis.

Hungry, Claire and Guy stopped for lunch at a Greek taverna and ordered a popular type of fish covered with a lemon-garlic-potato sauce and also Souroti—mineral water. The server set a basket of hard bread and fresh olive oil on the table as a starter. "Enjoy," he said. The repast sated them, and it felt good to sit down.

Because the retail stores would soon be closing for the remainder of the afternoon, Claire suggested they head back to the hotel, make a few phone calls, and take a nap so they would be rested for the night's activities. On the walk back to the hotel, both of the investigators took notice of several groupings of birds, and even of children and teenagers throwing food to them, but still they observed no old lady feeding the feathered creatures.

"Keep your fingers crossed that Kostas will be willing to share important information about George Zenonakis this evening," Guy said.

"I will. And information about *the old woman who feeds the birds*, too," Claire said. "I'm hoping he'll open up about both of them."

Due to the time change, it would be very early in the U.S., but once they were back in the hotel room the two decided to make some telephone calls just the same. First, Claire placed a call to Mr. Otto to update him on what had happened since they had arrived in Crete. She reached his answering machine and left a message, along with their phone number at the hotel. Guy phoned the office in Miami to retrieve messages. Nothing seemed urgent. Thankfully, no emergencies had surfaced requiring immediate attention.

Next, Claire dialed Sergeant Massey, Miami-Dade Police Department, and left him a message. She asked for a summary on the son of Hillary and Chadwick Otto—William or *Billy* Otto. They knew virtually nothing about him, other than the fact that he was presumed to be dead, having been working on the books for the plastics factory the night of the explosion. "We'd appreciate anything you can dig up on him, Sergeant," Claire said. "We're trying to assist Mr. Otto. And by the way, thank you for referring him our way. Gaston Lombard and I are in Crete, as I speak, working on the case, trying to see if we can locate the missing-in-action George Zeppano, known here on the island as George Zenonakis. Oh, and find out the approximate amount of money Mr. Otto kept in that internal vault, will you please? And also, see if the insurance company has made a decision yet regarding Mr. Otto's claim. I look forward to hearing back from you." She left the number where they could be reached, thanked him, and hung up.

As with any new investigation, there were more questions than answers. At this juncture, if only Kostas Michaelakis would steer them in the direction of George Zenonakis, or at least toward *the old woman who feeds the birds*, then the mission might start to unfold in a triumphant manner. If only…

"We have some time before we go to meet Kostas," Guy said, turning his full attention to his lovely lady.

"Hmmm. What did you have in mind?" Claire asked. "Were you thinking of a nap, perhaps?" She twisted her face into a look of puzzlement. "Or is there something else you'd prefer to do with our time?"

"I could think of a couple of things…." Guy said.

Clutching Claire and pulling her close, he placed his lips on hers and kissed her slowly and seductively. Scooping her up in his arms, he walked over to the bed and gently laid her on top of it. As he continued to plant unhurried and passionate kisses on every inch of her face and neck, he disrobed her. They made love, and afterward crawled in-between the sheets, staying cradled in each other's arms while they napped in blissful contentment.

Two hours passed like so many minutes, and Claire awoke with a start.

"Guy, what time is it?" she asked, gently nudging his upper arm.

He opened his eyes and looked at his wristwatch. "It's time to go," he said. "We overslept." He and Claire leaped from the bed.

They quickly readied for the evening and rode the elevator to the lobby. As they walked toward the door that connected the hotel to the attached parking ramp, they talked.

"I'm hoping for a big break tonight, honey," Claire said. "Kostas told us we could ride along in his car, but quite frankly, I'd feel more comfortable following him in our own car. That way we can leave if and when we want to. Besides, we are in a foreign country. We know no one else here, and who knows if we can trust these brothers? I mean, I think we can, but we don't know for certain, and we'd be putting ourselves in a terribly scary and vulnerable position without having our own vehicle at our disposal, don't you think? I don't want to do that."

"You're right, of course. I couldn't agree with you more. We'll trail behind Kostas in our rental car. We'll insist on it. It's safer that way," Guy said. He looked over at Claire. "We really don't know exactly what we're getting ourselves into tonight, do we? I just hope it proves to be productive in our search for George Zenonakis."

"It's our best hope, yet," Claire said.

The investigators walked into the parking garage, located the rental car, and set off on the exciting adventure of the evening, Guy behind the wheel. A few moments after he exited the ramp, the yellow Volkswagen Beetle pulled out of the same ramp, quickly falling into place behind them, several car lengths to the rear.

Guy raced the rental car along the streets of Heraklion as he headed in the direction of the jewelry store. Blessed with a keen sense of direction, he drove to the destination straightaway. They did not want to be late. Soon they would meet up with Kostas Michaelakis and follow him to the village where he was raised as a child. Exploring unknown territory evoked great curiosity in both Claire and Guy. With any luck, this very evening they would learn valuable information about the target of their search.

That night Claire Caswell and Guy Lombard were to be given a rare and intimate glimpse into life in a hillside Cretan village—an opportunity rarely afforded tourists or visitors to the island. For unless a member of the village, or a family member of a member—an *insider*—brings one to see a village, there is no chance the community will permit entrance to a stranger.

Rounding the final corner, they pulled up curbside directly across the street from the jewelry store and walked to the front door of the establishment. Kostas beamed when he saw the two Americans and waved them inside.

"I'm almost ready to leave," he said. "Give me a minute. Panos will stay on and close up later."

Panos grinned and the Americans smiled back at him. The brothers appeared to be two of the most kind-hearted men either Claire or Guy had come across in a long time. Within minutes, Kostas was set to go.

"You come with me," he said. "In my car."

"We talked it over before we got here and decided it would be best if we drove separately, in case we have to leave early for any unexpected reason," Guy said politely.

"Are you sure?" Kostas asked. A look of disappointment covered his face and was immediately evident in the tone of his voice.

"We'll stay close behind you. We promise. We're thrilled to go to your village with you!" Claire said exuberantly. Traveling in a car with someone they hardly knew, especially in a foreign country, carried with it the obvious risk factors, and despite the overwhelming goodness Kostas and Panos had exhibited, Claire felt so much more comfortable having a *getaway* car if they needed it. Baby Face Nelson looked kind and innocent, too, she reminded herself.

"If you insist. But I must first stop along the way and pick up my wife, Martha, at our home in the city, and also my father-in-law at his job. Martha and I are sleeping at the village tonight. Just stay with me and before long we'll be on our way to the village. Now, where are you parked?"

"Just across the street," Claire answered. "We're in a small red car."

He agreed to drive around to the front so they could pull out in back of him.

"I've got a dark blue car. See you in a minute," he added. "Is there no way I can convince the two of you to ride with me?"

"Thank you again, Kostas, but we really should drive separately," Claire said.

Guy nodded in support.

"Okay, then," Kostas conceded.

Claire and Guy traded good-byes with Panos and headed to the car. After an insignificant wait, the dark-colored car appeared on the street. Kostas drove by slowly and waved as he passed, sounding the car's horn in a succession of rapid beeps.

The night was young, and the little voice inside Claire let her know they were in for a night they would not soon forget.

18

CLAIRE MANEUVERED THE rental car away from the curb and pulled in line behind Kostas. His car was the smallest vehicle she had ever seen, and the two sleuths tried to imagine the possibility of five people somehow wedged inside. Canned sardines would consider their quarters spacious in comparison. Claire and Guy commented on the most sincere generosity of Kostas, however, to even offer to take them along in his car with the others—especially since that would have required him to drive the two back to the city at the conclusion of the night's activities, only to return again to the village thereafter. They felt doubly happy they had opted to follow their instincts and drive separately.

Kostas first drove to his modest city home. An amiable woman of light complexion and flaxen hair ran out to meet the dark blue car. She waved vigorously at the American visitors to Crete before jumping into the front passenger seat, making certain to pull her white print dress fully inside the tiny vehicle before slamming the door shut.

Kostas's second stop was in front of a dry cleaning business. When they arrived, an older man walked out. Dressed in a three-piece suit, he carried a medium-sized suitcase in his arms. He loaded the bag into the back seat of the small blue car and rapidly climbed in after it. Claire surmised aloud that the father-in-law probably spent days in town with Kostas and Martha, and then, in return, they all spent days together at the village. Now the investigators were even happier they had chosen to drive the red rental car, imagining the cramped quarters of the itsy-bitsy car filled to capacity with people and a suitcase.

Kostas sped off and dutifully Claire and Guy followed his lead. Before long, the lights of the city twinkled behind them and they found themselves passing an airport. With Claire at the wheel, the red rental car trailed behind the dark blue car as if attached by an invisible wire. Together, the automobiles traveled up and into the darkening hillsides that quickly became pitch-black, brooding hillsides. One hour passed, and Claire and Guy both began to wonder just how far away from the city they were venturing. A twang of apprehension occupied Claire. Where exactly was this village, she wondered?

"You know, Guy, we never did ask Kostas the exact location of his village. For smart people, that wasn't a very smart move."

"Yeah. I guess I assumed it wasn't this far away," Guy said.

"Me, too. But you know what they say: Never assume anything. We should have asked."

"I see that," Guy said.

"What if we can't find our way back later tonight?" Claire shuddered. "My, but it's dark out here. I can barely see the turns Kostas is making until he's right on them. It's unsettling to think we'll be on our own to make our way back out of this maze. It's one thing to be dropped into the middle of a maze in the daylight; it's another thing altogether to be dropped into the middle of a maze blindfolded. And this black of night certainly has the effect of a blindfold."

"We'll be okay," Guy responded. He failed to admit he was thinking nearly identical thoughts. "I'll be the driver going back to our hotel tonight to give you a break, anyway."

Claire grimaced. Fleeting thoughts of making a sharp U-turn and heading straight back toward the city entered her mind. But they had traveled too far to turn around now, she reasoned. And her curiosity at seeing an actual Cretan village outweighed her common sense by at least tenfold. Who said common sense wasn't all that common? She couldn't remember. Besides, this was their big chance to do some intense questioning of a native Cretan regarding the whereabouts of George Zenonakis, and that meant it was an opportunity they had to take. The option to retreat quickly left her mind. Yet, a big part of her remained hesitant. She drove on in silence for several minutes.

"What if Kostas plans to get us out into the sloping hillsides and kill us?" Claire asked in a sinister tone, attempting to inject a touch of humor to the building tension of not knowing what they were getting themselves into. "No one would ever find our bodies because *no one* knows we're even on this road or where we're heading. The only people who even know we're in Crete are Mr. Otto and Sergeant Massey."

"Claire. Claire. We'll be fine. Really," Guy said in a firm, reassuring voice, actually trying to calm himself as much as her. He had to admit that the situation was a bit touch-and-go the more he thought about it. Was it crazy for them to be following people they hardly knew into the inky, isolated hills of Crete? Claire was right.

No one would ever have a clue where to start looking for the two investigators if they disappeared. Once the fear had been verbalized, of course it was all either could think about. If only they hadn't forgotten their cell phones in the chargers at home. At least those might have provided a source of help if they needed it. If only...

Another half hour passed as Claire bravely followed the dark vehicle just a few feet ahead of her, venturing deeper into the remote and desolate hillsides, making turns whenever Kostas turned, slowing up or down whenever he did the same. The darkness became darker, and a silent, almost sinister, hush seemed to fall on the area like a blanket. No other cars traveled the road that night, except for one other in the far rear distance—evidenced by a set of dim headlights.

Claire manned the wheel like a soldier on a mission. Eight-thirty came and passed, and she felt pangs of hunger. Would they eat soon? She wondered. Guy's stomach growled loudly.

Silhouetted against the intimidating ebony sky, Guy noticed what appeared to be two giant radar devices strategically placed atop a nearby hill. "Wonder what *those* are?" he queried, more to himself than aloud. "Out here, in the middle of nowhere?"

Claire gave the apparatuses a quick glance and then returned her gaze to the difficult task of driving. "No doubt they're in that location to detect the presence, distance, speed, or direction of *something*—maybe approaching ships or aircraft?"

"Yeah, probably. Just seems strange way out here."

Minutes later, Kostas signaled a right turn and pulled onto a roadway seemingly much longer than it was wide. Claire followed faithfully behind. The extreme narrowness of the dirt road made it next to impossible to navigate the rental car without scraping its sides on both of the bordering embankments. But she held her own, traveling down the path with enviable skill. She realized at once why

Kostas drove the car that he did and concluded that the path was definitely not designed with automobiles in mind. Perhaps cattle, goats, sheep, or even narrow carts or wagons, but certainly not cars.

They had arrived somewhere because they observed signs of life. Soft and sporadic lighting emanated from centuries-old houses, built in close proximity one to another, within the concentrated hillside settlement. Claire lowered the driver's-side front window. The evening air was crisp, but not cold, and as she inhaled deeply an enticing and alluring aroma entered her nostrils. She had never smelled anything like it before and was immediately intrigued. The mysterious odor was intensely pleasing and simply overpowering in its intensity.

"Aaah! What is that curious fragrance in the air?" Claire asked.

"No idea," Guy said. "I can only hope it's food because I'm ready to keel over. I was starving an hour ago. Now, I'm ravenous."

"Me, too," Claire said. "Let's hope Kostas has that covered."

Kostas slowed almost to a halt, then opened his car window and pointed to the ground, signaling they had, at last, reached their destination within the village. He pulled over and parked his car. Claire followed suit, aligning the small rental car adjacent to his minuscule one.

"Sorry it took us so long to get here," Kostas said, alighting from his car. "I should have warned you ahead of time about the distance. It's a long way out here, isn't it?"

"We didn't notice," Guy lied. "Hope we'll be able to retrace our path when we leave tonight."

"You should have no problem," Kostas replied, grinning. "Just don't wander off the main road or you will find yourselves in a rather baffling snarl of confusion." He chuckled. "Now, I'd like you to meet my wife, Martha, and my father-in-law, Eugene."

Claire and Guy introduced themselves and exchanged warm

handshakes with Martha and Eugene.

"*Yassou,*" Eugene bellowed out.

"He says, 'Hello,'" Kostas translated.

"*Yassou,*" Claire repeated.

"*Yassou,*" Guy echoed.

Everyone laughed in unison.

Martha spoke English, but Eugene did not. He spoke only Greek.

Martha's face could not contain the enthusiasm she felt in meeting the couple from the United States, and she could not stop smiling at them. "I am thrilled to meet you and have you come to our village," she said. She grasped one of the hands of each visitor and held on tightly, exhibiting warmth usually unknown at a first-time meeting.

"This is where Eugene lives now, and where Martha and I grew up," Kostas said.

They walked the equivalent of one very long block to Eugene's dwelling and dropped off his suitcase. Then, together, they took a short stroll around the village. The invigorating, damp nighttime air magnified the aroma that Claire had noticed earlier.

"What am I smelling?" Claire asked. "It's incredible!"

Kostas and Martha chuckled.

"It's olive tree wood burning in the many fireplaces in the village homes," Martha said. "I'm glad you find it pleasing. We hardly notice it anymore."

"I've never smelled *anything* like it before," Claire said. "It's calming . . . almost hypnotic. I can't seem to get enough of it."

Now Kostas and Martha broke into hearty laughter.

The quaint village immediately evoked memories of days gone by. The many family apartments within its boundaries were built of a light-colored stone and situated just so on the slope of the hill-side. The structures stood proud in their simplicity. As the group wandered up and down the pathways of the village, Kostas pointed out several buildings and establishments, including a church, a taverna, and other business edifices important to the functioning of the community.

Soon they had circled back to Eugene's home and walked in through an open-air white arched entrance. His apartment—typical of the single- or double-storied apartments of the community—appeared stunningly basic in its construction and inner appearance. Immaculately tidy, the small studio apartment contained a single cot adorned with a handmade quilt and embroidered pillows. Two simple straight-back utilitarian chairs sat in front of a wood-burning fireplace, and framed family photographs, including childhood and wedding shots, covered one wall. The unit contained a washing machine, refrigerator, and small oven, and a separate outdoor entrance provided a washbasin, shower, and toilet. The kitchen took up one wall within the apartment, and Kostas pointed to several five-gallon containers filled to the brim with freshly processed olive oil that covered most of the space on the kitchen floor. If asked for a single adjective to describe the studio unit, Claire would say *pristine.*

"Eugene will stay here and unpack, and you'll come with us," Kostas said. "He'll catch up with us later."

Eugene tilted his head to the left and right, indicating *yes,* and waved good-bye.

The two couples walked several blocks together through the fragrant and brisk evening air until Kostas stopped suddenly in front of a building.

"Please, come in. This is our *kafenion,*" he said proudly. "You are safe here with us."

Claire and Guy exchanged fleeting glances and then followed Kostas and Martha into the establishment. The place was quite dark inside, and a good amount of heavy smoke hung above the tabletops as if frozen in place, making it difficult to see, at first. Once Claire's eyes adjusted to the miniscule amount of lighting, she looked around and considered her surroundings. She swallowed hard and felt the lump travel slowly down her throat. What had they walked into?

19

THE *KAFENION* WAS a gathering place filled with swirling, dense smoke and elderly Greek men. Thick-topped dark wooden tables, capable of seating four to six patrons each, appeared crowded together as if too many tables and chairs had been ordered for the limited space and the owner had decided to use them all nevertheless. Room to walk freely did not exist.

The buzz within the four walls instantly piqued Claire's interest, and once her eyes adjusted further to the dim lighting she took a closer look. Like snapshots taken in rapid sequence from one side of the room to the other, she panoramically considered her surroundings in an unbroken view. The incredible scene that unfolded before her eyes locked her internal curiosity mode into the on position, and she could not look away.

Elderly Greek men sat at the tables playing card games, downing shots of *raki*, smoking cigarettes, watching a Greek soap opera on a television screen mounted high on one wall, and bantering incessantly with one another. Claire had never witnessed anything like it before and immediately felt as if she had wandered into a secret society of sorts … for members only.

The only female in the place, other than Claire and Martha, wore two hats—that of server and bartender. She scurried around the establishment replacing empty carafes of the potent alcoholic spirit *raki* with full ones. This task alone would have kept the woman exceedingly busy, especially because she had to wedge and push her way through the few narrow spaces in and around the room to reach all of the tables, but she also had the responsibility of serving food.

Suddenly, Claire became aware that all sounds within the *kafenion* came to a screeching halt, as one by one every man sitting at the tables took note of the strangers who had entered the room—the American-looking couple who had invaded the private party. Each pair of eyes fell squarely on her and Guy. Claire felt an instantaneous wave of uncertainty wash over her. She nudged her way toward Guy until she felt his body next to hers. For a daunting moment, her response was to flee, but she held her ground and dismissed the thought.

As soon as the men realized the outsiders were with Kostas and Martha, they quickly looked away, continuing on as before. Admittance was permitted to the strangers without question because relatives of Eugene had brought them in, and that fact was clearly all the men needed to know.

Claire exhaled.

The private society, tucked away so securely within the remote location of the hillside Cretan village, appeared to be a refuge for the elderly men of the community. It was a combination pub, coffee shop, and tavern rolled into one; it was a place for the males of the village to yarn about local legends, play games, eat, drink, and be lively.

Waiting to be seated, Claire studied the villagers to the best of her ability. The men seemed to be dressed exclusively in black clothing, and she noticed clumps of thick silver or white hair poking out from underneath most all of the black woolen skullcaps. The inadequate lighting within the *kafenion* allowed her but a mere hazy glimpse into the swarthy, weathered faces of its members; but the amber glow emitted sporadically by numerous cigarettes being inhaled at the same time revealed more clearly the poker faces of the card players—faces that failed to reveal whether the men held good or bad hands. Black eyes glistened in the dim lighting.

"Come on," Martha said, breaking Claire's temporary trance. "The server is waving us to a table."

Martha and Kostas led the way to the only unoccupied table in the place, against a sidewall toward the back. Claire and Guy followed closely behind as together the foursome squeezed its way through the overcrowding of tables and chairs. Once seated, Claire felt somewhat less conspicuous.

"These places are common in the villages," Kostas said, seeing the fascination on his visitor's faces. "Each village has one or two of them. Most here drink *raki*, but you can also order brandy, beer, or a soft drink." His glance went to Claire.

The server walked by and set down a plate of green olives and feta cheese on the table.

"Bring us *raki*," Kostas announced to the waitress. "All around." The waitress hurried off using quick, short steps.

Claire gulped. *Raki*, yet again! "Kostas, I think I need something a bit milder," she pleaded.

"And bring the lady a Coke Lite," Kostas yelled at the waitress, several feet away.

He turned his attention back to his guests. "We will now eat as the villagers eat."

Before long, the server brought over four steaming-hot, round baked potatoes, a plate of freshly cut lemon wedges, and a shaker of salt. Then she placed two, five-inch-tall carafes of *raki* on the table, along with four thimble-sized shot glasses. Martha immediately filled the unusually small cups to the rim with the clear liquor.

"Drink up," she said. She downed hers in one gulp and refilled it immediately. Kostas and Guy did likewise. Claire forced a tiny sip of the burning alcohol into her mouth and down her throat.

"Strong stuff," Claire said. A moment later, she shrieked, "I'm on fire!"

Kostas and Martha chuckled wholeheartedly.

"You get used to it," Martha said, beaming. "I no longer notice the burn."

The immensely thick wooden tabletop came in handy. Like a pro, Kostas took each potato, one at a time, and pounded it decisively with his fist, artfully breaking it into two parts. Then, he squeezed fresh lemon juice and sprinkled salt on every section before apportioning them out. The four ate the delectable potatoes with their hands, very quickly, relishing every bite.

"Delicious!" Claire managed to say.

"Unbelievable!" Guy chimed in between bites.

The server brought over a plate of just-picked tomatoes, cut into chunks, and also a smaller plate containing dark ripe olives the size of large raisins.

"Please, eat," Martha said. "Enjoy the tidbits."

And they did. Before long, the plates sat empty.

The server pulled a fifth chair to the table, and Eugene surprised them all with his appearance. Without delay, a fifth shot glass arrived, and Martha filled it to the rim with the ubiquitous *raki* before she passed it to her father. At the same time, a second plate of warm potatoes—this time sliced and grilled—was added to the feast, again accompanied by fresh lemon wedges and salt. The five devoured the morsels in no time. Next came green legumes, each about seven inches in length. In-between chain-smoking cigarettes, Eugene took the time to pop out what appeared to be rather large-sized beans from each pod. He passed around the plate for all to enjoy. The marvelous flavor amazed the visitors.

Moments later, the female server carried over a plate of leafy green vegetables drizzled with a hint of vinegar and also a small dish containing hard, bite-sized biscuits. All was finger food and disappeared with great immediacy.

"I don't know what to say. I love it all!" Claire said. "Food has never tasted this good."

Kostas and Martha started to chuckle, and Eugene chimed in. The merriment became contagious, and before long Claire and Guy also broke into hysterical laughter. Sated and happy, the new friends enjoyed the camaraderie immensely.

"No wonder you're all so healthy here," Guy said. "If I ate like this every day, I'd probably get down to my ideal weight in no time."

Out of the blue, Martha pushed her chair away from the table. "I'll be back," she said. She got up and abruptly walked out.

"Is everything okay?" Claire questioned Kostas.

"My guess is she left because of you."

"*Me*?"

"You'll see, shortly."

Guy shrugged his shoulders at Claire.

The group continued to drink *raki* and engage in captivating conversation. Eugene listened and watched the Americans with interest, but was unable to contribute to the conversation. He smiled from time to time—that universal gesture that everyone everywhere seemed to understand.

Claire's eyes again scrutinized the crowd. She blinked. Her eyes smarted from the amount of blue smoke hanging just above each tabletop. She glanced at Guy and noticed that his eyes seemed to be bothered as well. As hard as she tried, she could not find a single man who did not have a lit cigarette pursed in his lips or clamped between his index and middle finger. She noticed the server walking to a wall cupboard, every few minutes or so, to pull out additional packs of unfiltered, popular American brand cigarettes for the *kafenion* patrons.

"Lots of smokers here in Crete," Claire said.

"Most all of us smoke," Kostas said. "But our cancer rates are low."

Thirty minutes had passed, and still Martha had not returned. Where had she gone in the dark and in such a hurry? Claire wondered. Neither Kostas nor Eugene seemed the least bit concerned.

"Tell us more about the Cretans," Guy said to Kostas. "How do you all manage to smoke so heavily and yet have such low cancer rates?"

Both of the sleuths hoped to eventually steer the conversation toward the Zenonakis family and *the old woman who feeds the birds*. As seasoned investigators, however, and based upon what they had already witnessed thus far on the island, they knew that rushing into the questioning prematurely could result in disaster. They would wait for the perfect opportunity.

"Our secret is olive oil," Kostas said.

"*Olive oil*?" Claire and Guy asked in unison.

"Yes. Olive oil."

All of a sudden, Martha stood alongside the table. She held a bag overflowing with large oranges in one hand, and a fistful of just cut, sweetly fragrant, white flowering orange blossoms in the other. She extended both her hands in Claire's direction.

"For you," Martha said. Her face beamed with pride.

"I'm touched," Claire said, accepting both. "I'm relieved you returned, Martha, and I'm taken aback by your generosity. You are a wonderful person, and a friend. Thank you." Claire set the gifts down in front of her and reached for Martha's hands, squeezing them tightly. "I will never forget this evening."

"I hope you like them," Martha said. She made a puffing noise through pursed lips, accepting the thoughtful words Claire had spoken. "I climbed up a ladder to pick the very best oranges near the top of the tree. For you."

Claire shook her head from side to side in astonishment. "Thank you, again, Martha. You're the best!"

Martha's face turned beet red.

Kostas looked at his visitors and began to inform them about the many researchers and biologists who continually visit Crete to study the wide variety of plant life growing on the island. "It's like no other place on earth," he said. "Our growing conditions are *nearly perfect* for fruits and vegetables, and plant life, as well."

And he spoke of the fact that most Cretan villagers live to be eighty-five to ninety-five years old with almost no diseases such as cancer, heart problems, or diabetes.

"As I told you, we consume much olive oil in our diet. And we drink mostly *raki* and wine. We eat fresh vegetables and fruits, relatively small amounts of meat, and we consume no butter," Kostas said. "And while most Cretans are heavy cigarette smokers, as you've noticed—the unfiltered varieties, no less—we are the healthiest people in the world." He paused. "Of course the clean air quality doesn't hurt us one bit, either." The corners of his mouth turned upward.

Claire and Guy exchanged quick glances. It was obvious to them both that Kostas clearly had to be referring to the quality of the *outside* air.

"Can we assume then that the mass quantities of olive oil, and perhaps even the *raki*, help negate the health problems associated with smoking?" Claire asked.

"No one seems to know for sure. But, you can't deny the facts," Kostas said. He took a long drag on his cigarette.

"Is there much crime here in Crete?" Guy asked.

"Oh, yes. The island is riddled with crime. *Many* murders," Kostas said. "All villagers carry guns, knives, and other weapons. Fact is, any size gun can be found here, from the very small to the very large. Even Kalashnikov and American rifles … and maybe even a tank or two." He stopped talking to take a drag on his cigarette. "Cretans are famous for their love affair with guns. But keep in mind, bearing arms provided the means for us to survive our many enemies in the past." He chortled.

"The many villagers know one another and are welcome in each other's homes at any time, night or day, early or late," he continued. "Any member who shows up at another's door will never be turned away. They are welcomed in and offered food. Even at midnight or in the early morning hours, it doesn't matter, the owner of any dwelling will invite a neighbor in if he knocks. The owner will go to the back of his residence, kill a chicken, and cook it right then, on the spot, while his neighbor waits. And I know this will surprise you, but they drink *raki* together until the meal is ready." He looked from Guy to Claire and a broad smile appeared on his face. He started to laugh. "I'm just having fun with you two, but fact is they do drink *raki* until the food is cooked and ready to eat." He took another drag on his cigarette. "Afterward, they'll start shooting guns together. A tad dangerous, perhaps, but all in good fun.

"In the village, by the way, if a man flirts with your wife," Kostas went on, "he will be shot dead. If a man sees someone's daughter without first asking permission from her father, the man courting the daughter will also be killed. Shot dead. The rules are simple and everyone follows them. We do not play around."

"Apparently not," Guy interjected. "Our laws are not quite that clear-cut."

Kostas and Martha chuckled under their breath.

"*Raki*, in case you've wondered, is distilled from the dregs—the wine must—after the wine is pressed from grapes," Martha said. "Everywhere, the whole island over, people are making *raki*. Even many of the small villages have a distillery, and they make the best *raki* around. You will be offered *raki* wherever you go, as you've probably already experienced—especially if people like you. More *raki*?" she asked. Her eyes twinkled, and she refilled each of the tiny cups. Claire slid hers toward Guy.

"One night, in this very place, I sat with three other villagers," Kostas said. "Between us, we consumed seventy-two carafes of *raki*—eighteen apiece. One man left to buy a half-side of a sheep, and it was cooked right here at this *kafenion*. We gorged ourselves on the delectable mutton some time around four in the morning." He laughed, reliving the event in his mind. "It was a night I remember vividly."

More stories and conversation continued, and the hours passed. Claire stifled a yawn. The efficient server had replaced the carafes of *raki* whenever they had appeared to be close to being empty the entire evening, and as she approached with two more full carafes, Claire and Guy each ordered a cup of strong Greek coffee.

"I hate to be the one to break this up," Guy said, after he and Claire finished the coffees, "but we have a long drive back ahead of us. As much as we have thoroughly enjoyed hearing about your village and spending time together, I'm afraid we should probably get going, and continue this later."

Reluctantly, the others agreed.

The two couples walked Eugene back to his place, and Kostas asked Claire and Guy to wait until he got his father-in-law settled in for the night. Eugene and Kostas went inside. Seconds later, Eugene reappeared holding a liter of pure olive oil in his right hand and a plastic container filled with *raki* in his left. He handed both to Guy.

"Eugene, thank you," Guy said humbly. "It has been a pleasure to meet you and spend this time together. Like Claire said earlier, I will never forget it." He set one container on the ground and shook Eugene's hand vigorously.

Kostas stood next to Eugene and translated Guy's words into Greek. Eugene broke into a smile from ear to ear.

Claire thanked Eugene for allowing them the privilege of seeing his village. "This memory will stay with us for as long as we live, Eugene," she added.

Again, Kostas translated, and a pleased and kindhearted expression took up the space on Eugene's face. He waved good-bye and retreated to his abode.

Kostas and Martha walked Guy and Claire back to their rental car.

Just as Claire and Guy were about to exchange good-byes with the lovely couple, and thank them for an enchanting evening, Kostas spoke up.

"Before you leave, there is something I need to show you. Follow us in your car. I'm afraid I have to insist. It is not far away."

20

AGAINST BETTER JUDGMENT, Claire and Guy agreed to follow the dark blue car to yet another unknown destination. Midnight had come and passed some time ago. The darkness of the night, coupled with the lateness of the hour—not to mention the *raki* consumption by Guy—and the fact they had a long drive back to the city, should have triggered the sleuths to head back to the hotel at once. But they did not want to appear rude to Kostas and Martha and refuse his last offer. Convinced that Kostas would ultimately help on their search for George Zenonakis, or at least point them in the direction of *the old woman who feeds the birds*, they persevered. The friendship needed to be solidified before they asked the important questions. Besides, they thought the world of Kostas and Martha and did not want to be responsible for any hurt feelings.

Once again following behind the dark blue car, this time with

Guy at the wheel, the two investigators made their way along more unfamiliar and curvy roads, leading them even farther away from the city and the hotel. Both Claire and Guy felt fatigued and in the worst way wanted to be back in their room, falling into bed. Making the return trip, reversing the drive out to the village in the hills, and traveling back through the unfamiliar blackness and terrain to the city, was of great concern to them. Yet they realized this supplemental experience might somehow be important to their mission, and this realization forced the two to stay alert. Like déjà vu, Guy thought he saw a set of dimmed headlights in the far rear distance, but when he blinked, they were gone. How many cups of *raki* had he consumed, he wondered? Funny. He didn't feel any adverse effects whatsoever from the clear alcohol, or he would have insisted that Claire be the designated driver. Perhaps the food had helped.

"Where *are* we going?" he asked.

"I only wish I knew," Claire said.

Approximately twenty minutes passed, and Kostas suddenly pulled his car off the road. Guy followed, pulling up just beside the dark blue car. Some thirty feet straight ahead, the sleuths spotted a substantial but grossly dilapidated building.

Kostas rolled his window down. "This is it," he yelled, pointing to the structure with the index finger of his left hand.

The little voice inside of Claire—the one that always warned her when a situation was not right—did not speak to her. This was a good thing.

"Stay close to me," Guy insisted.

The walk to the building was uphill, and it required a good amount of strength and vitality to ascend the steep embankment. Before long, however, the four found themselves standing in front of the building's main doorway. Claire looked at all parts of the structure critically and observed that the place was in desperate need of repairs and paint. In fact, but for the occasional spattering of light sneaking through the deteriorating boards, one would assume it to be an abandoned property in need of demolition. Faded gray boards hung loosely on certain sections of its facade, many by a single rusty nail, and upon closer scrutiny it became apparent that numerous patchwork repair attempts had been made to preserve the integrity of the old building.

The shock came when they stepped inside. Claire and Guy gaped in wonderment. Everything looked to be in brand-new condition and ultra-modern in design. It felt like stepping from an old attic, filled with antiques and cobwebs, into a thoroughly modern high-tech-in-every-aspect room. The startling operation was clearly not what either of the sleuths had expected.

Claire and Guy scanned the interior with a keen spirit of inquiry, at once realizing they had walked into some kind of active factory. Sleek and shiny stainless steel machinery took up most of the space within the walls of the large warehouse. The facility looked extraordinarily clean, and an interesting and enticing odor permeated the place.

"Martha and I want to walk you through an olive oil processing plant," Kostas said. "*This*, my friends, is how we make olive oil." A look of enormous pride beamed across his face. "The procedure for making olive oil is something few Americans will ever see. This plant runs for four consecutive months every year—day and night, November through February. Small green and black olives—leaves, vines, and all—are collected in large old burlap coffee sacks. They are then transported to this location and poured into this large vat, over here." He walked a few steps and pointed to one end of the intricately connected machinery. "From here they travel up this V-shaped conveyor belt where the olives are separated from the leaves and vines and washed in water." Again, he pointed. They walked a few steps farther.

"After that, they enter this section here." Kostas indicated a different component. "This is where the olives are pitted. The pits are then transferred to this area. Right here. They are ground up by an auger—a boring tool—and removed from the process, bagged, and sold as fertilizer."

"Okay. This is fascinating," Claire said, not missing a thing.

"Next, the olives are crushed in the pressing machine. This action produces heat," Kostas said.

They followed Kostas to the end of the elaborate processing chain.

"Here, in the final stage, fresh, warm olive oil, not too hot, pours into this very large, stainless steel vat. The vat is connected to a hose with a nozzle, much like that at a petrol station. Large plastic jugs are placed on the computerized scale sitting right next to the vat, and each container is individually filled until an identical weight is achieved. The olive oil made any given year is stored until the following year, when it is best to be consumed." Kostas said. He watched the reactions of the two Americans with interest and seemed pleased they appeared to be impressed.

Two middle-aged Greek men stood nearby, overseeing the operation of the processing plant. One wore a ragged blue sweater and the other a tattered brown sweater. They smiled at Claire and stared at her, each stroking his chin with a finger.

Kostas said, "They think you are very pretty, Claire. That is why they stroke their chins in that manner. It's part of our culture. No worries, though. They are just admiring you. They have never been in the presence of such a beautiful woman before." He paused and looked at the Americans. "Come with me." They walked a few steps, and Kostas introduced both workers to Claire and Guy. The men beamed with delight at the visitors to the plant, and by doing so revealed many missing front teeth. They spoke no English, but were obviously quite jubilant to have onlookers from another country admiring the facility. Claire guessed visitors to the plant had to be a rarity.

Speaking to Kostas, who then translated into English, one of the workers remarked that Guy looked *Italian* in heritage, and Claire looked of *French* descent. They also wondered if Claire was a movie star. Kostas informed the men that Claire and Guy were tourists from the United States, and that knowledge appeared to trigger even greater and wider smiles of pleasure on the face of both men. They giggled and acted silly, almost childlike, in their behavior.

Martha leaned over to Claire and whispered in her ear. "They don't know how to act. They are honored by your visit."

The two couples stood at the end of the line and watched the perfectly heated, fresh olive oil pour into the large, stainless steel vat, not unlike water running into a bathtub. Claire realized that the incredible fragrance saturating the air outside of the building was the very smell of freshly pressed olive oil. The odor was alluring in its essence.

"Smells so good," Guy said, leaning in closer to the vat and inhaling deeply.

The employee in the tattered brown sweater disappeared into the back room. He reappeared moments later carrying a long, narrow loaf of fresh, warm white bread. His hands and fingernails looked filthy with dirt and grime. Without washing them, he pulled off a chunk of the bread and held it under the steamy fountain of olive oil until it was saturated. He walked to a nearby counter, grabbed a shaker of salt, and sprinkled the seasoning liberally on top of the sample. He passed it to his opposite hand, and unexpectedly offered the choice food to Claire. She accepted it graciously, and, with all eyes on her and with olive oil dripping down her arm, she sank her teeth into the delicacy.

"Umm. The flavor!" she said. "And the distinct aroma! It smells like a mixture of olives . . . and apples . . . and *grass*." She took another bite and nodded in approval to both workers. The sparkle in her eyes and grin on her face told the workers without words how much she enjoyed it.

The worker then prepared and handed a similar sample to Martha, Guy, and Kostas, in that order. Before long, all four had tasted the mouthwatering warm luxury.

"Magnificent!" Guy declared loudly.

The worker offered a second portion all around, and everyone accepted. Then, the workers treated themselves. Afterward, the worker in the blue sweater passed around a well-used community cotton rag for hand wiping.

Kostas leaned over to Guy and whispered in his ear. "Tonight, Claire will wake up in the middle of the night in a *very* friendly mood. You will see." He winked at Guy. "It's the olive oil."

Guy looked at him and grinned his famous grin.

"Why not have another taste, Claire," Guy suggested. "We may never get a second chance to experience such special olive oil." He had an ulterior motive, of course, and wanted to make certain she was eating enough of the *liquid gold* to do the trick.

Kostas and Guy exchanged secret smiles, and suddenly all of the men started winking at each other. Although this did not go unnoticed by Claire, she thought better about asking what was humoring the men to such a great degree. She'd ask Guy later, in private, if she remembered.

Minutes later, out of the blue, Claire started to feel very romantic. Her gaze fell upon Guy, and she shot a teasing grin his way. She was unable to take her eyes off him.

"It's working already," Kostas whispered to Guy.

"Is it difficult to get an accurate reading on the amount of oil in every vat?" Claire asked Kostas, still looking fixedly in Guy's direction.

"Excellent question," Kostas said. "After each batch is completed, one of the workers uses a squeegee to remove all of the excess olive oil that clings to the sides of the vat ... in order to get a totally accurate weight."

Suddenly, Claire turned to Martha. "We can't thank you and Kostas enough for bringing us here, for showing this to us. The whole evening has been unforgettable. I mean it. We'll treasure the memories always. Thank you."

"*We* are the ones privileged to spend time with the two of you," Martha said. "It's not often we have visitors from so far away." She wrapped her arms around Claire and hugged her tightly.

The workers reached for the investigators' hands and shook them vigorously. As the four departed, the workers waved good-bye.

Guy and Claire were overwhelmed by the generosity and bigheartedness of Kostas and Martha, Eugene, and the olive oil factory workers. The night had been one of those rare times in life that would live on in Claire's and Guy's memories forever. As the couples approached the two cars, Kostas lowered his voice and spoke quietly to Martha, words that Claire and Guy could not hear. Martha answered back.

"I don't know what to say, Kostas," Guy said. "To see your village and this plant ... it was just an unbelievable evening!"

"We so much enjoyed your company," he replied. "By the way, Martha is staying here at the village tonight with her father, but I decided I'm driving back to the city. That way, you can follow behind me and you won't get lost. It's late, it's dark, and I insist."

"No. We will not hear of it, Kostas," Claire said. "We are great navigators and will have no trouble finding our way back. Thank you, anyway. You enjoy your time here with Martha and Eugene."

"The decision has already been made, my friends," Kostas said. "Just follow me in your car. I will drop Martha back at the village on our way."

"Is there no way we can change your mind?" Guy asked.

"There is no way."

Claire embraced Martha and thanked her again for the oranges and orange-tree blossoms.

Claire and Guy followed the dark blue car to the village and, thereafter, trailed close behind as Kostas wheeled his way back to Heraklion. The deep dark of the hour felt sinister. The many twists and turns along the return route required knowledge of the area, and, without a doubt, Claire and Guy would have made numerous, time-wasting wrong moves if they had been on their own. As much as they regretted having Kostas lead the way back to the hotel, they were grateful he had insisted. Exhaustion had claimed both of the investigators, and the return drive seemed interminable. As Guy manned the wheel, Claire reached over and put her left hand on his right thigh. He liked to drive that way.

Guy glanced into the rearview mirror for a long moment. Was that a set of faded headlights in the far back distance, once again? He couldn't be certain. Why would another car be out on this road so late, anyway? It didn't make sense. Perhaps the *raki* was playing games with his mind after all. Yet, strangely, he still felt no effects whatsoever from drinking it.

The two cars traveled onward.

At last, they spotted the welcoming lights of the city of Heraklion up ahead. Guy expelled a sigh of relief. It was three o'clock in the morning, and he could not wait to be back in the hotel room, dropping his heavy head onto the feather-stuffed pillows that awaited him. Again he thought he noticed diminished headlights in the far rear distance, but he was not sure. Kostas drove into the hotel's entrance area and pulled over. Guy followed him in. Both he and Claire jumped out of the rental car to say goodnight to Kostas.

"Kostas, again, many thanks for everything," Guy said. "We'll stop at your shop tomorrow and pick up the money clip." A hearty handshake was exchanged.

"Can you wait here for just a minute, Kostas?" Claire asked.

"Sure," he said, a questioning look in his eyes.

Claire looked at Guy. "I'll be right back. Keep Kostas company until I return." She ran to the front doors and disappeared inside.

Kostas gave Guy a questioning look.

"No idea," Guy said.

Claire rode the elevator up and quietly sprinted to the room. She needed to find something to give Martha, some kind of gift. Suddenly she remembered the purse from the market. It was still in the bag and the tags were still in place. She grabbed it, locked up the room, and hurried back to Kostas and Guy.

"Kostas. Thanks for waiting. Will you please give this to Martha from the two of us?" she asked.

"Of course. What is it?"

"A small token of our appreciation."

"Please. You don't have to give her anything. It is our way."

"I insist. And, again, thank you."

"Yes, I second that," Guy added, shaking Kostas's hand a second time.

"See you tomorrow, then," Kostas said. "And sleep well tonight." He winked at Guy and drove off to his home in the city.

"What was that wink about, counselor?" Claire asked minutes later, climbing into bed. "It's the second time tonight I noticed him winking at you."

"Nothing, my dear. Nothing. Goodnight, my love."

They fell asleep quickly, spooning as one. At about four a.m., Guy awoke to Claire stroking his muscular arms, kissing him tenderly on the neck, and uttering sweet nothings into his ear. The olive oil had taken effect and was working its magic. Guy pulled her close and things progressed rapidly and passionately. Afterward, they relaxed in total comfort, sinking into deep, heavy sleep.

Guy smiled in the dark as he drifted off. Kostas had been right.

21

CLAIRE AND GUY awoke refreshed.

"I had the strangest dream last night," Claire said. "I dreamed we . . . in the middle of the night we . . ."

"You dreamed we . . . what?" Guy asked.

"Oh, never mind," she said. "It was just a dream."

Guy smiled slyly.

"We need to talk to Kostas *today* about the whereabouts of George Zenonakis and *the old woman who feeds the birds*. We can't put it off any longer," Claire said. "If anyone can help us, it will be Kostas. It's time to be frank with him. It's time."

"You're right, of course. We have to pick up the money clip today, too."

They took turns showering and dressed for the day in comfortable, loose-fitting clothing and walking shoes. As Claire buttoned her blouse, she noticed the message light on the telephone blinking.

"Somebody tried to reach us, Guy." She pointed to the telephone. "Wonder how long it's been flashing? I didn't notice it when we got home last night."

"You mean, this *morning*, don't you? I don't think either of us noticed much of anything when we walked into the room this morning. Check it out, will you?"

Claire pushed the appropriate numbers to retrieve messages and learned one message had come in the evening before from Sergeant Massey. She listened.

"Ms. Caswell, I got your message and found out what I could about William Otto. Afraid there's not much to report. Sounds like he was a regular kind of fellow—thirty-four years old, hard working, an accountant for his family's plastics business, did the books for many years. Never married. No children. No known enemies. And that's about it. State Fire Marshal's office established that the explosion was an intentional act. The modus operandi matched that of every past explosion George Zeppano is suspected of causing. No surprise there. But solid evidence is lacking. No eyewitnesses. No DNA survived the fire. You get the picture. Yeah, yeah, yeah." He cracked his knuckles. "Oh, and the Otto fortune kept in the vault was right around four million dollars, including some multi-generational family money. We assume it was incinerated in the blast along with everything else. If I can help you further, let me know. Hey, enjoy Crete if you two have any free time. And try some of that renowned olive oil they're so famous for if you get the chance." He snickered, cracked his knuckles, and ended the message.

Claire summarized the call for Guy. "That's a lot of money. Makes me wonder what the *real* motive was for that explosion. Was it control of the neighborhood or theft of millions disguised as control of the neighborhood? Maybe George Zenonakis or his goons yanked the money out of the safe before the blast?" Claire stared straight ahead, deep in thought. "If that did happen, if George Zenonakis and his men entered the building before they leveled it to pull out the money, now I'm wondering if they walked in on Billy Otto. And if they did, maybe he was murdered before the explosion and did not die from the blast? It sounds like the Miami–Dade Police Department never even considered the possibility."

Guy looked at her. "You are remarkable. I mean it Claire. You are a born sleuth. I think your theory seems very plausible. Maybe you should discuss it with Sergeant Massey."

"Not just yet. I'd like to see if I can come up with some solid evidence first."

"Four million dollars is a hell of a lot of money, Claire. People have died for much less."

"And m-o-n-e-y spells *m-o-t-i-v-e*. Perhaps controlling the neighborhood was the big picture goal, but theft of millions made the job a whole lot sweeter. Maybe George Zenonakis heard about the safe and decided to help himself to the Otto family fortune." Claire thought for a moment about what she had just said. "Yeah. The whole thing makes more sense now. Either way, Billy Otto was at the wrong place at the wrong time."

"You might be on to something, Claire."

"Sergeant Massey ended his message by saying I should try some of the olive oil that Crete is so famous for. Then he chuckled. Wonder what that was all about?"

"I have *no* idea, honey. Perhaps because it's so healthy, he thought it might be a good idea for you to consume lots of it while you're here. I don't think it's a bad idea, either." He turned and smiled to himself. Some secrets were best kept secret.

"Oh, and another thing. Mr. Otto never called us back. Hope he's okay," Claire said.

"We'll try him again later," Guy said. "And by the way, as I said, that is one large pile of money." It was obvious that Guy still pondered Claire's theory.

"Yeah, it is. And then you have the question of what George Zenonakis would have done with all that money," Claire said. The cogs in her mind had not stopped turning. "Putting it into a bank account would be out of the question as police could always subpoena those records if they became suspicious of where the money went. So, that would never do. He couldn't buy real estate with it, as those written documents could always be reviewed, as well. What would you do with all that money if you wished to put it into something portable for purposes of leaving the country? Buy diamonds?" At this point Claire could not know how close she was coming to putting together the pieces of the puzzle surrounding the explosion at the Otto's plastics factory.

After a quick breakfast in the lobby coffee shop, the investigators walked a few blocks and ended up at the Michaelakis family jewelry store. When they walked in, Kostas left the customer he was working with and rushed over to greet them.

"Please. Come in, dear friends. Look around. I will be with you shortly."

Claire and Guy happily browsed the display cases that surrounded the perimeter of the store. Claire spotted a thin band set with a single red ruby. It immediately caught her eye, and Guy noticed her interest.

Kostas approached them. "What a *wonderful* evening we had with the two of you last night!" He embraced Claire and then Guy. "I told Martha you had given me a present for her, and she made me tell her what it is. So, I looked in the packaging. It is a beautiful handbag! She is so excited to see it! Many thanks from her to you, Claire. And, by the by, how did you sleep last night?" Kostas asked, looking directly at Guy with keen interest.

"Quite well, thanks for asking, my friend," Guy replied with a wink that Claire observed.

Claire rolled her eyes. She had come to the conclusion that the men had some kind of guy thing going on between them—something they were not about to share with her, a top secret something that had started at the olive oil factory the evening before.

"Kostas, can I see that stunning little ruby ring?" Claire asked, pointing to it.

"Oh, you have exquisite taste, Claire," he said. "That is a Burmese ruby. The finest ruby you can find. It is the best of the best, the icing on the toast."

"That's *cake*, Kostas," Claire said. "The icing on the *cake*."

All three laughed robustly.

She slipped the delicate ring onto her right ring finger, and it fit perfectly. No sizing would be necessary.

"Nice," Kostas said, admiring the ring on her finger. "When your eye catches hold of a particular ring, and it fits you exactly right, we say it is *meant to be*."

"How much?" she asked, afraid at what his response might be.

He looked at the tag carefully. "For you?" He looked at the ring and then at Claire and quoted a most reasonable price. "This ring was clearly designed with you in mind," Kostas said. "You know what the Americans say: If the ring fits, wear it."

"I think that's *shoe*, Kostas. If the *shoe* fits, wear it," Claire said, laughing again. "I have to admit, though, I do love it." She again admired the brilliance of the tiny red stone.

"Write it up, along with the money clip," Guy cut in. "It will be Claire's memento of our lovely trip to your incredible country, and also a gift for Valentine's Day tomorrow."

"I almost forgot that tomorrow is Valentine's Day, Guy," Claire said. She kissed him on the cheek.

"Such love, between the two of you," Kostas said. "I saw it immediately when I met you." He disappeared to the back room to wrap the purchase.

He reappeared a few short minutes later and handed the package to Claire. "Wear the ring in good health, my American friend."

"I intend to." She smiled. "I'll treasure it."

"Before we go on, I'd like to take you both upstairs to our workroom," Kostas said. "Panos is up there working right now, applying the final touches to your money clip, Guy. It won't be ready until around five or six o'clock this afternoon. Please, follow me. I'll show you our operation."

He led the Americans up a steep and narrow spiral staircase, to the upper floor of the business. Panos and another goldsmith sat hard at work. Panos looked up when he saw the visitors and nodded warmly. With Kostas interpreting, Panos confirmed the money clip was coming along just fine and should be ready later in the day. He gave Guy the American thumbs-up sign, and Guy returned it to him. Both grinned.

Kostas walked his new friends around the entire upstairs workshop area, explaining all aspects of the impressive enterprise in detail.

Claire thought the time was ripe to ask the important questions. "Kostas, we need to talk to you about something very serious," she said.

"Anything, my dear, anything at all. Let's go back downstairs."

The three cautiously made their way down the steep set of steps.

The showroom was empty for the moment. A young employee worked dutifully, spraying and wiping clean all fingerprints and handprints left by customers and browsers alike on the many display cases.

"Come with me," Kostas said, showing Claire and Guy to a back viewing room. "Please, sit," he said, indicating the chairs surrounding a small table. "What is it?" he asked, looking Claire directly in the eyes. "It sounds important."

"Well, Kostas, it is important. You and your family have been so generous to us, and we've enjoyed meeting you and spending time with you so very much," she began. "We hope it's the beginning of a wonderful friendship."

"I have many American friends," Kostas said, "but none I like as well as the both of you. I used to take my American friends bowling when they visited me here, but since the nearby American military base all but closed, several years ago, I don't see too many of them anymore. Now, fewer American military personnel remain on the island. So I have little, if any, opportunity to speak English with anyone these days, other than Martha. That is why I welcome you with open arms."

"Well, your English is *very* good," Claire said. "And your hospitality tops the charts."

His face reddened.

"Kostas, Guy and I are private investigators in the States." She paused momentarily to let the jeweler absorb the disclosure. "We were sent here on a case. We've shared this with no one, but we trust you and want to tell you all about it and maybe get your input."

His gaze changed from jovial to grave. "*Private investigators*? I had no idea. How could *I* possibly be of help to *you*?" he asked. "I do not understand."

"Let us explain," Claire began. "I'll tell you who we're looking for here on the island. He is a man who goes by the name of George Zeppano in the U.S. Here, he uses his family name: Zenonakis. *George Zenonakis.*"

All color drained from Kostas's face.

"The man has committed many violent crimes in the U.S., Kostas," Claire said. "Most recently, he arranged to have a plastics factory in Miami blown into small pieces because the owner would not succumb to his threats of extortion: his pay-for-protection scam. The business owner's only child—a grown son in his thirties—was killed in the explosion, and there was nothing left of his body to recover from the smoldering remains. The owner's wife died a short time later, presumably from a broken heart after losing her son." She paused.

Kostas remained silent and hung his head.

"The family's life savings, a rather large sum of money, was kept in a vault within the building. That, too, was presumably lost in the blast, although I'm not convinced," Claire said.

"The man has nothing left. Nothing. He is destroyed," Kostas said, visibly sickened by the accounting. "George Zenonakis did this. And he took the money, too. I can guarantee it."

Claire and Guy exchanged long glances.

"The suspected perpetrator of the disaster, George Zeppano—George Zenonakis—ducked out of sight immediately after the incident. It is strongly believed that he returned here to Crete, his homeland, to the protection of his grandfather, the infamous Nikos Zenonakis," Guy said.

Kostas listened intently.

"Kostas, Claire and I are experienced investigators. We were sent here by the owner of the factory to track down George Zenonakis and bring him back to the States to stand trial."

Kostas shuddered. "You have *no* idea *who* or *what* you are dealing with." His eyes drilled into Claire's and then into Guy's. "These are *dangerous* people. George Zenonakis is a fierce opponent. He will never be taken down."

"We understand," Guy said.

"You understand *nothing*!" Kostas blurted out.

His sudden outburst startled the investigators.

"*No one* in these parts has dealings with that family. George Zenonakis is a treacherous soul. The entire island sighed a collective breath of relief the day that man left to go and live in the United States years ago. He is an unpredictable, double-crossing, double-dealing, savage renegade! Go nowhere near him if you value your lives."

Claire and Guy did not stir.

"Cretans thought we were finally rid of that man and his deeds of evil for good. But I, too, have recently heard the rumor that George Zenonakis has returned to Crete. I just didn't know what brought him back, until now."

Kostas again hung his head and held it in his hands.

"Heed my warning, American friends. Abort your mission now, while you still have the chance." Perspiration streamed down Kostas's forehead, and he moved uncomfortably in his chair. "If George Zenonakis finds out you are after him, he'll turn the tables and come after you. And our law enforcement will not help you. They steer clear of the man and his family. Always have. Always will."

Confining silence filled the room.

"Excuse me," Kostas said abruptly. He hastily left the room, attempting to pull the door closed behind him, but unintentionally leaving it slightly ajar.

Claire got up and peeked through the slight opening.

"What do you see?" Guy whispered.

"Strange. He just got on his phone."

22

THE SQUADRON-OF-FOUR ORDERED an early breakfast at an outdoor café. Today was the day to nail down the location of their target. They had already wasted far too much time attempting to learn the location of the Zenonakis mansion.

Lastner reiterated his grave concern regarding the American couple *on island* also searching for the same infamous criminal. This fact was an added complication they did not need. If the couple located George Zenonakis before the vigilantes did, Lastner and his men could not execute their plan, and that would never do. Dark justice remained the only way to deal with the ilk of lawbreakers like George Zenonakis, Judge Lastner reasoned. Finding their mark first, before the others, assured the vigilantes the opportunity to rid the world of an infected blemish on society. Based upon what they had learned, the couple was a day or two ahead of them in their search. That was not a good thing.

"I want each of you to come up with a plan to ascertain the whereabouts of the elusive Mr. Zenonakis. Time is running out. The race is on between the American couple and our team. Who will ferret out the monster first? Today I want you all to be aggressive with your questioning. Offer to distribute money liberally to people who cooperate with you. Refuse to put up with people who play the silence game. We need answers, and we need them now. Do what you have to do to get them. No more Mr. Nice Guys. No more excuses. It's time we go for the jugular. We'll meet in the room I share with Teddy at 12:00 noon. I want answers!"

The men disbursed in different directions. It would be their last great chance to search out the information they needed in the city of Hania. For once word got out publicly that the men were searching for George Zenonakis, there lives could be in certain jeopardy.

BACK IN his room, minutes before the noon meeting, Kyle Teddy dialed his home number. He needed some alone time to think. Nothing seemed to be going right. His team had only been wasting time and effort since arriving in Hania, Crete. Everyone they had talked to, and everything they had tried, produced not a single lead. His efforts that morning had produced nothing new, and he assumed the story would be the same with the rest of the group. Maybe this time they had truly undertaken an impossible mission. Maybe they had finally met their match. If only the four could just board a plane, fly home, and forget about the whole thing. If only the team would leave justice to the courts. If only the blood pact could be dissolved once and for all. If only master Lastner could forget about vengeance. If only…

Teddy yearned to be surrounded by his family in the familiar sanctuary of his regular environment. As the phone rang, he formed mental images of his life in Tennessee. Was it his imagination or could he actually smell the aroma of his favorite dish—a specialty his wife always made to welcome him home when he'd been away for an extended time—as well as fresh bread baking in the oven? Thoughts of his cozy abode, fireplace blazing, and his precious lifestyle momentarily numbed him with contentment. In his mind's eye, he conjured up a picture of his children gathered around him, tugging at his arms and hugging his legs, competing for his attention, begging him to read one more story, wanting more and more of his time. And of his beautiful wife standing in the doorway watching the scene unfold before her, eyes sparkling, a look of happiness embedded on her girlish face.

This was the world where Kyle Teddy fit so snugly and rightly. This was the place where he flourished as a man and where his soul felt nurtured and fulfilled. This was Kyle Teddy's kingly realm. Soon, if all went well, he would return home and never again be forced to jump aboard the venomous vendetta vehicle driven by Thomas Lastner. He would pray for divine intervention.

He raised his eyebrows and shrugged his shoulders. He allowed thoughts of sheer serenity to implant firmly in his inner being, and it sated him, at least for the time being.

The phone rang and rang, but his wife did not answer. He felt sad and alone.

JACK MANNING ran to his room to phone Melissa before the meeting. More than anything he desired to return to his home, and as soon as this current caper could be completed, and the situation *corrected*, he'd get there as quickly as possible. For now, however, he felt trapped. Worry and anxiety plagued him. Everything seemed to be going wrong. He and his team had not even been able to locate the target of the hit, and the longer they stayed on the island, snooping around, the greater their chances were of getting caught. They had spun their collective wheels since arriving in Crete, with no results. Oh, how he longed for it to be over and done with, and for this to be the last time he'd ever have to partake in such nonsense. He felt fretful and nervous.

More and more, he was thinking that Teddy shared similar thoughts. He wanted badly to broach the subject with Teddy soon—to discuss the possibility of working together to find a way out of the bloody blood pact. But if he were wrong about Teddy, the price would be high.

GEORGE ZENONAKIS'S thoughts were unexpectedly interrupted. A bodyguard announced that Ambrose had returned to see him. George instructed his personal protector to send the visitor in. Righting himself in his chair, George combed his hair straight backward using all fingers on both hands and took a long swig of ice water. He pulled a small hand mirror from the top desk drawer and glanced into it. He did not look good. And he did not feel well, either. He should probably see a different doctor, he thought; yet doctors did not impress him to a great degree. After all, the last one he'd seen had given him that dreadful medicine that seemed to only make matters worse. Ambrose walked into the room and cut short George's pensive mood.

"Ambrose, come in," George said. "Come in. Have a seat, my friend." He gestured to the same chair Ambrose had sat in on his last two visits and nodded to the bodyguard indicating he was free to leave.

"I assume you are here to confirm that the purchase price we agreed upon has been transferred to my account. Am I correct in my assumption?" George asked. His steel cold eyes cut into his caller's.

"Well sir, not exactly. I have been informed that the buyer needs additional time to liquidate some assets before he can come up with that kind of money. He needs three more days."

"*What?* What went wrong, Ambrose? What changed?" George asked. He spoke in an unusually quiet tone that sent chills up and down Ambrose's back.

"I do not know the *precise* problem, sir … Mr. George. He only said it would take a bit longer than he initially thought to raise the necessary funds."

"This is not good. Not good at all. I want this transaction wrapped up, and I thought you were the man to do it for me, Ambrose. Perhaps I am wrong."

"I *will* close the transaction, Mr. George. I give you my word. It will take only a few days longer," Ambrose pleaded. "Please let me do this for you."

"Very well, Ambrose. I will grant you three additional days to finalize this transaction. That is all. Three days. See that it happens." With his hand, George waved off his visitor and called out loudly for the guards.

"But Mr. George, sir, with all due respect, we have not yet discussed my cut of the deal." He spoke politely, but with obvious concern. "What is my cut?"

"Get him out of here," George ordered his bodyguards. The whites of his eyes turned yellow, and he refused to address the question.

George's defenders grabbed Ambrose by his arms, hoisted him from the chair, and led him from the office.

"*Three days, mothafucka!*" George boomed.

"I'm wondering how Mr. George treats his *enemies*, if this is how he treats his *friends*," Ambrose muttered to the guards.

Neither responded.

NOON ARRIVED, and the team gathered in Lastner and Teddy's room. The mood appeared grim. As predicted, no new information had been obtained through the diligent morning efforts of the members. It seemed that the harder each one tried to solicit information from people, the worse the situations became in every instance.

Two days had turned into three, and still they had no more information than when they had started. It was time to regroup and change course.

"As you all know, our plan of action has not worked," Lastner began. "Usually we have no problem getting people to talk and cough up information. Crete, however, is another matter altogether. Basic fear of the Zenonakis clan inhabits the good citizens of this city. We are not going to change that fact. Seems even the police are too afraid of the family to do anything about them." He took in a deep breath and exhaled slowly. His head had started to throb in a fierce way.

"It's time for a change in venue," he continued. "I have studied the maps and decided that the four of us will travel to Heraklion this afternoon. I've arranged for a rental car. Heraklion is the other major city along the northerly coastline of Crete, and it's the capital. There is nothing left for us to do here in Hania, and maybe we'll have better luck in Heraklion. The majority of Cretans live in one or the other of these two cities. Somebody out there will talk to us if the price is right."

Lastner, a man used to getting what he wanted when he wanted it, acted incredibly irritated. With each passing hour, the situation had incessantly gnawed away at him. They needed to locate the object of their search, make the hit, and get the hell out of there. Spending too much time in the area would certainly not be a good thing. It meant more witnesses that could potentially identify the quartet, and that possibility concerned him to no end.

"Another thing," Lastner said. "And I repeat myself here. We must determine the identity of this American couple getting in the way of what we have to accomplish. If we find them, we learn exactly what information they have gleaned before we take necessary action against them. We must keep our eyes and ears open at all times. The fact that the twosome has a lead on us raises my ire. We locate our competition, and we could very possibly learn vital information to help our cause. Remember, though, the couple can never see us or know the reason we are here. *That* would most assuredly cause us insurmountable problems. We must find out who they are and what they're up to, but the reverse can never happen."

THE GROUP checked out of the inn and piled into the small rental car. These cars of reduced dimensions, ubiquitous on the island, afforded tourists great gasoline economy and ease of parking; yet, the benefits came at the expense of comfort. With the four men crammed inside, little or no elbow room remained, and barely enough breathing room. The level of discomfort made the drive nearly unbearable, and all four became annoyed and highly irritated. A mere one half hour into the journey, the car began to sputter and smoke. Numerous warning lights on the dashboard lit up just as Lastner pulled the vehicle over onto the shoulder. He turned the key off to let the engine cool, waited a few minutes, and then tried several times to restart it. All attempts failed.

"*Shit!*" Lastner yelled. "This is exactly what we damn well didn't need." He tried to use his cell phone. There was no service in the area.

The men waved their arms at every passing car, hoping some good Samaritan-type would stop and assist them. Finally, a small dark green car pulled over behind them. A man jumped out and walked over to examine the smoking car. He looked over the engine intently.

"Me mechanic," he announced. "This over," he said. "Dead." His broken English was clearly understandable. He pointed to Lastner. "You ride with me." He pointed to the passenger seat in his car. "I take. Help you."

The others agreed to wait by the side of the road while Tom Lastner went with the man to get help. Some thirty miles down the road, the mechanic pulled into a petrol station. Lastner thanked the man and tipped him. The station had no mechanic on duty to assist him. Of course, that would have been too easy.

Lastner pulled the car rental agreement out of his shirt pocket and called the Hania agency. The employee who answered the phone apologized for the inconvenience and informed Lastner that the company had no other vehicles to offer him that day. One would be available the following morning, if needed. However, he was happy to send a tow truck to the area of breakdown and bring Lastner and his passengers back to Hania. Tom grimaced. What next?

After pinpointing as best he could the location of the stalled rental car, he had no other option than to hitchhike back to his friends—a situation he would rather have avoided, but under the circumstances could not. Numerous autos and many minutes passed before a kindly tourist couple picked Lastner up and agreed to take him to the location of the breakdown. If only the mechanic that stopped to help them initially could have fixed the problem. If only. So much time could have been saved. But it seemed luck had not been on the side of the vigilantes since the day they arrived.

Once Lastner finally reached his team, they waited another forty minutes for the tow truck to arrive. When it appeared, a collective sigh could be heard from the group. The driver hooked the rental car to the back of the tow truck and shifted the auto into neutral. The men piled into the cab of the tow truck—Lastner on Harriman's lap and Manning on Teddy's. While the space in the rental car had been cramped, the space in the tow truck was barely endurable, causing the driver and passengers to feel as if a boa constrictor encircled the lot and squeezed with no mercy or pity. The drive back to Hania seemed doubly as long as the drive out of the city to the place where the vehicle had stalled.

When the driver at last reached the city, he delivered the quartet and their luggage back to the inn they had checked out of earlier in the day. Pushing and prodding each other, one by one each man pried himself free from the tow truck's front seating area. Exonerated at last from the extremely tight space, every one of the foursome shook his arms and legs to make certain all parts still worked.

Tom Lastner walked to the front desk and asked for a local business listings phonebook. He took a seat in the lobby and used the house phone. While the others looked on, he called every other car rental agency listed in the book, trying feverishly to locate another vehicle. All cars had either been spoken for or were already out on the road that day. The final company he phoned had a car to offer him in four to five hours. The group would simply have to wait.

"Dammit!" Lastner bellowed. "Dammit!" He slumped deeper into the chair and punched its arm several times. He was an angry man. "This fiasco is costing us an entire day, and we do not have the luxury of a day to lose." A low, guttural sound of utter frustration emanated from his throat, and the pain in his head intensified. He let his head roll back so that the chair top could support it. He closed his eyes.

"Let's go have a libation … while we wait," Scott Harriman

suggested. "Might as well make the best of a bad situation."

With the exception of Tom Lastner, the others followed Harriman's lead and trailed behind him into the inn's bar.

The hours dragged on as if in slow motion. The men ate and drank, but engaged in little conversation. The mood of the group appeared somber. Nothing was going the team's way. Lastner remained glued to his chair, trying desperately to manage the growing pain in his head.

Finally, a young man walked into the lobby and called out the alias name Lastner had used to rent the car. "Car for Bradley Rentsal," he announced.

Lastner yelled out, "Here!"

The man informed Lastner that the rental car was parked out front. All he had to do was sign the rental form. Another employee of the rental agency had followed the car deliverer over to the inn, and the two would drive back to the agency together. Rentsal was free to take the car once he signed on the acceptance line. Lastner scribbled *Bradley Rentsal* on the form, grabbed the keys, and grunted a thank you.

He walked into the pub and found the others. "Let's go," he ordered his men. "We can still make it to Heraklion this evening."

"Red-dee," Scott Harriman said, slurring his word. As usual, he had consumed three times more alcohol than the others.

"Good thing we ordered some food to go along with the drinks," Jack Manning whispered to Kyle Teddy. "Otherwise, Harriman would be on the floor."

23

CLAIRE WATCHED KOSTAS carefully when he returned to the room. What had made him dart out so quickly? Who had he called?

"We understand your warning, Kostas, but we have a job to do," Claire said. "We'll be careful and watch our every step."

Kostas only shook his head from side to side. "You're not hearing me, Claire. Your lives are in danger . . . even now, as we speak . . . word may already be out that you are here looking for George Zenonakis."

"Do you know where the Zenonakis family lives?" Claire persisted, not about to be dissuaded by Kostas's words.

Kostas exhaled a sigh of deep exasperation. "You won't give up, will you?"

"We will not," Claire said.

"I tell you this against my better judgment. Nikos Zenonakis owns a country estate high up in the mountains, somewhere south of Hania. It is positioned on the side of a cliff and is quite inaccessible. That's all I know. I do not know the exact location, and I have never seen the place. Like most of us on the island, I would be afraid to go anywhere near it. You two must never approach that mansion. The bodyguards are told to shoot anything that moves, and it's rumored they have a virtual arsenal up there for the specific purpose of keeping strangers away. Whether they do or not is unclear, but the rumor certainly keeps anyone from venturing too close. No one *ever* travels near the Zenonakis homestead. I don't know a person who has seen the place. No one dares approach it—not even the police."

"As we suspected, and more," Guy said.

"I must repeat myself. George is a wicked man with a dastardly heart. Stay far away from him and from the estate. I would advise you to abort your plans this very minute and return to the United States at once—while it is still an option." Again, the alarm bells rang loud and clear.

"We hear your warning. We do," Claire said. "But we have a job to do. Now, Kostas, I have one additional question for you. Have you heard of *the old woman who feeds the birds?*"

Kostas stared at Claire for one minute without uttering a word.

"Ah, indeed, I have," he said. She is a true enigma in these parts—a captivating mystery that no one can really explain. She's here, and then she is not. She appears, and then she disappears ... almost like a vanishing act. No one knows who she is, where she lives, where she came from, or how she survives. But she is spotted from time to time and from place to place around this island, most often sitting on a bench or chair somewhere in or near the city of Heraklion. People say she is aware of everything that goes on in these parts, both currently and from time immemorial. She speaks both Greek and English." He paused suddenly as if deep in thought and then began again. "It is said she is old beyond her age, yet timeless; present, yet absent; simple, yet shrewd. She is a true paradox of nature who most recently has been spotted wandering. . . ."

He stopped short and took in a deep breath before slowly letting it out. "I have said too much already. Now forgive me for being rude, my friends, but why do you ask about this woman? How do you even know about her?" Without waiting for an answer, Kostas stood. "Leave her alone, too," he said. He walked from the room.

THE BEHAVIOR of Kostas stumped Claire and Guy. They had definitely struck a nerve of some kind with him, and he had reacted strangely. Was he being protective of them? Or of George Zenonakis and *the old woman who feeds the birds*? They couldn't be sure.

After listening to him, however, they were more certain than ever that they had to locate the bird woman. She could lead them directly to George Zenonakis. No doubts remained. They spent the remainder of the day continuing to search for the old woman.

In the late afternoon, the sleuths returned to the jewelry store to pick up the money clip Guy had purchased. A salesclerk informed the two that neither Kostas nor Panos were in that afternoon, but Mr. Lombard's money clip was finished and wrapped for pickup. She walked to the back room, returned with the small parcel, and handed it to Guy.

The investigators went to sleep that night, filled with uncertainty. Kostas's behavior distressed them greatly.

THE FOLLOWING morning, Claire opened her eyes to see Guy staring at her like a leopard intently fixed on its quarry. His was the face she loved to wake up to each morning, but this day the intensity of his gaze aroused her curiosity and set in action a dominating silence. Guy supported his head on a propped pillow as he held his fixed look only inches from her smooth, tanned face.

"Good morning, my beauty," he said, breaking the quietude. "How'd you sleep?" He kissed her gently on an exposed shoulder.

"I had jumbled dreams all through the night." She was still observing him and wondering what occupied his mind.

He smiled at her with that mysterious smile, the one that told her without speaking exactly what was on his mind. "Let's get married when we return to Florida. No big to-do. Just in front of a justice of the peace. What say ye?"

This was the second time he had proposed.

Claire stretched. "I say we wait until we resolve this investigation, Guy, and then we talk about it. We shouldn't rush into tying the knot without first planning the details that are important to us, should we?"

"We need to get married, Claire. I want you to be my wife. I want us to be legitimate life partners … for as long as we both shall live."

"Sounds like you've been practicing the lines," Claire said. She furrowed her brow. Then a loving expression appeared on her face, and she cocked her head to one side. "Guy, you know I love only you. Never doubt that. And marriage will happen, when it happens. Just—not now. We're far too busy with work to throw the planning of a wedding into the mix." She leaned over to kiss him.

He turned his head away from her and leaped out of the bed, leaving the room without saying another word.

Claire rolled her eyes. Now she'd done it. She could almost reach out and touch the tension remaining in the air. Why was he making this *so* difficult? How she wished he would stop asking her to get married. She had said, "Let's think about it," in response to his first proposal, and now she'd put him off again. She knew at some point she would need to succumb to the legal fusion. But standing in front of a judge and exchanging I do's certainly would not change the solid and committed relationship they now shared. So it seemed like much ado about nothing.

Yet, despite all of her hesitations, more and more frequently these days she envisioned herself walking down a rose petal-covered aisle, wearing a shell-pink tea-length silk wedding dress and carrying a bouquet of white roses mixed with fragrant white stephanotis. And Guy, standing firm and tall, looking dignified and elegant in his black tuxedo, directing his gaze solely into her eyes as he walked in her direction, reaching out his hand for hers. Then, the two of them publicly exchanging promises to love, honor, and cherish one another ... until the end of days. It would happen. And, truthfully, she wouldn't mind it so much if it did. But she detested the societal pressure that surrounded the whole concept of the institution of marriage. It came at her from all directions. Why could two people in love not simply commit their lives to one another privately, before God, without the necessity of a public marriage ceremony? She didn't understand.

The fear of taking that permanent step and seeing it have a negative impact on the two of them, changing everything they had built together, was her innermost fear—one she refused to verbalize to anyone, but one that kept her wide-eyed and awake through many a night. But what if she put the matter of holy wedlock on hold for too long? Would Guy get discouraged and walk away for good? This distressing thought often resurrected its ugly head, making her realize that a probable D-Day loomed on the horizon. It was time ... or wasn't it? Should she make the leap ... or not? She hoped things would only get better if she did, but what if things got worse? On and on her inner turmoil debated, as if half of her was on each side of the issue.

It felt good to take a long, hot shower, and Claire ended it with a spray of icy cold water pulsating down her back. She stepped out and stood in front of the mirror. She dried her hair and applied quick touches of makeup, finishing with a swipe of her signature coral lipstick over her full lips. She sneezed, and immediately she sneezed again.

"Bless you. Bless you," Guy yelled out in quick succession from the main room.

"Thank you. Thank you," Claire answered. She threw on a white terry robe provided by the hotel, walked over to him, and gently kissed him on the side of his face. He looked at her, and their eyes locked. At once, all tension lifted, at least for the time being.

"I say we need to locate *the old woman who feeds the birds* as quickly as we can, Guy. When we first heard about her, I knew she would be the one to give us the help we needed. The little voice inside of me confirmed it, and that voice gets louder every day. We must find her. Kostas almost told us where to look for her yesterday, but he stopped short of revealing that information. His behavior was so strange at the end of our visit, and I keep wondering what happened."

"Me, too. He acted as if someone got to him. If we knew the identity of the recipient of his sudden phone call, we would probably have the answer."

"If George Zenonakis gets wind that we're on his trail, he could disappear for good," Claire said. "Something's got to give, and soon." She thought for a moment. "Our sense of direction on investigations has always been pretty right on, so let's follow it now. I say we pay Kostas another visit this morning and see if we can coax more information out of him regarding *the old woman who feeds the birds.* Kostas told us she knows everything that goes on here on the island. It is imperative that we question her. She *will* steer us to George

Zenonakis. I know it. She holds the key to this whole thing."

"You will get no argument from me, Miss Crack Investigator," Guy said. He flashed a winning smile her way. "Let's track her down *today*."

"Good. I like your optimism," Claire said. "And once we locate the criminal we're after . . . I guess at that point, I would suggest we go straight to the local police, explain exactly what we're doing here, and ask for assistance. We'll need logistical help getting Zenonakis back to the U.S."

"What makes you think the authorities will make any move against the Zenonakis family?"

"Because George Zenonakis committed murder. We both know that. How can law enforcement ignore the facts? Besides, it would not bode well for relations between the U.S. and Greece if the government refused extradition in a case of capital crime. Once we present them with all the details, how can they refuse us?"

"Well, I guess we cross that bridge when, and if, we get to it," Guy said. "Maybe your friend Sergeant Massey in Miami will be of some help to us in that regard—as far as making the initial contact with the local police here, when that time arrives."

"I certainly wouldn't call that man my *friend*, but I know he'll help us if we need him. He and I have agreed to cooperate with each other, despite his unstated belief that women should be home raising children, cooking, and doing the laundry—barefoot and pregnant, of course. Everything about that man silently screams out his true feelings."

Claire and Guy readied for the day and telephoned Kostas. The salesclerk who answered the phone said he would not be in until later in the afternoon. The investigators agreed to make the most of the day until they could visit with Kostas. Claire kept her fingers crossed that he would come through for them and provide the information they so desperately needed.

The sleuths stopped in the lobby coffee shop for a quick breakfast. As they ate, they discussed the case.

"I think we've done everything we should have so far, Guy," Claire said. "Between us, we've checked local phone directories and other Cretan public sources in hopes of finding the physical locale of the Zenonakis estate, to no avail; questioned countless numbers of people as to the whereabouts of George Zenonakis; attempted to find the old woman on our own; developed a friendship with a native Cretan in hopes of learning insider information; and recorded all of our efforts each day in our journal. We've checked Hania, and now Heraklion. Quite frankly, without Kostas leading us to the old woman, we're running out of possibilities."

The Zenonakis clan was a family everyone seemed to know all too well; yet, no one would discuss anything about them. Was it the element of fear that kept the people of Crete so quiet when that last name was spoken? If so, fear of what? It seemed as if a thief crept up and snatched away the voice of each Cretan whenever he or she was questioned about the infamous family. Had the Zenonakis dynasty exhibited such a ruthless behavior code in the past that the mere mention of the name silenced the masses, not unlike dealing with the Mob—the Cosa Nostra? Whatever it was, it seemed to be working like a charm.

Guy pulled out his map of the area. "Where to, my hotshot sleuth?"

"Let's walk back to the old city again," Claire said. She finished her Greek coffee and thought for a moment. "I say we go in that direction," she said, pointing to an area on the map near the waterfront. "Birds seem to be thick in that area."

"Let's hit it, then," Guy said. "It's time to track down that old woman."

The day was young and hopes ran high for closing in on the elusive bird woman of legend.

As the two walked from the hotel, the stranger followed a respectable distance behind.

TOM LASTNER and his group had arrived in Heraklion late the evening before. Now, the four men were rested and eager to pursue their hunt in the new territory. While they sat at breakfast, Lastner glanced at his wristwatch and then supplied each of his team with a sequential leer. He was not happy. Things were moving way too slowly for his liking, and something had to change. Mercifully the pain in his head had lessened, and he was ready to hit the ground running.

"I want to see results *today*," he demanded in a low, deep voice. Then he gave his men a warning. "I need to review what we've already discussed. The longer we stay here, the greater the risk of being identified by some do-gooders who want to help the police or score big points with the Zenonakis family. We stick out as obviously different than the norm on this island. We're instantly recognizable as Americans, and you can bet your ass that some nosy people will wonder what the hell the four of us are doing here in Crete—especially since we do not look like typical tourists. And for sure, when George Zenonakis is suddenly found dead, a lot of questions will be raised. There will be many to point their fingers directly at us—the ones asking oh-so-many Zenonakis questions of oh-so-many people—directly before his demise. So I suggest we ..."

"Then maybe we should *look like tourists*," Scott Harriman broke in. "That way no one will give us as much as a second glance."

His comment silenced Tom Lastner, who turned his full attention directly upon Scott Harriman.

"Did you just interrupt me, Scotty?"

"Excuse me, Tom, but yes, I did. Your comments suddenly made me realize that right now we *look* like four Americans on the prowl for someone or something. We need to get our act together real quick and pose as legitimate tourists. That's the only disguise that might get us what we want and keep us out of trouble."

Tom Lastner glared at Scott Harriman for one additional minute before saying a word. His cold fierce eyes could put the fear of eradication in any human being, and right now they were doing the trick on Scott Harriman. Scotty swallowed hard, but refused to look away from the ferocious and steady gaze of the conductor. He held his ground until the bedeviling eyes of Lastner darted off in another direction.

"You're right, of course," Lastner said.

All three men expelled a silent and collective gasp of relief that went unnoticed by the unpredictable head of the group.

"How about bird-watchers?" Kyle Teddy suggested.

"What the hell are *bird-watchers*?" Lastner blared.

"They're people who scout areas for rare and interesting birds native to a particular area or country," Kyle Teddy explained. "I did some quick research on Crete before we flew here and recall reading about the exotic birds that live in these parts and about how bird-watching is a common sport on this island."

"I'm listening," Tom Lastner said. He scratched his forehead. "Your ridiculous suggestion may just have some merit, Teddy."

Kyle Teddy took offense at the adjective *ridiculous*, but dared not say anything for fear of once again erupting the great Mount Lastnerius.

"Yes, indeed. Bird-watchers we will become," Tom Lastner said. "Let's get some red plaid shirts, binoculars, notebooks and pencils, doltish looking caps, and bird books. Then we will look like bird-watchers. That will be our cover."

The three men were not certain if he was serious or jesting.

"We can probably skip the red plaid clothes and foolish caps, if you ask me," Jackson Manning said. "We don't want to look too conspicuous, do we? I thought our goal was to fit into the mix and not stand out in the crowds."

"We are all very smart today," Tom Lastner said. "So very smart." The sarcastic tone dripping from his words portrayed his utter contempt for ideas that did not issue from his own lips.

After gulping down the remains of breakfast, the group went shopping. Two hours later, and dressed in Bermuda shorts, khaki shirts, hiking boots, sunglasses, and baseball caps, all members of the quartet actually looked every bit the part of bona fide bird-watchers. Binoculars hung around the neck of each man, and between them they toted a variety of books on the subject of Cretan bird-watching—each title illustrated with vivid color pictures revealing the myriad of birds native to the area.

The vigilantes took on the role of bird-watcher most seriously. Costumes in place, the performance was about to begin.

24

"WHERE TO NEXT?" Guy asked. "This random walking around by the water's edge, questioning whomever is speaking English, is producing absolutely no results."

"Well, I'm not sure," Claire said. "If you were an elderly woman who wanted to feed some birds, where would you sit? We need to start thinking like she might think." She paused and pondered. "I would find a place where birds gather, where humans would not bother me, a place where I could simply feed those warm-blooded vertebrates in peace and enjoy my day. Or better yet, let's think of it from the perspective of the birds. If you were a bird, where would you go if you were hungry?" She paused again. "I guess I would fly to a place where other birds gathered in numbers on a regular basis—a place I had found food in the past or could be assured of finding food in the present. Or, if I needed to scout out a new area,

I would look for a crowd of birds from my aerial perspective and when I spotted a large number of them in one spot, I would assume they were near a food source."

"Okay. Good. I'm following your line of thinking," Guy said. "They do say, birds of a feather flock together, so I agree, let's find areas that attract lots of birds. I think we may be on the right track."

"I believe that saying refers to *people,*" Claire said. "People with the same interests or tastes are often found together. But the adage came from somewhere. I've noticed so many times that birds tend to huddle together on telephone lines. Several adjacent lines will be empty, and yet great numbers of the same type of bird will converge together on one particular line. It's strange. So, I agree with your thought process. Let's look for flocks of birds."

After walking around for two additional hours, looking for groupings of birds, it appeared that the majority of local birds seemed to gather in most or all of the outdoor courtyards, in and amongst the many streets of the city. But these areas were also filled with many tourists and locals, bustling in and out of the surrounding shops, talking and laughing, loudly and freely.

Claire stopped cold in her tracks. "She's not here. There is too much activity here. The noise level is too high. We're looking in all the wrong places."

Guy looked at her, puzzled. She was staring straight ahead. He would not question her instinct.

"We will not find the old woman around here," Claire repeated decisively. "We will find her away from the heart of the city—in a more serene spot—where birds flourish in less inhabited places."

She looked around. One block away, she spotted several parked tour buses. "Let's hop on a bus and check out the outlying areas." She pointed the buses out to Guy. "We can cover more ground that way."

"Great idea. And my feet thank you," Guy grinned his famous grin. "This endless walking has taken its toll on them."

Claire looked down and noticed that Guy had put on dress shoes, instead of tennis or walking shoes, that morning. "That's why the old term *gumshoe* described detectives," she said. "Gumshoes are sneakers—shoes made for secretive sleuthing. Looks like you forgot to wear your gumshoes today, honey." She made a face of distress. "Let's give those poor feet a rest." She smiled a kind smile.

They hustled over to the head tour bus and stepped aboard, thankful for a comfortable seat and appreciative that they could concentrate their combined attention on searching for the old woman while someone else drove them around the outskirts of the city.

Tooling along, they noticed that many of the sites reminded them of what they had seen in and near the city of Hania, yet Heraklion definitely had its own distinctive flavor. Birds could be spotted virtually everywhere—in the sky, on the ground, up in the trees. Small ones even flitted right past the windows of the tour bus.

Crete seemed to be comprised of an interesting mix of beaches, mountain ranges, gorges, fields along the coastlines, deserts located high in certain mountains, and rivers created during the rainy season. The amazingly diverse topography lured a wide variety of flying creatures to the island—a land comprised mostly of limestone.

"It's funny," Claire said. "You never really notice the birds, unless you're looking for them, and then they seem to be everywhere."

As the bus rolled slowly along, both of the investigators agreed to search for an outright haven of birds.

About three miles outside the city limits, the driver announced they were passing the ruins of the Palace of Knossos. Just then, rain began to pelt the windows of the bus, dissuading tourists from getting out to take a closer look. Sitting inside the dry motor vehicle seemed to hold greater appeal.

Unexpectedly, Claire grabbed Guy by the arm. "We're getting out," she said.

She hollered out to the driver. "Please, stop the bus!"

"Sure you want to walk around in the rain, miss?" the driver asked.

"We are. In fact, we'd like to spend some extra time looking around here," Claire said.

"If you want to poke around the place, that's just fine. You'll miss the rest of the tour, but it's your money," the driver said. "I'll be driving back this way in exactly one hour. Make sure you're out here, and I'll pick you both up. That way you won't have to walk back to town."

"Great. Thank you," Guy said to the driver as they stepped from the bus. "We'll see you in an hour then."

"Hey, take these with you," the driver called out. He tossed Guy two portable black umbrellas. "You'll need them."

"You're a lifesaver," Claire yelled back. "Thank you."

"One hour. Enjoy yourselves," the driver shouted before closing the doors.

As the bus drove off, Guy turned to Claire. "What is it? What did you see?"

"Follow me," she said. "This way." She ran across the road.

Guy moved at top speed to keep up with Claire. A minute later, she stopped abruptly and pointed to something. "Look at this," she whispered. "Just look at this!"

THE DISINGENUOUS bird-watchers sat in restless eagerness as the rental car whirled its way to an outlying area of Heraklion—to a place filled with local serious bird-watchers and tourists alike, to a spot the hotel clerk had recommended as being one of the best locales to catch sight of rare and interesting birds. "A natural aviary, of sorts," the clerk had told the group. He also advised the four to look closely into the dense foliage of the area, as most of the elusive flying creatures sat concealed and did not perch out in the open for all to see.

Upon arrival, the quartet mingled in, around, and through the crowds, pretending to be glancing upward and about with rapt expressions, piercing the tree foliage with four sets of eyes, presumably probing the dense green leaves with insatiable curiosity, scanning for unusual species of Cretan birds, all the while scribbling unintelligible notes on writing pads and peering through binoculars for minutes on end while listening with impatient interest to the conversations of nearby birders.

The men were hoping to discover English-speaking Cretans to engage in quiet conversation that would eventually lead to questions about the infamous Zenonakis family, a seemingly simple task that to date had become a surprisingly prickly endeavor. Determining an exact location of the Zenonakis family estate—the home of these people so infamous on the island—was turning out to be an amazingly difficult undertaking. Asking too many overt questions simply did not work. So the team of four set about to use a grand amount of discretion this time as they attempted to elicit information from fellow bird-watchers in the area, hoping that someone—anyone—would slip out a morsel of helpful particulars to assist them in zooming in on the target of their search.

The birder disguises seemed to be working, as legitimate bird-watchers sporadically grabbed the arm of one or another of the foursome and pointed at trees or toward limbs to share the experience of viewing an uncommon species of the bird world. Each specimen perched majestically, seemingly conscious of the individual dignity and uniqueness it alone possessed. No one suspected the quartet of being anything other than what it appeared.

Soon it became apparent that the ability to speak a common language was not important amongst the many genuine bird-watchers; rather, only the capability of pointing and smiling broadly. It was a cult, of sorts, and sharing the discovery of a recherché bird seemed to be a reward in and of itself. Because language was not a barrier, tourist birders speaking a myriad of languages co-existed beautifully with local Cretans.

Kyle Teddy took to the sport with flying colors and actually became keenly interested in locating examples of the species so vividly portrayed in the books he carried. This was a hobby he could sink his teeth into, if circumstances were only different. Then, out of the blue, a sharp stab in his side brought him into high alert, and he winced in pain. Tom Lastner stood next to him, holding his right arm at waist level with the fingers on his right hand held tightly together in a horizontal position. It became instantly apparent to Teddy that Lastner had inflicted the physical jab intentionally.

"What was *that* for, asshole?" Teddy asked. He immediately regretted the noun he had used, but was unwilling to take it back.

"Do not excessively luxuriate in the ruse, Teddy," Lastner commanded in a tone spitting forth unfriendliness. "At all times, remember the mission. You're getting lost. And clean up your speech. You're a man of the cloth, aren't you?" Lastner leered at him maliciously and then laughed. As a second reminder, Lastner leaned in closer to Teddy's face and whispered a disquieting message to him. "Don't you enjoy it! You'll regret it if you do." Coupled with the icy darts bolting from Lastner's eyes, Teddy got the message loud and clear. "And don't *ever* refer to me as an *asshole* again!" Lastner said. Then, so unexpectedly, Lastner threw his arms around Teddy and hugged him. "Let's get on with it then, my friend."

Teddy would never understand the ever-present dichotomies

dwelling within the mercurial and controlling judge. Returning to the task of listening and looking for people to pump for potential information, Teddy felt Lastner's eyes penetrating him for several long minutes. This incident acted as a turning point for Kyle Teddy. It became the catalyst that signaled once and for all that he must find a way out of the hideous college pledge. Once upon a time he had admired Tom Lastner, but now he detested the man. This last caper would be it for Kyle Teddy.

Hours passed mingling and feigning birding, and while the four men talked with countless people, whenever the topic of the Zenonakis family was raised, no matter which one in the group broached the subject, the result was always the same. Mouths slammed shut, and those being questioned turned on their heels and walked briskly off in a different direction. All Cretans seemed to know the subject was strictly off-limits. But Teddy, Manning, and Harriman did not lose heart. They continued acting as birders and talking to legitimate individuals engaging in the sport.

Lastner took a time out. He was fed up and quickly running out of patience with this silly bird-watching gig. He thought long and hard and came up with a new plan of action to obtain the information they so vitally required to accomplish their mission. The plan was risky, but it had to be attempted. He would share the specifics of it with the others in a short while. Nighttime would work best for his scheme.

A MINUTE after Claire and Guy stepped away from the tour bus, the rain came down harder. They quickly opened the umbrellas, thankful to have some shelter as they walked around the grounds. Birds took off en masse, flying to nearby trees to escape the downpour.

"Never have I seen so many birds in one place at one time," Guy said. "Actually, it's a little unnerving."

"I noticed it from the bus window—this congregation of birds," Claire said. "I know it's raining, but the ruins are ours to explore. I'm wondering if this influx of birds might attract an old bird woman, perhaps?" She looked at Guy. "Let's take a look around. Besides, we have an hour to kill before the bus returns. Let's take advantage of this great opportunity."

"This is the stuff I live for," Guy said. "Look around. Red columns, a palace chamber, a million hints of what used to be. We may never get the chance to see this place again. What a time in history it must have been when the Palace of Knossos was in full operation. I can only imagine."

Claire picked up a multi-panel folded brochure sitting inside a primitive wooden roadside stand and started to read about the site. She gave Guy a quick synopsis.

"We're standing on the excavated ruins of the once majestic Palace of Knossos, the center of the ancient Minoan civilization that thrived on the island of Crete during the Bronze Age—2700 to 1450 BCE. Apparently, little is actually known about the Minoans, or of their demise, whether it was triggered by earthquake or fire, but there is much conjecture. It is thought that over 100,000 people lived in and around this palace at the high point of the Minoan civilization.

"The Myth of the Labyrinth may have started here, with the structure's intricate and confusing layout of approximately 1,300 rooms, all interconnected by corridors. Legend has it the elaborate structure was built in a mazelike network by King Minos of Crete. It was multi-storied, with inner and outer staircases, and had rooms strategically placed around courtyards. It had aqueducts to hold fresh water, sanitation drainage, water-flushing toilets, porticos, airshafts, frescoes decorating the walls, and on and on. It was thought to be the political center of that civilization, and maybe the ceremonial center, too."

Instantly, Guy's interest heightened to grand proportions. "I'm hooked. Tell me more." His insatiable intrigue with all history had been ignited.

"We'll have to read all of this when we get the chance. There is so much history associated with the Minoans and this Palace—and this entire island."

Together the two sleuths walked slowly through the fascinating ruins, appreciating the historical magnitude of the unearthing.

"This palace was a labyrinth, Guy," Claire said, referring to the handout. "The Minotaur of legend supposedly lived inside. Confined. It could not find its way out of the maze."

"The Minotaur is the half-man, half-bull creature of Greek mythology," Guy said. "Daedalus created this labyrinth, if my memory serves me correctly, and the Minotaur fed on human flesh, legend claimed. Eventually, the creature was slain by Theseus."

"Your memory is flawless, my great master of history," Claire replied, smiling. "That's precisely what it says in the pamphlet."

"Ooh. Scary. What was *that*?" Guy spun around wildly.

Claire turned quickly and looked in the direction Guy pointed. She saw nothing unusual. Her heart pounded.

"Just kidding. I thought perhaps you'd think the Minotaur had returned to the scene to grab us." He grinned a sheepish grin.

"Funny, Guy. *Real* funny. Remind me to laugh." It was clear Claire did not find his nonsense one bit amusing.

They paced through the ruins, taking in everything, intrigued by the obvious sophistication of the civilization that thrived so long ago. Tall, colossal, earthenware jugs—*pithoi*—once used to store wine and oil, stood proudly in place, and remnants of still vivid orange and blue murals remained as evidence of the once great people. A trough for running water, steps to rival anything of the current age, a public underground bath, and so much more. The ruins seduced them.

The overcast sky had turned the day gray and hazy. Within minutes, the rain came down even harder than before.

Claire and Guy stepped underneath an overhang to escape the inclement weather.

Suddenly, Claire screamed. "What was *that*?"

"Good try, my love," Guy said. "But you can't fool me."

"I'm serious, Guy. I swear I just saw a shadow ... moving ... over there." She pointed. "I thought we were alone in here. Let's check it out."

"After you. I'm right behind you," he said.

She gave him a disappointed look.

"Okay. Okay. Follow me," he said.

Together, under the cover of umbrellas, they ran in the direction of the shadowy form, but found nothing when they reached the area from which it had emanated. Just then, Claire spotted another shadow and ran toward it, only to be let down again. Once more, she saw a shadow and chased it, too, but to no avail.

"It's her," Claire said. "I feel it."

Guy's eyes darted to the right and he spotted a cat walking atop a ledge in the ruins. "Claire, it's only a cat. Look, over there." He nodded with his head in the direction of the small mammal that gracefully but rapidly moved away from them. "Probably coming for the birds."

"No. The shadow I keep seeing is much larger than that of a cat," she protested.

25

"IT'S A *LABYRINTH*, my celebrated sleuth," Guy said. "A complex entanglement. Things probably appear as they are not—especially under this cloud cover."

"I don't know," Claire said. "I don't buy it. I know what I saw." She glanced furtively in all directions, not the least bit convinced that a mere cat had caused the humanlike shadows she witnessed. Yet, with all the birds in the vicinity she guessed there probably were lots of cats nearby.

The investigators continued to walk amidst the ruins of the Palace of Knossos, under the rain of the day, fascinated by the ancient history.

"I can close my eyes, Guy, and imagine this area brimming with people busily at work leading productive lives. It's easy if you try."

"It is. I envision a thriving urban center dominated by this incredible palace. What a time it must have been to be alive."

The tour bus would soon return to pick them up. The hour had passed quickly. Claire and Guy walked back across the road to wait.

"Funny. When I saw all the birds, I thought we might find the old bird woman here," Claire said. "My famous sixth sense failed me. I can't understand it. That little voice inside me yelled out so loudly." Then, suddenly, Claire's eyes darted to yet another shadowy image of movement appearing on a portion of a wall within the ruins. The object crouched low, and it seemed to move with deliberate speed. But when Claire ran back across the road to check it out, she returned with a look of frustration on her face. "Whatever it was, Guy, it disappeared into thin air."

Behind a clump of trees, many feet away from where they stood, the stranger dressed in brown concealed his presence, his eyes riveted on the sleuths. He had parked his yellow car out of sight.

The tour bus returned on time, and Claire and Guy boarded and rode it back to Heraklion. They agreed to grab a late lunch and then walk over to the jewelry store to see Kostas. Hopefully, he would be in by then.

"LOOK!" KYLE Teddy said in a low, muffled tone. He pointed upward toward an Eleanora's Falcon perched high near the top of a large tree. "Listen!" he whispered, as the rare bird whistled its usual *ke-ke-ke-ke-ke*. "It sounds like a child is making that noise," he added softly. At once, all surrounding bird-watchers aimed their binoculars in unison to see the impressive medium-sized bird. Time stood still as the crowd quietly and voraciously inhaled the magnificence of the unique species.

Twenty minutes later the falcon flew away, displaying its broad wingspan for all to see. Once again, the birders breathed normally.

"Good spot, by the way!" a tourist shouted loudly to Teddy. The man clapped his hands.

One by one the other birders joined in with the clapping, each looking at Teddy and smiling broadly or giving him the thumbs-up sign.

Teddy nodded back, embarrassed by the praise, yet acknowledging the kind gestures. But he feared retaliation from Tom Lastner for calling attention to himself. It was something he had not meant to do.

An English-speaking couple with a European accent walked over to Teddy, carefully stepping around a patch of wild orchids to reach him, and started up a conversation.

"How'd you spot it? We've been looking for his kind for several days now," the woman of the couple said. "Actually, several *years* now, to be honest. I guess we've just been at the wrong place in the right season, or at the right place in the wrong season." She shrugged her shoulders. "Certain places in Crete are better than others for spotting a variety of birds, you know. For example, the huge Samaria Gorge, south of Hania—that place is absolutely renowned for gathering a wide variety of birds. You should go there while you're visiting the island, if you haven't already."

"We live in France," the man of the couple said. "And every year, over the past several, we've come to Crete on holiday—specifically to bird-watch. We've seen birds of so many species. For example: the Griffon and Bearded Vulture; the Golden Eagle, the Buzzard, and the Sardinian Warbler; the Blue Rock Thrush and the Fan-Tailed Warbler; and the Crested Lark and the Italian Sparrow, to name a few. But never the Eleanora's Falcon, until today." He pondered for a moment and scratched his forehead. "On second thought, I guess we did see one in the far away distance on an occasion outside of Hania, up near Omalos, after that never to be forgotten drive, now that I think about it." He stopped momentarily, as if remembering. "But we've never before seen the likes of that impressive beauty up close. *Merci beaucoup* for the great sighting!"

"I'm sure you've come to this spot for many years yourself," the woman chimed in.

"Not really," Teddy replied chuckling. "I'm actually quite new to this sport of birding. Beginner's luck, I guess."

"I don't believe you," the woman said. She looked at him quizzically. "Not for one second."

Teddy seized the opportunity to engage the couple in further conversation, hoping to work his way into asking questions about the Zenonakis family. Suddenly, he became aware that Tom Lastner stood only feet away from him. While pretending to be looking upward, Lastner craned his neck to hear all of the conversation. Teddy proceeded to draw the couple in, making statements and asking questions, knowing full well that his work would be fully critiqued by Lastner later on.

The couple seemed fascinated to hear all about Kyle Teddy, the humble preacher who, together with his wife, was fully engaged in home-schooling the couple's four young daughters. The level of contentment, so evident in his voice when he spoke of his calling and home life, appeared to hit a tender spot in the woman. Teddy was such a genuine person—one with values and morals—and she liked that in an individual; it seemed so unusual to find nowadays. The threesome quickly fell into easy conversation, enjoying each other's company.

At once, Teddy felt a pair of dark eyes boring into him. It was Lastner, of course, now standing directly behind the French couple. Without words, Lastner's penetrating glare told Teddy to stop wasting time and get on with the mission.

"So, you've visited Crete *many* times before?" Teddy asked, looking from the man to the woman. "Tell me, have you ever heard the name George Zenonakis?" The step was bold, and Teddy held his breath, afraid the question would scare off the pleasant couple.

The man and woman exchanged quick glances, turned, and walked off in the direction of a line of trees some thirty feet away. Teddy noticed the couple whispering to each other and then staring back at him in a curious way.

"Great work, Teddy," Lastner said, brushing past the defeated pastor.

"At least *I'm* trying," Teddy retorted. "How are *you* doing, Tom?"

"Zip it!" Lastner uttered. "Just *freaking* zip it!" He growled and walked away.

Jack Manning and Scott Harriman peered through binoculars into the surrounding trees, desperately attempting to mix the purported bird-watching with coaxing other birders to give up information about the infamous family. Trying to appear as legitimate birders, it became a fine balancing act. Physically, the two stood about fifty feet away from Kyle Teddy. Jack and Scott gazed upward, mechanically, speaking softly, fully acting the part of tourists hoping to spot and appreciate the rare species of native island birds. After each had approached a dozen legitimate bird-watchers and pumped the folks for information, the two had ended up with only a healthy serving of frustration. Now, together, they had decided to actually spend time looking for the birds pictured so brilliantly in the books they carried. Maybe that way, birders would engage *them* in conversation that would flow more smoothly. And that approach seemed to be working until Tom Lastner caught up with them.

"What the hell are you two doing? Looking for Tweety Bird?" Lastner asked snootily.

Kyle Teddy had followed Lastner over to the other team members.

"Well, forcing questions on people doesn't seem to be doing the trick," Manning said. "As if we haven't learned that by now."

"Yeah. Nobody's talking," Harriman said. "This is a grandiose waste of our time."

Manning and Harriman felt like screaming with frustration.

"How about *you*?" Harriman asked Lastner. "How are you doing with this?"

"Let me get this straight. You're asking *me* about *my* performance?" Lastner boomed. "Must I review the rules, here?"

"No, Your Highness," Harriman said. He bowed down. "We stand corrected, O Great One." Harriman was the only one of the three able at times to get away with giving it back to Lastner. "I need a stiff one." Clearly, Harriman was greatly annoyed. He walked a few steps away. It was late in the afternoon, but the sun was still high in the sky. The day had been tedious and unproductive, once again, and truthfully he had had this pretend bird-watching activity up to his eyeballs.

"I hope you mean a strong *coffee*, Scotty, because the four of us need to sit down at a taverna and have a clearheaded talk. I'm calling a meeting of our team now."

The men dutifully loaded into the rental car, and Tom Lastner drove to the waterfront area of Heraklion. He parked the vehicle, and the men followed him to a nearby outdoor café. Lastner ordered black coffees all around.

"I've figured out a way to obtain the whereabouts of George Zenonakis," Lastner began.

Over thick demitasse cups of strong Greek coffee—the grounds settled to the bottom—the men listened carefully to what their leader proposed.

After Lastner explained his planned strategy, Teddy pushed his chair away from the table and sighed deeply. "I'm not sure I like this idea. Sounds fraught with danger to me. Too many variables we cannot control."

"I'm in agreement with Teddy," Jack Manning piped in. "What if we get *caught*? Then what? That's the last thing we need to happen."

"We will see to it that we do not get caught," Lastner said. "Getting caught is *not* an option." He looked around the group, eyeballing each man with intensity. "Do I make myself clear?"

"Clear as water," Scott Harriman said. "*Crystal* clear."

"Or mud," Teddy mumbled under his breath.

"I'm sorry, Teddy. We all missed what you said. Can you repeat it, please? Louder this time for the whole group to hear?" Lastner glowered at Teddy with a look that could melt steel.

Put on the spot, Teddy improvised. I said, "Not *mud*dled . . . very clear."

"Good," Lastner said. "Then we will carry out the mission tonight, as soon as it gets dark. We will move swiftly, get what we need, and make a hasty retreat."

After further discussion about appropriate dress, materials needed for the caper, and the role each would play, an evening rendezvous time was agreed upon and the meeting ended. Lastner picked up the tab, and the four calmly exited the sidewalk café, but not before agreeing to meet for dinner prior to the escapade to discuss final details.

THE LATE lunch sated the two investigators. Now it was time to visit Kostas. They walked the few blocks to his family jewelry store and stepped inside. A female employee greeted them. She was someone they had not seen before.

"We are here to see Kostas. Please tell him Claire and Guy are here to see him," Claire said.

The woman disappeared into the back room and reappeared a short time later.

"He is not able to speak with you now. Please try him another time."

"What?" Claire asked. "We only need a couple minutes of his time. It will not take long. Surely he will see us."

The woman shrugged her shoulders. "I'll ask him a second time." She turned and again ambled into the back room to speak to Kostas. When she returned, the look on her face gave Claire and Guy the answer they feared.

"He will not see us, correct?" Claire asked.

"No, he will not. He requests that you do not bother him again."

Claire's expression froze, unable to believe what she had just heard. Feeling saddened by the circumstances, the two walked back to their hotel. The best hope for finding the old woman had just disintegrated before their eyes.

"I'm tired, Guy. I'm going to lie down and take a nap before dinner," Claire said. She disrobed and crawled in between the sheets, saying nothing more.

The sound of total despair evident in her voice cut to the quick in Guy. After all, she was the optimistic one ... the one who always said, "Persevere. The answer is here if we look long enough and hard enough. Don't give up. Stay with it." He had heard her say those words a thousand times if he had heard them once. Now, it seemed as if she had thrown in the towel, admitting certain defeat.

Guy undressed and climbed in next to her. The time had come for *him* to encourage *her*. "The answer is right in front of us, Claire, if we look long enough and hard enough," he whispered in her ear. "Don't give up. Stay with it."

She did not respond.

26

"MY BIRDS, MY birds, my flawless friends. How lovely are your feathers. Your eyes … so caring. Your songs … so majestic. Ah, yes, my delightful, exquisite birds. How you brighten up my days."

The old woman sat in isolation on a primitive bench, birds clustered around her feet, perched upon her arms, and nestled on top of her head. Together, the multitude of feathered friends twittered and whistled a melodious symphony for her ears only. She joined in from time to time, harmonizing with the characteristic chatter of the creatures—her only companions in the cruel and pitiless life that had been dealt to her. When she sang, she felt young again. As her pleasant sounding voice overflowed with rhythm and emotion, the deep creases embedded in her downcast demeanor seemed to all but disappear.

Nothing had ever worked out in her life, and as the decades passed she found herself bitter, forlorn, and reclusive. Now, in the twilight of her years, she actually preferred to be alone—seldom and only out of sheer necessity having any dealings with other human beings. At this stage, her birds provided the peace she could find nowhere else.

The bird woman, petite in stature, appeared much older than her years. Deep, unordered wrinkles had been delivered to her at an early age, and she looked gaunt and haggard. Using her knobby fingers each morning, she worked her fresh-snowfall-colored hair into a single long and thin braid that wove its way down the center of her back. Tiny hazel eyes twinkled with a fierce strength and seemed somehow out of place on her otherwise weather-beaten face. Whenever she sat near her beloved wild birds, the intensity in those powerful eyes intermixed with a look of genuine and undisputed love. The rare onlooker, able to grab a glimpse of her singing to and with her many feathered friends, never forgot the unusual sight they beheld. The undeniable natural harmony of a human communicating so purely and absolutely with wild creatures left an indelible, almost eerie, imprint on the observer.

"Oh, my special one," the old lady said to a reddish bird that hopped onto her shoulder and seemed to look her straight in the eyes. "In a short while, I may have to leave for a time, but I'll be back again." She leaned over and kissed the little bird gently on its beak. Strangely, the bird appeared to bob its head up and down in understanding to the old woman. "You take care of the others while I'm gone," she continued. "Warn them whenever danger is near. And fly with them to find food each day." Again, the red bird raised and lowered its head, in rapid succession, in apparent assent.

CLAIRE LOOKED over at Guy. "I want to go back to the Palace of Knossos. Don't ask me why. But, there is something there that will help us."

"What, Claire?"

"Not sure. I need to look the place over a second time ... this time with a closer eye."

"I won't question you, Claire. Let's walk to the center of the city and find a tour bus to drop us there. Hopefully, you're correct."

Claire did not comment further. She was staring straight ahead, deep in thought. Whenever Guy observed her in this mood, he knew the wheels were turning in her head, and he also knew not to disturb her. She was alone with her thoughts and needed to dissect them.

In silence, the investigators walked to the shopping area of the city. Soon they spotted a number of tour buses parked end to end along one of the streets. They approached the lead bus, paid the appropriate fare, and stepped aboard. As fate would have it, the same driver from their previous excursion was behind the wheel once again. In a short time, Claire would have her second opportunity to scan the area of the ruins of the famous palace. A powerful inkling was calling her to return, and she had to comply. Riding the bus for the minutes it took to reach the tourist attraction seemed to take longer than it should have.

"Driver," Claire called out when she spotted the familiar area. "We would like to get out here, please."

He pulled the bus over to the side of the road. "Same routine as before, madam?" he asked.

"Exactly the same," Claire replied. "See you in about an hour."

"Don't forget about us," Guy said, as they stepped from the bus.

Claire and Guy crossed the road, walked past another tour bus parked in the opposite direction, and strolled into the area of the ruins. Several tourists slowly paced the area that day, taking photographs and oohing and aahing to each other over the breathtaking, surviving fresco remnants—in shades of brick, caramel, teal, and white. One by one, or two by two, the onlookers finally walked back to the bus that had brought them there and boarded to continue the tour.

"At last we're alone," Claire said. "Let's sit down. Over there." She nodded her head to indicate the direction. As they walked, she pointed to a flat-topped rock ledge. They took a seat on the hard surface, and Claire turned her attention to Guy. "Now, let's watch and listen. We must sit in total silence."

Minutes passed and nothing out of the ordinary occurred. Guy began to talk, and Claire held an index finger to her puckered lips, signaling he must remain quiet. Almost as if on cue, birds started to arrive out of nowhere and out of everywhere—first a couple, then ten ... thirty ... a hundred. Before long birds dominated the entire area in numbers too voluminous to count. All species of the feathered animals met and merged together on the ground in front of the two investigators. A small one hopped up onto Claire's lap and looked up at her.

"I wish I had something to feed you," Claire whispered. "What a darling little bird you are."

"I have food," an elderly voice crackled from somewhere behind them.

Startled, Claire and Guy whirled around in the direction of the utterance.

Ten feet away stood an elderly woman. Her clothing had frayed to tatters and draped loosely over her gaunt frame. Her hands were covered with old, worn canvas gloves. In each arm, she held a green burlap bag. She inched her way toward the pair and sat down on the same ledge. She placed both bags on the ground by her feet.

"Hello my darlings. Mama is here," she said, looking out at the birds. "They're magnificent, aren't they?"

"Yes, they certainly are," Claire said. "I've never seen so many birds in one place in my life. Do you feed them often?"

"Every day," she said with a slight smile. "They are my children. If I do not feed them, no one will. They have come to rely solely on me."

At once, the investigators realized they had finally found the old woman for whom they searched.

Sitting in quiet amazement, Claire and Guy watched an astonishing scenario unfold before their eyes. One by one, birds beat their wings in the air and flitted up to a different spot on the old woman and landed. Before long, her head, shoulders, lap, arms, upper legs, and feet were covered with her feathered friends. They billed and cooed, chirped and warbled, trilled and whinnied, squawked and whistled, and twittered and tweeted. Simple and complex songs melded with musical and harsh tones to fill the air with a pleasant mix of strange and glorious sounds. Some melodies varied in pitch, while others seemed to repeat the same note over and over. Certain tones trumpeted clear, others were opaque. The elaborate ensemble rivaled a musical composition of full orchestra.

The sleuths sat in wonderment, taking in every bit of the mystifying phenomenon.

When the birds completed their private performance, the elderly woman reached down to retrieve one of the bags sitting at her feet. She opened it carefully, with birds still clinging to her hands. Reaching inside, she grabbed a handful of the seeds and tossed them gently on the ground in front of her. Birds flocked to that spot to indulge in the welcomed food. Next, she threw handfuls out in several other directions. Other birds followed that nourishment, gobbling it up quickly. Before long she had emptied one entire bag, and all the birds, except for one—a red bird—had left the comfort of her body perch to gorge hungrily on the gratifying sustenance.

The old woman reached down to retrieve the second bag, opened it, and scooped out a portion specifically for the scarlet bird. Propped on her lap, the bird ate directly out of her hand.

"You always wait until the others have eaten, my friend," she said. She stroked its head tenderly. "This has never gone unnoticed by me."

When the red creature had sated itself, the old woman threw the remainder of the second bag's contents out into the wind. The birds whipped themselves into a frenzy, fighting for and overindulging in the tasty small bits of food.

Guy stood and extended his hand toward the woman. "I am Guy Lombard, and this lovely lady with me is Claire Caswell."

"I know who you are," she thundered. "You have been searching for me. What is it that you want?" Her small eyes betrayed a rebellious nature.

"We are searching for a man," Guy began. "A man we believe has returned to his homeland of Crete."

"It is important that we find him," Claire said. "He has done terrible things, hurt many people, and needs to stand

trial for his actions." She looked directly into the eyes of the old woman. "We were told you could help us pinpoint his location. His name is…"

"Stop!" the woman cried out. "I know for whom you search." She looked away. "What are your plans for him?" Her gawk returned to Claire.

"We are private investigators from Miami, Florida. Our job is to return him to the United States, so that he will stand trial for what he has done," Claire replied. "We were hired by a man gravely damaged by the actions of George Zenonakis—a man whose life George destroyed." She went on to tell the woman exactly what had happened to the Otto family: the explosion, the death of their only offspring, the loss of the family money, and the subsequent death of Mrs. Otto.

The elderly woman took it all in and then sat still for a time, seemingly absorbed in her private thoughts. The two investigators did not interrupt her. Repeated, sharp, high-pitched chirps from the red bird, sitting so proudly on the old woman's lap, eventually snapped her back to reality. She turned and faced Claire, once again.

"I will help you," the old woman said. "But I need to think this over. Meet me back here tomorrow at the same time. I will propose a plan."

Guy glanced at his watch. "I'm afraid we must leave now. The tour bus will be here in a minute to pick us up."

"Thank you," Claire said to the old woman who feeds the birds. "Thank you."

The old bird woman refused to look at either of the investigators.

Guy grabbed Claire by the hand. "We must go or we'll miss our ride."

THE FOLLOWING day, the sleuths arrived back at the site of the ruins, precisely at the same time as the day before, anxious to talk with the old woman. They waited for the full hour, until the tour bus again stopped to retrieve them, yet she never appeared. Strangely, neither did the birds.

"CLAIRE? CLAIRE? You're dreaming. It's just a dream," came a familiar voice seemingly far off in the distance. As she listened, the voice became louder and louder. "It's a dream, Claire. You're dreaming. Wake up."

Claire opened her eyes and rubbed them.

"Honey, you're been napping for a long time," Guy said. "You became so restless I had to wake you. Are you all right?"

"I had the strangest dream," she said. "You won't believe it. I saw her … the old woman … at the ruins. We have to return to the Palace of Knossos first thing tomorrow. It's imperative!"

"Okay, I'm with you. But tonight let's go out for a nice Italian dinner. I think we could both use a break."

27

THE INVESTIGATORS DRESSED for dinner and stopped to ask the concierge his recommendation for the best Italian restaurant within walking distance of the hotel.

"Oh, that is easy. It's three short blocks from here—an effortless walk. I will call ahead and make a reservation for you." He jotted the name and street address of the eatery on a piece of white paper and handed it to Guy. "I send all of our guests to this restaurant if they are in the mood for authentic and delicious Italian cuisine. It's *superb*! Patrons simply rave about it!" He gave them walking directions and wished them a delightful evening.

The establishment was cozy and welcoming. Marine-blue sconces decorated the yellow walls, and decorative Venetian chandeliers dangled at irregular lengths from the ceiling, drawing every eye upward. Glowing votive candles encased in attractive wrought iron holders provided ambient lighting on each table, and clusters of burgundy plastic grapes hung from arched doorways.

The meal was delectable—just as the concierge had promised. But Claire's mood seemed edgy and her appetite was minimal. Her dream had been all too real, and she couldn't put it out of her mind. In fact, it was all she could talk about throughout the entire dinner.

"She's there. We will find *the old woman who feeds the birds* at the ruins of the Palace of Knossos. I know it. *Her* shadow is the shadow I saw when we visited the site. My instinct was correct after all, Guy. I still have it," Claire said.

"Yes, and your dreams are always reliable. So I would say you haven't lost your touch one bit, my love. You're right on your game." He smiled warmly. "You're still a top notch, crack investigator. The absolute best I've ever worked with."

Claire didn't smile back. All of Guy's niceties that evening appeared to be in vain. The vision had obviously shaken her considerably, and now she felt more urgency than ever to find the old woman and seek her help. Stress mounted within Claire and made her world sway back and forth. Something was about to happen. Soon this case would take a mighty turn.

"I won't relax until we go back to the ruins in the morning," she said. "I'd ask you to go with me tonight, but in the dark it would probably be an exercise in futility."

Claire and Guy ordered lattes after dinner and split a chilled chocolate-filled cannoli.

Unbeknownst to the sleuths, and as fate would have it, the team of four men had just been seated in the same restaurant in an adjoining room.

Guy excused himself from the table. As he wandered down the corridor in search of the men's room, he heard a strange, almost eerie, chant emanating from an adjacent private room within the establishment. The voices were muffled, and while he couldn't make out the words, he was sure they were being spoken in English—not Greek or Italian. Moreover, the accents in the voices definitely sounded American. He pressed his ear to the hall wall just in time to hear the men's voices repeating the chilling chant a second time:

Justice, justice, we will undertake.
Make things right, make no mistake.
They can run, but they can't hide.
We will do our jobs with pride.

That's odd, he thought. The loudest voice seemed uncannily familiar to him. It was a voice he had heard before, but to whom did it belong? He could not remember. On his way back to the table, he walked past the room and without slowing his step shot a furtive glance inside. The lighting in the room was too dim to see anything clearly, but the meeting had all the earmarks of a clandestine gathering. Guy made out four figures sitting at the table, whispering in the dark setting. The hush-hush backdrop, combined with the sinister chant, pelted instant misgivings into Guy. What were these Americans up to? Nothing good he assured himself.

Back at the table, Guy shared what he had just heard and seen. "I know that voice, Claire. But I cannot recall where I've heard it before."

"It will come to you, when you least expect it," she said.

On their way out, Guy stopped and asked the maître d' for the name of the person who had booked the private room for the evening. "I think I recognize the voice of one of the men," Guy said, "but I can't be certain."

The host checked his reservations book. "That would be the Bradley Rentsal party, Mr. Lombard. The four men are visiting from the United States. Mentioned they are here on a diving trip. You're an American, too, yes? Do you know Mr. Rentsal? Shall I tell him you are here?"

"No, sir. That's not a name I recognize. I must have been mistaken. But I do have one last question for you. Is Mr. Rentsal the one with the loudest voice?"

"Oh, yes, he is the one with the, how do you say it … with the *thunderous* voice!"

Guy chuckled. He was intrigued to say the least.

"But now the whole party is very quiet in there," the host continued. "Lots of whispering going on, according to the server. It's like they're having a top secret meeting. They even asked the waitress not to come back once she served the food. She found the request strange, so she came to tell me about it. I told her as long as they pay their check, they can dance on the tables in their underwear for all I care." He half-suppressed a laugh.

"Well, thank you kindly," Guy said. "We had a wonderful evening."

THE VIGILANTES wined and dined and enjoyed themselves, but they also discussed the logistics of the plan Lastner had concocted earlier in the day. Soon it would be time to put the scheme into play. It was late, and the darkness of the night would aid and abet the group activity nicely.

BACK IN the room, Claire yawned twice in rapid succession.

"Tired?" Guy asked, sympathetically.

"No, I'm exhausted," she said. "But I can't turn my mind off. I don't know if I'll be able to sleep tonight, or not."

"I understand. We took on an onerous task when Mr. Otto hired us to bring George Zenonakis back to the U.S. Making headway in this case has been difficult to say the least. And to tell you the truth, you're much better at this investigative stuff than I am."

"Not so, Guy. We make a great team. Always remember that. One without the other would only be half as good."

"I think we got pulled into this matter not realizing just how tough this case was going to be. We had nothing to go on, initially, and still have very little."

"Yeah. But that's always the case, isn't it, when you really think about it?" Claire asked. "We never really know what we're getting ourselves into, until we're in it up to our eyeballs. In the end, though, we've always been able to put enough of the pieces together to solve the investigation. This case will be no different."

Guy thought for a couple of moments. "I know you're probably right. It just feels like we're in a spin class, pedaling as fast as we can and going nowhere. It annoys me to no end." He sighed deeply. "I'm not a patient person. I like to get things done."

"Persevere, Guy. Good things come to those who wait." Claire said, recalling the words of her late grandmother.

Guy looked at her and saw great determination on her weary face. He grinned his famous grin. "Welcome back, my dear. For a while there, I thought you had lost your staying power. Glad to see it's back."

She hugged him tightly. "Goodnight, my love." She kissed him gently on the lips and then on his forehead. "I love you. Pleasant dreams."

GEORGE ZENONAKIS pulled a notepad and pen from the top drawer of the large desk. His thoughts seemed foggy again. Grandfather Nikos had changed. He seemed to have little or no time for his grandson these days. For an old man, he kept very busy with his own life, as if his grandson did not exist or matter in the slightest. In fact, since George had returned to Crete, his grandfather had spoken with him only on rare occasions and out of sheer necessity.

Upon further reflection, it seemed that not even Papou could be counted on anymore. So much for family. Very soon, when the sale of the ruby was finalized, George would be rich in his own right and would never again have to beg the old codger to wire him money. Then, when his grandfather died, George would inherit the family estate—the generations of Zenonakis money—as well. He would have more money than he could spend in a lavish lifetime. He daydreamed. Perhaps he would remain in Crete permanently and make the Zenonakis mansion his home. He wondered if that would finally make him happy. But, alas, he did not think so.

Absentmindedly, he doodled on the top sheet. He drew an outline of the Miami plastics factory he had studied so diligently in order to pick the precise spots to place the plastic explosive compound—in order to ensure a total collapse of the building. The unusual design of the old construction had complicated matters.

In the murk of his mind, George muddled through the mayhem of that night. He recalled walking into the building through the side door that had strangely been left unlocked. He remembered climbing the stairs to the second level and seeing a light glowing in an internal office. He relived walking toward the light and observing that an employee was hard at work, late, and so unexpected, and how that young man had presented an obstacle that had to be dealt with in a quick and decisive manner. As he let his mind meander through the memory, he continued to scribble. George drew an office on the margin of the paper and a stick figure sitting in a chair with his back to the doorway. Then, in his mind's eye, George recalled stepping quietly into the room and slipping the high-carbon steel piano wire over the head of the unsuspecting employee who sat so engrossed in his work. George remembered crisscrossing the fine wire behind the man's neck and pulling on it in a violent, uncontrolled rage as the worker struggled for his life. The whole incident had ended in seconds. The piano wire George always carried in his pocket had served its purpose.

As George restored that critical moment to life, his pen drew a loop around the employee's neck. Then George placed a large X over the man in the chair, denoting the problem had been resolved.

Next, George Zenonakis envisioned his brisk walk through the building looking for the safe Mr. Otto had so loudly boasted was stashed with cash. George had so easily located it, and placed a small amount of the soft, hand-moldable plastic explosive over its combination lock, backing far away before detonating it. How easy it had been to blow the sturdy door wide open. George remembered signaling his men who waited outside, and how, in no time flat, the strong cabinet with the complex lock had been thoroughly emptied of its cache—the glorious, thick bundles of green paper money. Replaying the scenario in his mind, George scribbled a rectangular strong box on the sheet, drew a dollar sign on it, and wrote the word *kaboom* over it.

Then he sketched numerous tied-up parcels of cash, placing a dollar sign on each chunky bundle. He smiled wildly as he looked over his masterpiece. Finally, he remembered being the last living man to walk from the building and detonating the plastic explosive to level the structure. The blast had produced a brilliant display akin to pyrotechnics in the nighttime sky. It was a sight that burned permanently into George's recall.

He smiled as he scribbled *BOOM* in large letters across the entire sketched edifice and added a large exclamation point after the word. When he completed his simple diagram, he placed his signature in the bottom right corner, so proud he was of his fine work. But then, suddenly, a surprising feeling of self-loathing and revulsion washed over him. He had done a lot of horrible things in his lifetime, but he had never committed murder before—at least not with his own hands. He needed to go to bed. He grabbed his drawing, crumpled it up, and threw it into the wastebasket under the desk. He struggled to raise himself from the chair, swooned, and collapsed onto the floor.

Seconds later, a hand snatched the wadded sheet of paper from the receptacle.

TOM LASTNER and his avenging squadron were in place, ready to go. The main police department in Heraklion had been locked up for the night. In case of an emergency, an intercom placed near the front door allowed for individuals to buzz the nighttime officers on duty to request assistance.

"You all know the plan," Lastner whispered to his men. "Teddy, you and Manning go first. We'll follow behind and do our thing. Make it look good."

Manning put on dark, horn-rimmed eyeglasses and pulled his cap low onto his forehead. Teddy did the same. Manning approached the intercom, pushed the call button, and waited to talk.

"What is the problem?" a deep male voice asked.

Manning held down the talk button and in a frenzied voice cried out that a man had been following him. He screamed that the person was still tailing him and he needed help. The policeman agreed to come outside immediately, along with the other officer on night duty. Manning and Teddy staged a fistfight twenty feet from the entrance door. The officers exited the stationhouse and approached the skirmish, each grasping a nightstick. But neither man had the opportunity to use his black baton. Tom Lastner and Scott Harriman crept around behind the unwitting enforcement agents and jumped the two, pulling them to the ground and pummeling them with sound punches to the jaw, until both policemen were out cold.

"We have three minutes tops," Lastner said. "Spread out and find the file."

The four hoisted the officers to the side of the building, out of view, and yanked latex gloves from their pockets, pulling them on as they ran into the building. Two minutes later, Harriman located the thick Zenonakis file. The gang fled the scene, with Harriman toting the prized folder under his right arm. They loaded into the rental car, and headed back to the hotel. Once at their destination, the team gathered in a quiet corner of the lobby and Lastner scanned through the file materials, summarizing the information contained therein for the others.

"You did good tonight," Lastner said, praising his men. "It's all here. Everything we need—photographs of the estate, members of the Zenonakis family, and bodyguards, the precise location of the estate, with a map and clear driving directions, etcetera, etcetera." He passed the photographs around so that the men could familiarize themselves with all of the players and paused introspectively. "The poor officers never knew what hit them, and I doubt they'll figure out what's missing from the storage cabinets until we're long gone from here." Lastner looked from man to man. "The last thing we need is police searching for us. We're going to wrap this thing up posthaste and get out of here. Now let's get a good night's sleep, men. Tomorrow we have much planning to do."

28

CLAIRE AWOKE WITH a start. She turned her head to the side and glanced at the alarm clock. It was later than she imagined. Guy was sound asleep and looked so perfectly at peace. Pulling herself close, she kissed him tenderly on the lips. He opened his eyes a slight crack.

"Tired," he murmured. "Fifteen more minutes."

"Oh, honey. We need to get moving. Today's the day. Today we find the old woman. Today we get the information we need to find George Zenonakis. Today we start to wind things up. I can feel it. And I can't wait to have this case behind us and be back at home in our own bed." Claire seemed highly energized and motivated to start the day. It became instantly clear that additional sleep was not in the picture.

"Come on, honey. We need to get moving," Claire repeated, rolling out of bed. There was an unspoken sense of urgency in her voice.

Guy opened his eyes a bit more. She had roused him from deep slumber. He instantly fell back to sleep.

"Get up," she pleaded. "If things go the way I hope they will today, we'll be returning to Miami soon. Please wake up."

"I love you," he uttered.

"I love you, too," she said. "But we must get going." She jumped into the shower. When she stepped out, Guy was just getting up.

"I'm tired this morning," he said. "*Unusually* tired. The schedule we have been on has been merciless."

"I know. And I barely slept at all last night. We've kept up quite a pace since we arrived in Crete. It's no wonder you're feeling beat."

While Guy showered, Claire again attempted to reach Mr. Otto. Still no answer. She left him a message. Maybe he wasn't taking calls. When someone is in mourning, that is often the case, she reasoned. The two dressed for the day, took the elevator to the main floor, and walked into the café to order a quick breakfast.

The stranger who had tailed the investigators for several days now sat in the lobby, eagerly waiting to resume his position as soon as the two walked from the restaurant. He lit up a cigarette and pulled a magazine onto his lap. His fake facial hair continued to itch him relentlessly, and he reached up and scratched each piece with his fingernails. The situation was dragging out far too long for his liking. Things needed to reach a climax, and soon.

After each consuming an omelet, wheat toast, orange juice, and coffee, the sleuths felt ready to start the workday. Claire had a renewed sense of vigor and seemed sure the day would produce monumental results. Guy remained unsure.

In silence, the two walked the several blocks to the shopping area of the city. They passed the jewelry store owned by Kostas and Panos and peered in through the windows. Neither brother was on the showroom floor. Rather, they spotted only the woman who had informed them on their last visit that Kostas would not see them again. When they waved to her, she did not return their friendly gestures.

In a short time, the investigators spotted the line-up of tour buses parked end to end along one of the main streets. They approached the lead bus. Standing by the open front door, the driver collected tickets. Guy paid the fare for the two of them and followed Claire up the steps to board.

Tourists, in vacation mode, seemed to be taking their sweet time stepping onto the bus and finding a seat that morning, and the delay frustrated Claire to no end. Finally, however, the bus began to roll. Because the driver had to slow down several times to answer questions of the more-than-curious riders, reaching the Palace of Knossos took longer than it should have. At last, the driver made the announcement that the remains of the famous palace would soon be visible.

"Is anyone interested in getting out and walking around the ruins for fifteen or twenty minutes?" he asked, looking into the vehicle's rearview mirror.

The Cretan day was magnificent in its splendor. Sunny, clear blue skies summoned the riders. Most every person taking the tour raised a hand. Claire and Guy piled out along with the others, greatly disappointed to have to share the site for any length of time. If only it had been raining that morning. If only...

As the inquisitive onlookers plodded around the ruins of the excavated palace and surrounding area of Knossos, they dallied longer than the driver had suggested, but due to the outstanding quality of the day, he allowed it. Just as in Claire's dream, the tourists moved with the speed of turtles—taking one photograph after another, and oohing and aahing over the breathtaking, surviving fresco remnants in shades of brick, caramel, teal, and white. At last, one by one or two by two, the onlookers returned to the bus and began to re-board, eager to continue the driving tour. By then, forty-five minutes had passed.

Claire walked over to the driver and explained that she and Guy would like to spend additional time at the amazing archeological discovery site. She requested he stop on the return trip and pick them up. He agreed with no problem.

"You both paid for a full tour, and I cannot refund your money," he said. "But if that is what you wish to do, be my guest. Make sure to stand out on the road in an hour then. Enjoy!"

The bus drove off as soon as the last of the tourists found a seat.

"Finally, we're alone," Claire said. "I thought they would never leave. Now we stand a reasonable chance of spotting *the old woman who feeds the birds*. With so many people mulling around, even the birds stayed away, in case you didn't notice." She pointed to a rock ledge similar to the one in her dream. "Let's sit down over there."

They walked to the spot. "Let's watch, listen, and see what happens," she said. "We must be very still."

Long, uneventful minutes passed, and then, like in her vision, birds began to arrive and land all around the two sleuths. A small red one looked up at Claire and then flew to her lap.

"I wish I had something to feed you," Claire whispered. "What a darling little bird you are." Her dream seemed to be coming true step by step.

The bird stayed for only a minute or two before flying away to be with the others.

"Guy, that tiny red bird was in my dream! Only in my dream it flew to the old woman's lap. It seemed to know her. Parts of this are like an instant replay."

The feathered creatures soon realized that neither Claire nor Guy had any food to throw to them and started to leave in droves. The full hour came to a shocking close with no sign of the old woman. "I'm afraid it's time for the bus to return," Guy said. "We'd better leave."

"No! It isn't supposed to be this way," Claire said, disheartened beyond words.

She was so sure that her dream had been a premonition of things to come. What was happening? Her sixth sense, always flawlessly reliable, had failed her miserably. As she stood to leave, her purse dropped to the ground. When she bent down to retrieve it, she spotted a piece of cloth wedged into a narrow crevice at the bottom of the natural rock bench. She tugged at it, and pulled out a folded green burlap bag.

THE BODYGUARD announced the arrival of Ambrose.

George sat, slouched over his desk. He did not feel well this morning. "Send him in," he replied.

Ambrose entered the room and quickly took his usual seat across from George. George stared at his visitor who appeared edgy and overly ill at ease. Beads of sweat poured from Ambrose's face, and he fidgeted uncontrollably in his chair.

"Ambrose," George said calmly, observing the unexpected behavior. "Please tell me the money has been wired into my account."

At first, no response came. The lump in Ambrose's throat was too large to swallow and did not allow him to speak. A long minute passed. Then, with great effort, Ambrose shot out words. "The buyer reneged."

"*What?*" George asked. His too tranquil tone sent shivers riveting through the body of the already-on-edge visitor. "He *reneged* on the purchase altogether?"

"Yes, Mr. George," Ambrose said, "The man had a problem raising the necessary funds."

"What problem would that be, Ambrose? You told me we had

a deal. In fact, you gave me your word on it. What are you telling me now?"

Ambrose reached into his briefcase and pulled out the packet.

"I am returning the magnificent Burmese ruby to you, Mr. George. The deal is off. I can look for another buyer if you'd like."

George did not speak. Rather, he bore his dark eyes into Ambrose.

Ambrose fainted.

George summoned his guards. "Get him out of here." He gestured to the visitor. "When he comes to, teach him a lesson before you release him."

The bodyguards nodded obediently.

GRANDFATHER NIKOS sat in his secret chamber, listening to the entire conversation.

He shook his head from side to side. His mood was pensive.

CLAIRE AND Guy talked as they walked. Back near the waterfront in Heraklion, they commiserated. The case was simply not progressing. Retreating and forgetting about the entire matter, although it remained an option, was not a good one. The two had never yet given up on an investigation. But more and more, it seemed that nothing was going their way to bring the matter to conclusion.

"We need to take a cab back to the palace grounds again and wait for the old woman to appear," Claire said. "The green burlap bag tells me that she has been there. It's just a matter of time until she returns."

"Are you sure you want to do this, Claire?" Guy asked. "We could sit there for hours on end with no results."

"I think we have to. We're plum out of other options."

They hailed a taxi and returned to the site. Three hours later, they walked back to Heraklion, disappointed beyond measure.

Claire's great hope for finding the old bird woman at the palace that day had been dashed.

They stopped for a quick bite, and then, at Claire's suggestion, agreed to split up in an effort to cover more ground—to once again ask around and see if anyone could lead them to the old woman. After settling on a place to rendezvous in two hours, Guy embraced Claire, holding her close for some time. The sleuths walked off: Claire heading east and Guy meandering west.

Claire walked in and out of every establishment the two had not previously entered. She conversed with numerous clerks, patrons, restaurant owners, wait staff, and business owners. After a time, she purchased a cup of Greek coffee and stood still on a heavily trafficked sidewalk, sipping and watching. Four stores down, a man lingered in an adjacent alleyway. He peered around the edge of a building and gawked fixedly at her. Dressed in agitation, he tapped his foot as he eyed the sleuth and smoked a cigarette.

Quickly and unexpectedly, Claire turned and looked directly at him. He darted his head back, out of sight.

Who was that? Claire wondered. The man seemed to be staring directly at her. She hurried toward the alleyway, but when she got there the individual was nowhere to be seen. For days now, she had experienced the feeling that someone was following her. Maybe it was not her imagination, after all. Thoughts of the yellow VW raced through her mind, as well as the set of faint headlights that seemed to be ever present in the rear distance. Had they been tailed since they first arrived in Crete? Is so, who was shadowing them? And why? The thought made her very uncomfortable, and for the first time on the island she felt vulnerable.

Claire spent the remaining time conducting the same detective work. In half an hour, she would meet up with Guy. Hopefully, he would report greater success than she could. She yearned to tell him her thoughts that they were being followed. She itched to get his take on who might be tailing them.

The two desperately needed a break . . . a new clue to follow . . . something . . . anything to point them in a different direction.

Spotting a real estate company across the street, an idea came to Claire. Maybe, she thought . . . just maybe. She walked over and stepped through the front door of the office. Numerous photographs of properties listed for sale took up most of the wall space. She studied the photos one by one, acting as a potential purchaser.

An agent approached her.

"How can I be of help to you today?" the lady asked in English.

"Oh, I'm really just looking," Claire said. "Your island is very beautiful."

"Thank you. Are you from the U.S.A.?" the lady asked.

"I am. It's my first visit to the island."

The agent chuckled. "So many first timers come in to look at properties for sale. Travelers fall in love with Crete and think about purchasing a small villa for their return visits. Happens all the time."

"Your English is very good," Claire said.

The woman turned a shade of red. "Thank you, kind lady. We have properties listed in all price ranges."

"Even really high-end properties, I'm sure," Claire chortled.

"Oh, yes."

"What property on the entire island is the most valuable?" Claire asked in a light-hearted manner.

"That's easy. But I'm afraid that property has never been for sale."

"Where is it? I'd love to drive by and see the place just to satisfy my curiosity."

"No, you would not want to get close to this place. It is heavily guarded, and visitors are not welcome."

Claire acted curious. "Do you at least have a picture of it that you could show me?"

The woman looked around and then gestured for Claire to follow her to a back room. The agent pulled a folder from a desk and took out a photo. She handed it to Claire.

"Wow! This is quite an estate. It's simply gorgeous," Claire said. "Where is it?"

"Southward from Hania," the woman said. "Up in the mountains, built on the side of a cliff. An unscrupulous family owns it. It is dangerous for me to even have a photo of the mansion, but I do. It intrigues me to no end, and I'd love to get a peek inside of the place myself someday. But I know that will never happen."

"Who owns it?" Claire asked. She feigned interest in the woman's story.

The woman again looked around to satisfy herself that no one was within hearing distance. "The Zenonakis family—an evil clan," she whispered.

"I have a silly request," Claire said. "Could you make a photocopy of that picture for me? I'd love to have it as a souvenir of my vacation here—to show my friends back home." She smiled excitedly. "If it's not too much of an inconvenience."

Suddenly, the agent appeared perturbed and jittery. She eyed Claire in a manner that suggested the real estate professional was attempting to assess the truthfulness of the visitor's request. "You would be bringing it back to the United States as a souvenir, you say?"

Claire nodded.

"Well, I don't know," the woman said, scratching her head. "I just don't know." Clearly, the request upset her.

Claire reached into her purse. She walked toward the agent as if intending to shake her hand and covertly handed the woman a wad of euros. "This should cover any copying expenses," Claire said softly. She smiled kindly.

The agent turned to face the wall and inconspicuously counted the cash. She made a copy of the estate photo and handed it to Claire.

"What is the exact location of the property, in case I decide to drive by despite your warning?" Claire asked.

The woman spoke in a whisper. "You do *not* want to go anywhere near that place. Understand?"

Claire nodded. "Let me do some more thinking about whether I'm interested in purchasing a small villa, and I'll get back to you. Thank you for your help. I enjoyed meeting you."

The woman gave Claire her business card, and the two exchanged a handshake.

Claire ventured back outside, and for the first time in this case she felt a real ray of hope. We have a picture of the estate, she screamed silently. *Finally* we have something concrete to go on! Now all we need is a better fix on the location.

She ran to the spot where she and Guy had promised to meet, arriving ten minutes later than the agreed-upon time. He was not there. She waited anxiously, so eager to share the news with her partner and love. But ten minutes turned into thirty, then forty-five, then an hour. Guy would never be this late. Ever.

All at once, emergency alarms sounded inside Claire. Bells, horns, and whistles alike competed in her head to be heard. *Something is wrong ... terribly wrong*! Then her eyes darted to a dark substance on the flat stone walkway—only feet from where she stood. She moved in nearer, stooped low, and examined the splattering more closely.

It was blood.

Her worst fears were realized, and she shrieked in horror.

29

CLAIRE GRABBED FACIAL tissues from her purse. Cautiously, she placed several over the trail of blood spots and soaked it up. She folded the absorbent pieces of tissue carefully, several times over, thereby protecting the dark specimens should DNA testing be required. She held the bundle of soft material to her heart. "I'll find you, Guy. I'm on the way," she said. Tears welled in her eyes as she carefully wedged the tissues into a deep pocket of her bag.

She raced down one surrounding block after another, frantically searching for a sign of Guy. He was hurt and needed her. Where had they taken him? Where? He was nowhere to be found. She ran until her chest tightened, and she started to gasp for air. Forced to stop, to catch her breath, she hoped for the best but imagined the worst. What if they planned to kill him? "Please God, don't let anything happen to Guy. I love him. Protect him. Help me find him," she pleaded aloud.

Taking in a deep breath, she impelled herself to run several more blocks to find Kostas and Panos. They would surely help her. How many times had a Cretan told her if she ever had trouble, or needed help or advice, not to hesitate to ask any one of them? Traditional hospitality and generosity of spirit seemed deeply ingrained in the people of the island. Kostas and Panos would be there for her. She depended on them. But when she neared the jewelry store, to her chagrin she saw that it was closed.

Panic rolled in, and the severity of the situation hit her in a direct and uncompromising manner. She had to locate Guy and free him from his abductors. Think, she told herself. *Think*! George Zenonakis must have discovered the sleuths were on his trail and wanted to put an end to it. So much for her brilliant plan of separating to cover more ground. "I'm sorry, honey. Hang in there. I'll find you and get you out of this mess. I promise," Claire said softly. She knew he couldn't hear her. Or could he? She would keep talking to him anyway.

Apprehension and dismay draped her being, and she turned ashen. What should she do? She forced back tears. The police would never help. They would go nowhere near the Zenonakis estate. But she had to give it a try. There were no other options. She'd make an emotional appeal for help to the local law enforcement officers. Maybe they would assist her when she identified herself as a private investigator from the U.S. She spotted a tavern about two blocks away and knew it would be open for business. There, she could use the phone to contact the police.

Drawing from an unknown source of energy, she sprinted toward the establishment as fast as her legs would carry her. As if a switch had been hit, the dark of night appeared in a flash. What had the abductors done with Guy? Where had they taken him? What were they doing to him? What were their plans? These questions, and others, spun around and around in her head, and the potential answers terrified her. About halfway to the eatery, Claire tripped over something on the sidewalk and sailed through the air. She landed hard on the cobblestone street.

"*Ouch*!" She screamed out in pain. "*That hurts*!" Her hands had broken the fall and prevented a worse injury, but she had scraped them badly, and now blood streamed from both her palms. Helplessness was not a feeling she liked or accepted, but it was right there waiting to grab her. *What next*? She fought back with everything within her and started to get up. As she did, she felt a walking stick lightly touch her arm. Peering through the darkness, she saw the outline of a decrepit elderly person.

"Grab the cane," the gravelly voice crackled.

Claire obliged and was surprised at the strength with which the older man hoisted her from the ground.

"Thank you," Claire said, whimpering. "I'm having a bad time."

"You have been looking for me," the voice hissed.

Suddenly Claire froze. Did this elderly man intentionally trip her with his cane? If so, she could have been seriously hurt—the last thing she needed right now. "Who are you?" she asked. "Did you purposely trip me?"

"I did," came the reply. "Now tell me what it is you want, as if I do not already know."

"I beg your pardon. Who are you?" Claire demanded.

"It seems to me that you need my help, missy, and I'm here to offer it. Follow me." The person turned and entered a dark alleyway between two shops. "Come along," the deep voice said, noting Claire's hesitation.

Claire followed the man against her better judgment. Guy

needed her, and she would try any means available to help him. The old man stopped at a door twenty feet down the way, unlocked it, and walked inside. Claire stepped in behind him and walked to one side, keeping her distance.

The figure that had followed Claire and Guy for days huddled outside on the dark street, waiting for Claire to resurface.

Claire heard the door lock behind her, and the elderly man turned on a low-wattage light. With her renewed vision, she stared in disbelief. It was not a man, after all, but a woman—an old woman, covered with more facial wrinkles than Claire had ever seen before. Suddenly, from all directions, birds began to chirp. Darting her glance around the room, Claire noticed numerous cages, together holding a wide variety of domestic birds.

"Mama is home," the old woman called out softly.

It was she! *The old woman who feeds the birds*! Claire had convinced herself that if the woman actually did exist, they would never find her. But here she was, in living color. Fear began to evaporate from the tearful sleuth as, in astonishment, she gaped at the old woman.

"I need your help! I'm desperate! They've taken Guy, my partner! You've got to help me," Claire shrieked. "Please, I beg you, help me."

"Calm down, missy. Your anxiety will not make this any easier. We must think as rational human beings." She looked old beyond her age as Kostas had related, but she seemed to have remarkable vim and vigor.

"Time is of the essence. Who knows what they'll do to him?" Claire grimaced.

"We have a little time. I will help you find him, missy. But we must be cautious. We'll do this my way, or not at all." She walked to a cupboard and took out a fresh towel, antiseptic cream, and bandages. "Here. Wash up in the sink." She motioned toward the kitchen and handed the items to Claire. "Wipe the blood from your hands, and bandage your wounds."

Claire obeyed and talked at the same time. "Anything. I'll do anything to help Guy. Do you know where the Zenonakis mansion is? We need to go there at once. George has him there. I know it."

"*My way*!" the old bird woman roared. "I will tell *you* what we will do! We will do things *my* way!"

Claire stopped talking and forced back greater tears. What an unthinkable situation she was in! Time mattered. She would not argue with the old woman.

"We will wait until the darkness of night is well established," the old woman said. "But first, there are things we must take care of, missy."

LASTNER AND his men drove the coastal route back to Hania and now had everything ready to carry out the night's mission. They had purchased basic climbing equipment and sturdy knives from a sporting goods store, and steaks to satisfy any guard dogs. Those items, together with night-vision glasses, high-quality binoculars, and thick gloves, provided the men everything they required to complete the task. The group's preference was always to use guns in an extrajudicial attack, but since packing them in luggage presented a high risk of apprehension, the team had opted to use different weapons on this occasion.

Dressed in black, with blades secured, the foursome sat in the rental car on a side street in the city of Hania. In the dim lighting, they discussed plans a final time and readied themselves internally to partake in the societal correction.

Each took a turn reviewing the stolen file contents one last time and memorizing the photos of both George and Nikos Zenonakis, as well as the two guards the estate employed. Then, turning their collective attention to the map, together they determined the best route to the Zenonakis estate. Situated high on a precipitous cliff, reaching the locale could present a significant problem in and of itself; and, once there, gaining access to the interior would present an even more onerous task. The thrill of the challenge seemed to greatly invigorate Lastner and Harriman, and it was decided unanimously that those two would lead the charge.

Inflicting deserved punishment would temporarily sate the emptiness Judge Lastner and Scott Harriman felt deep inside. But, as always, it would be a temporary fix. Punishment, after all, was not justice. As the time for the hit neared, the two smelled blood and now craved it. And nothing but a successful execution, eradicating the target, would relieve the pain increasing steadily in Tom Lastner's head.

"Remember, men," Lastner said. "dehumanize the target. George Zenonakis operates outside social boundaries and communal ties that make our society function. Think of him as an alien enemy who must be destroyed. Keep your eyes on the prize. We are bound by the spirit of the game."

The brotherhood set out on the road to Omalos, Lastner behind the wheel. They would approach the estate and lie in hiding to assess the situation, and then make their move when the timing proved perfect.

GUY LOMBARD was in trouble. Serious trouble. He opened his eyes a crack and saw only darkness. Soon his eyes opened wider, and he realized he was lying in a cramped closet or enclosed space of some kind. When he tried to lift his head, pain bolted through it and he winced. His mouth, gagged with a cloth, was extremely dry.

He wanted badly to swallow, but he could not. His hands, tightly bound behind his back, hurt desperately, and he struggled valiantly to free them. He tried to move his legs and realized to his horror that they too had been tied securely. Liquid trickled down the back of his head onto his neck, and he knew it could only be one thing—his own blood. Bound in the manner he was, he could barely move at all, and the stuffy atmosphere of the enclosure made it difficult to breathe. Never had he been in a greater nightmare. Then, an even more horrible thought possessed him. Where was Claire? Had they grabbed her, too? What were the abductors doing to her? Who were they? The Zenonakis clan? What did they want? He succumbed to the pain and passed out.

When he came to, minutes later, he strained his memory to recall what had happened. Slowly, the circumstances began to become clear. He remembered waiting for Claire at the agreed-upon meeting place. Soon it would be dark, and she was late. He had started to worry about her when, out of the blue, an object had cracked down on the back of his head with brutal force. All had gone dark.

Utter dread enveloped him as he realized he was the victim of an aggravated assault and kidnapping. And what about his precious Claire? He could not allow himself to think about it. He had to find a way out and help her.

Pain lashed through his head, and he again blacked out.

GEORGE ZENONAKIS paced back and forth in his office, smoking a cigarette. When he finished, he pushed the red button under his desk. Instantaneously, the two bodyguards appeared.

"Sit," he ordered. "Did this Lombard fellow utter anything when you brought him in tonight?"

"No, sir," both said in unison.

"He was out cold the entire time," one volunteered.

"I need to know who he is and why he and the blonde are after me. They look too American not to be. Check on him while I call my resources in the States. As soon as he awakens, bring him to me."

Both guards nodded at once.

GRANDFATHER NIKOS sat in his secret chamber, enraged. He would not have the blood of an American on his hands. He would not allow George to further dishonor the Zenonakis family name. No longer could Nikos Zenonakis turn a blind eye. He picked up one handgun after another, thoughtfully considering each piece of his stash. His arsenal sat clean, fully loaded, and ready to perform. Why had George turned out to be such a bad seed? Such a messenger of evil? He could have done so much with the life given him. He could have contributed to society in a positive way. Maybe Nikos had not been the best influence on George when the boy was a youngster, but the circumstances had been difficult.

He pondered the situation. The Zenonakis family had never been ruthless in a diabolical kind of manner—powerful and controlling, perhaps, but not evil.

Nikos stared straight ahead, unblinkingly. The time had arrived to correct the problem. Tonight, Nikos would make his move. "Forgive me, my son, for what I must do," he whispered.

GEORGE WAITED impatiently for the prisoner to rouse. He wanted answers and would get them shortly. Soon he would know why this American couple hunted him like relentless bloodhounds. He would demand answers, and if Lombard did not cooperate, he would pursue other means to make him talk.

Sweat poured down George's forehead and into his eyes, causing them to sting. He closed them and dropped his head to his desk, where it remained for a few long minutes. Then he sat upright and lit a cigarette. Unnamed forces were tightening a noose around his neck, and he wanted and needed exoneration. The tenacious Mr. Lombard would sing like a canary, or else. He took a deep drag of his Marlboro and put it out. He needed answers. Walking to the attached bathroom, he filled the basin with icy cold water and splashed the colorless liquid all over his face. He looked in the mirror and discharged a disgusting grunt. At that moment, the guards appeared at the study door carrying a struggling, still bound, Guy Lombard between them.

"Ah, yes. Bring him in," George demanded, walking toward the prisoner. "Set him down in this chair." He pointed to one of the chairs in front of the desk. "Leave his hands and feet tied, but remove the gag from his mouth."

The guards implemented the orders without hesitation.

"Close the door behind you," George said. "Leave us alone, but stay near. I will buzz when I need you." An unholy aura possessed George. He stayed on Guy's side of the desk and stood near him. Placing his left hand on his left hip, George used his right hand to stroke his chin. "Mr. Lombard … Mr. Gaston Lombard."

Guy struggled to remain cognizant. He felt light-headed and fought the urge to pass out. "What do you want with me, you sonofabitch?" He struggled to swallow, but the dryness in his mouth would not allow it.

"Oh, Mr. Lombard, I will ask the questions. And *you*? You will tell me exactly what I want to know. If you refuse, your lovely blonde-haired lady will pay the price. Do I make myself perfectly clear?"

"What have you done with her, you *fucking* sonofabitch?" Guy blurted out, mustering all strength within him. "If you lay one hand on her, I'll..."

"You'll what, Mr. Lombard? Please tell me." He chuckled under his breath. "I hardly think you're in a position to threaten much of anything. Wouldn't you agree?"

Guy scowled at the loathsome human being sharing his air space. The criminal stirred the investigator's anger to new heights.

"As I'm sure you have surmised by now, Mr. Lombard, I am the fox you have been hunting. I am George Zenonakis, also known as George Zeppano." He looked Gaston Lombard over as if attempting to assess the amount of fortitude the man contained. "I have done my homework on you, Mr. Lombard, and know that you and Ms. Caswell are the best private investigators in the Miami area. So I must tell you, I am most curious to hear who hired you. Who had the *brass balls* to send the two of you across the pond to my backyard to come looking for me? That is my question for you."

Guy glared back at the mobster. "Stick it where the sun don't shine, bastard."

George's eyes glowed in a strange, violently excited, manner. "You've got nerve. I like that. Now tell me who sent you, or pay the price." He spoke in a loud voice.

Guy stared back into the eyes of a maniac, but refused to answer.

George's tone changed suddenly, and he spoke in almost a whisper. "I said, tell me why you seek me with such dogged determination."

"Water," Guy demanded. "I need water."

"You'll get a tall glass of cool water just as soon as you answer my question, Mr. Lombard. Now, I'll repeat myself a final time. Tell me why it is that you and that lovely lady of yours have tried so desperately to find me? Who hired your services?"

Guy still did not answer, refusing to give an inch to the reprehensible man.

George Zenonakis moved in closer to Gaston Lombard. George raised his hand high in the air and brought the backside of it down sharply across Guy's face. Guy did not flinch. The second time, however, George struck Guy with such strength that he grunted out an involuntary gasp as the powerful impact threw him to the floor. Blood spurted from his severely cut lip. George walked behind his desk and pushed the red button. The door opened, and the guards stepped in.

"Bring our *guest* back to his quarters," George ordered. "No food. No water. And make sure you re-gag him. Return him to me every hour on the hour until I tell you to stop. We will see how long he refuses to give me information."

The men grabbed the prisoner by his arms and dutifully dragged him across the floor. Guy struggled courageously to free himself from the restraints and from his restrainers. He screamed out to George as they pulled him from the room, "I'll see that you spend the rest of your days behind bars, if it's the last thing I do." The guards reached the closet, twisted the dirty rag tightly over Guy's mouth, and shoved him back inside. They slammed the door and locked it, once again leaving him confined in the cramped quarters, and in total darkness.

Several more *meetings* took place between George Zenonakis and Gaston Lombard over the next several hours. Guy was alive, but barely. He had been beaten to within inches of his life. Each time he had refused to speak, he enraged his captor to an even greater degree.

In the stillness of his confinement, Guy pondered his predicament. The situation was not good. How much longer could he withstand the torture? How much longer could he refuse to give this monster the information he demanded? Blood seemed to be oozing from every part of Guy's face and head, and the restraints around his wrists and ankles had caused severe injury and bleeding in those areas, as well. He closed his eyes and dreamed of being reunited with Claire, of holding her in his arms and tasting her sweet lips. What a glorious moment that would be. He felt himself losing consciousness and blacked out.

Minutes later, he came to and again became acutely aware of his circumstances and surroundings. Although he had been threatened many times during his career as a Miami–Dade state attorney, he had never been captured and tortured. This was a first, and he vowed it would be the last.

He considered his situation and determined that he would be submissive to preserve his remaining energy, continue to withhold information, and when the opportune time to strike availed itself, he would make his move. In the meantime, he placed great faith in Claire Caswell. She would figure out who abducted him and where they'd taken him. If she were free, she would find him. Perhaps at any moment, she would burst into the mansion, police at her side, and rescue him. That is, if she was not being held prisoner herself. But the thought that she was free, and coming to get him, kept him going in the short run.

However, reality returned. Not knowing Claire's exact whereabouts caused Guy grave concern. If this George Zenonakis character was pulverizing him, and he had Claire, what was he doing to her? Then, a surprising thought entered Guy's mind. Maybe Claire was not, in fact, being held a prisoner like him. Perhaps they didn't take her by force after they captured him. Could that insinuation be nothing more than a wild-ass bluff to elicit information from him? Wouldn't they show him they had her, if they did? The longer he mulled it over, the more certain he became that George Zenonakis's thugs had not captured Claire. He breathed a bit easier.

In either case, however, Guy would not rest until this criminal was put behind bars where he belonged. He joined Mr. Otto's life quest.

Sometime later, Guy thought he heard someone unlock the door of his private quarters. He was right. The door opened slowly. He tried to swallow, but could not. Suddenly, a hand grabbed Guy's arm and squeezed tightly. Then the hand reached over and pulled his gag down around his neck. Something hard pressed against his lower lip and cool liquid ran onto his chin. Guy parted his dry lips a crack and drank. Water had never tasted so good. He took another sip, and a third, and one more as the stranger held the glass to his mouth. Before he could manage a single word, the gag was put back in place. The next thing he heard was the locking of the closet door.

"Claire," he shouted out silently. "Claire!" He struggled desperately to free his hands and legs.

30

"I SAW YOU in my dream," Claire said. "You looked exactly the same."

The elderly lady threw a compassionate glance toward the investigator. At that instant, any lingering apprehension within Claire dissipated. She no longer doubted the sincerity of the old woman and knew she would do her best to help Claire free Guy. All instincts told her to trust the old bird woman.

"Tonight will not be easy," the old woman warned. "You must prepare yourself."

Together, they walked to the hotel where Claire and Guy had a room. Claire went upstairs and retrieved the keys to the rental car, and in no time flat sprinted back across the lobby to the attached parking garage. She forced herself to take deep, rhythmic breaths as she drove the car to an outside street. Claire pulled the red car over to the curb, and the old bird woman placed bags into the backseat and then dropped her thin frame onto the passenger seat.

"Tell me your full name," the woman said.

"Claire Caswell."

"And the name of your partner?"

"Gaston Lombard. I call him *Guy*."

"Very well, Claire Caswell. I have an interesting story to tell you on our drive to Hania."

"What is *your* name?" Claire asked.

"My name is not important, missy. Now, when we get to Hania, we'll be taking the road to Omalos up to the mansion."

Claire froze. "*The road to Omalos*?"

"Yes, do you know of it?" the old woman asked.

"I've only heard of it," Claire said. "The day we arrived in Hania, the innkeeper told us to make certain to see the snow-capped mountains. He told us to follow the Road to Omalos signs."

"So you see, missy, it was right before your eyes at the beginning of your adventure. You just didn't know it then."

As Claire drove she fought back tears, hoping desperately they would reach Guy in time.

The bird woman shared the tale of her life with Claire as she tooled along the coastal route. It was a story that both stunned and saddened the sleuth.

"You poor dear. I had no idea," Claire said.

"Only one other does," the woman said.

As the two traveled onward, they discussed what each would do when they reached the estate.

"The road to Omalos may terrify you, young lady," the bird woman said, "but there is no other way up there."

"*Terrify me*? *Why*?" Claire asked.

"My dear, you will see for yourself as we travel the winding road for thirty-one miles. At first everything will be fine, but as we ascend higher toward the crowns of the White Mountains ... the

Lefka Ori ... on our way to the Omalos Plateau ... the spot where the vast Samaria Gorge begins ... things will change rapidly. Only the strong make it all the way up. Only the strong."

"You're scaring me now," Claire said. "Please stop doing that."

"I will be with you. And as your President Roosevelt said: 'The only thing we have to fear, is fear itself!'"

Soon Claire saw the city lights of Hania up ahead, and minutes later she drove the rental car into the city.

"Now," the old woman said, "just follow the road to Omalos signs and arrows. I'll help you find them all. It can be confusing as there will be many roads that branch off in other directions early on."

Claire traveled down the main street of Hania and soon noticed a sign on the left that read, "To Omalos." The arrow indicated a left-hand turn. She took the turn and began to notice sporadic signs saying "Omalos," with an arrow directing the traveler in one direction or another. The signs appeared quite frequently.

Way up ahead, in the far, far distance, Claire saw a series of craggy mountains outlined against the dark evening sky. As she looked more intently, she noticed what appeared to be tiny, itty-bitty lights moving somewhat horizontally, high, high up, near the very top of the mountain sitting straight ahead in her line of vision.

"What on earth are those flickering lights way up at the top of that mountain?" Claire asked.

"They are car lights."

"What sane person would travel *up there* in a car?"

"That is where *we* are heading, Claire. That road will take us to the village of Omalos. It is the location of the Zenonakis villa."

"*What*?" Claire shrieked. "*I cannot do this*! *I have a dreadful fear of heights*! *There is no way I can drive way up there*!" She slowed the car and said, "It's time to turn around." Claire had noticed that the road had started to elevate, but she had no idea what she was getting herself into.

"I'm afraid, Claire Caswell," the old bird woman said, "that once you are on this road you cannot turn around. Not until you get to the Omalos plateau, that is. There, you can turn around to drive back down."

Claire was clearly not doing well. She ripped the bandages from her hands to ensure a better grip on the wheel. Tears flowed down her cheeks—for Guy Lombard and for the horrific situation that now confronted her. Life had thrown unthinkable, dangerous, and inescapable hurdles her way. Guy had been kidnapped and desperately needed her help to stay alive; yet, to help him she had to confront her nightmarish and irrational fear of heights—an abnormal fear that paralyzed her. She held her breath. The feeling of overwhelming pressure to perform built within her like steam in a pressure cooker, and she let out a prolonged high-pitched wail.

The bird woman ignored her cry of despair. "The road is ample now, but very soon it will start to taper, and then rapidly become *severely narrow,*" the old woman warned. "When you drive around a curve, it will be nearly impossible to round the bend if you meet a car coming from the opposite direction. It can be done, but it requires considerable skill."

"*Why didn't you tell me?*" Claire yelled in an intense voice. Panic had set in, and she trembled in raw dread. *"I would have told you I could not do it! You should have told me!"*

"Claire Caswell, grab hold of yourself. You want to help Guy Lombard, don't you?"

"Of course!" she howled. "You know that! He is all that matters."

"Then face your fears head-on. You have no other option," the woman said. "We must travel the road to Omalos. It will take us about an hour, and I would advise you to keep a sharp lookout on the road directly in front of you, Claire Caswell. Do not take your eyes off the divider line. Especially on the curves. And under no circumstances ... I repeat, under *no* circumstances ... let your eyes wander from the road. No shoulder exists, and no guardrails. Look only straight ahead."

Claire whimpered. "*Shit*! I can't do this. Get me out of this."

"There is no way out. You will be fine, missy. Just fine. Keep your eyes glued to the road ahead, and hold your thoughts on Guy Lombard. He needs you."

Claire drove on in a state of heightened anxiety, groaning unconsciously. Soon the road narrowed dramatically, as she knew it would. Her stomach turned to knots and her hands trembled on the wheel. She felt hot and flushed, and her heart started to beat too fast. Her leg muscles tensed, and she felt so afraid.

"I can't do this," she wailed. "*I can't do this!*"

"Yes you can, Missy. Guy Lombard needs you. Just think of him."

In Claire's state of panic, she failed to notice the lemon Volkswagen Beetle, maintaining a safe distance behind, but steadfastly trailing her up the terrifying road to Omalos.

THE FOUR-MAN vigilante squad reached the area near the mansion after the perilous drive up the mountain. Lastner turned the headlights off and rolled the vehicle to within range of the estate, pulling it behind a thick grouping of trees. The men stepped from the car and pulled out the climbing equipment and other items purchased in preparation for the night's activities.

Kyle Teddy immediately dropped to his knees and kissed the ground. Then he looked upward. "Thank you, oh merciful God, for getting us here safely. I thought we would surely die," he said aloud.

It had been an even more traumatic trek for the passengers than for the driver—who had some semblance of control over the situation—and Harriman, Manning, and Teddy reeled from the experience.

"Never again." Jack Manning said in a low, slow voice. "Never, ever, ever. I felt certain we would all be killed. If you swerve at all and cross the line, a car driving in the opposite direction will knock you right off the road. You'd plummet more than a mile straight down to a horrible death. I wonder how many cars are at the bottom? And bodies, for that matter?"

"I don't think my nerves can take it again on the way back down," Kyle Teddy said. "I mean it."

"I thought it was a bit of a thrill, myself," Scott Harriman whispered.

Actually, he had gripped the door handle until his knuckles turned snow white and repeatedly taken swigs of *raki* from a plastic travel flask the entire way up.

"We'll have time for this talk later," Lastner said, breaking into the conversation. "Right now, we have serious work to contemplate. We need to assess the situation and make a plan for getting in there." He pointed upward to a magnificent villa, sitting proudly on the steep cliff just above them.

The others looked upward and took in the spectacular white stone dwelling. A sight to behold, the lighting within and without the estate together seemed to illuminate a good part of the entire upper mountainside.

"This is not going to be easy," Lastner said. "We need to get in, make the hit, and get out. It's a long way down, and we have no way around that. I want us back on flat ground as soon as possible. Arrangements are in place for the four of us to fly out of here tonight. Oh, and by the way, we do not want to harm Nikos Zenonakis or the bodyguards, only our target: George Zenonakis. You all know the plan. Now, let's get busy and figure out a way in."

GRANDFATHER NIKOS selected his Glock firearm. He loaded the magazine with bullets and slid it into place. He checked the weapon over, and everything looked to be in good working order. It would do the job nicely. He hid in his secret space, awaiting the perfect opportunity. Tonight it would happen. Tonight was the night he would finally take care of the longstanding problem, once and for all.

He waited until George had fallen into a deep sleep on the sofa in the den—a routine that occurred every evening lately. Then Nikos picked up his cell phone and called both bodyguards, one and then the other, extending the same offer to each man.

"I am giving you the night off. Leave now," Nikos said. "I do not want to see you again until tomorrow afternoon. There is no further discussion."

Both individually argued that George had ordered them to cover him around the clock. Nikos gently, but firmly, reminded the guards that *he* remained the one in charge at the Zenonakis estate … and not his grandson. He also informed the men that a gift for each of them waited just outside. "You can pick up the keys on the table by the front door as you leave," Nikos said.

Without further ado, the bodyguards left the mansion through the rear door, leaving it unlocked, and each man slipped into the driver's seat of his new black Mercedes S-Class sedan. Stealing away in the darkness of the night, Lastner and his team observed the sudden evacuation of the two young men—the bodyguards.

"According to the police records in the file we absconded with, that leaves only two inside—George Zenonakis and his elderly grandfather, Nikos Zenonakis," Lastner said. "That's a break we could never have hoped for or expected."

CLAIRE GRIPPED the wheel with all her strength, forcing herself into a near trance-like state in an attempt to endure the severe angst building within her. She steered the car upward and onward along the tormenting drive, while all self-preservation instincts within her bellowed out for her to stop. With no lighting on the dangerously steep cliff road, the headlights on her red rental car provided the only guidance she had in the blackness of the night.

Involuntarily, she inhaled deep breaths, each time holding the air in her lungs too long before exhaling, and having to gulp in more air to keep from blacking out. As Claire directly faced the enemy of fear, silence rode in the vehicle like a third passenger.

The narrow road leading up the side of the mountain allowed barely enough room for cars traveling in opposite directions to pass at any given point. As the route ascended, and as persistent hairpin turns confronted Claire, the treacherous trek became even more precipitous. Claire refused to allow herself to look off to the right, to view just how close her vehicle was to the edge of the cliff and to the sheer drop-off that promised certain and violent death.

"*How much longer*?" Claire screamed out in agony. "*How much farther*?" She winced in distress as her eyes stayed glued to the road ahead.

"We are nearing Omalos, missy. You are doing quite well."

The old woman seemed to have nerves of steel.

Just as the bird woman finished speaking, Claire approached another curve. She hoped beyond hope that another car would not be coming from the opposite direction. But fate did her no favors. Approaching headlights from oncoming traffic briefly presented, signaling a potentially critical moment. Suddenly, not only one black car careened around the curve at that precise point, but two identical cars, one immediately following the other.

"Hold your own!" the old woman yelled. "Hold your own! Watch the line on the road in front of you!"

Time slipped into slow motion as Claire did her best to stay on her side of the narrow curved road. Both black cars slid over the centerline, scraping her car as they passed. She closed her eyes for a nanosecond, thinking the end had come. In that billionth of a second, she envisioned the rental car plunging over the road and rapidly spiraling straight downward for more than a mile, gaining incredible speed before its final, fatal impact.

"Hold your own!" the bird woman yelled again. "Hold your own!"

The brief encounter was just that … brief. But just as the two black Mercedeses slid past her, the driver of the front car applied the brakes, and the driver of the second in line could not slow down in sufficient time. He smashed into the rear of the lead sedan.

Keeping her eyes affixed to the road ahead, and coupled by the darkness of the night, Claire could not see what happened behind her, but she could hear it. The deafening crushing of metal forcibly impacting other metal at high speed, and the resultant high-pitched squeals of the tires and grinding noises of the brakes as the drivers frantically tried to stop the inevitable, created sounds that implanted in Claire's psyche in a manner that she would remember for the rest of her life. Hooked together, the pair of Mercedeses crossed the centerline just behind the red rental car and blasted over the edge of the road, plunging headlong down the mountainside in an uncontrollable free fall.

Claire needed to vomit and tried in desperation to hold it back, but could not. The uncontrolled flow from her mouth splattered the steering wheel and dashboard.

The old woman spoke in an unruffled tone. "Keep going, Claire Caswell. Hold it together! There is nothing we can do about what just happened. Keep your eyes on the road ahead of you. It's just a bit farther."

Claire did not respond. She couldn't speak.

A minute passed. "I'm assuming the drivers of those cars were the Zenonakis bodyguards. That will make our job easier," the bird woman said.

Claire remained silent.

THE HOUR of reckoning approached. As George Zenonakis slept like an infant, in interrupted cycles, time was quickly running out for him.

THE VIGILANTES had decided it would be easier to drop down to the mansion than climb up. Since viewing the hasty retreat of the bodyguards, however, they had reassessed the situation and determined they could now storm the place by entering through the front windows—after first silencing the guard dogs with the meat they had toted along. The perfect opening to strike quickly approached.

CLAIRE CASWELL had miraculously completed the drive and now stopped the car a safe distance from the estate, across the way from where Lastner had hidden the vehicle that transported the vigilantes to the nearly same spot. Shaken to her very core, she could barely contain herself. Next to hysterics, she felt the old woman slap her across the face.

"I'm sorry to do that, missy, but you need to focus. If we are not careful, we will get ourselves killed up here. Be alert at all times. Think about Guy Lombard."

An image of Guy's face appeared in Claire's mind and stayed there. I'm coming for you, Guy, she said silently. Hold on. They would get through this ghastly ordeal and life would go on, she told herself. Oh, how she rued getting involved in the Otto family debacle. It was her fault that Guy was in danger—assuming he was still alive. She reached deep within her being and pulled up the strength she kept there for emergency situations.

"I'm ready," she said, regaining her confidence.

The old woman grabbed the two bags from the car's backseat and set off in the direction of the mansion. Steps later, she stopped cold and turned around.

"Coming, missy?" she asked.

Claire had frozen in place, reliving the ordeal she had just been through. She snapped to and followed directly behind the old woman as they inched their way up the steep incline toward the rear of the estate. When they got close, the old woman put her hand up in Claire's face.

"Wait here," she whispered in a voice Claire could barely hear.

The old woman proceeded to move in closer to the back of the dwelling. She reached into one of the bags and pulled out two juicy steaks. She tossed them into the backyard, and the dogs leaped at the fresh meat, ripping it to shreds. She dropped the bag and motioned to Claire.

Claire ran to her side, and the two walked to the back gate and entered the yard, walking around the dogs to the estate's back door. The old lady tried the handle and looked back at Claire with a smile. It was unlocked.

THE DRIVER of the rented yellow VW Beetle pulled up behind the red car and parked. He got out and followed after Claire.

GUN IN hand, and strangely calm, grandfather Nikos stood just feet away from the sleeping George. A small desk lamp illuminated the face of his grandson, and for an instant Nikos recalled with sadness the face of George as a young lad. How could a life have gone so terribly wrong?

ALL OF a sudden, without warning, all lights in the mansion went out simultaneously, plunging the Zenonakis estate into total darkness.

31

AT THAT PRECISE moment, night-vision glasses in place, the vigilantes used the blunt ends of their knives to crash through the front windows of the mansion and swiftly enter the premises. In haste, the team ascended the set of stairs leading to the upper floors in search of George Zenonakis.

At the exact same time, the old bird woman and Claire slipped into the house through the rear door. They moved stealthily along the main hallway on the ground floor until the old woman grabbed Claire by the hand and led her into a room. Then, crouching in one corner to avoid detection, they waited. As Claire's eyes adjusted somewhat to the darkness, she thought she spotted a human figure sleeping on the sofa. She pointed out her discovery to the old woman, who then tiptoed closer to take a better look. Reaching into the bag she still toted, the bird woman grabbed hold of its contents. The object felt cold to her touch.

Grandfather Nikos braced himself. From his vantage point behind the sofa, he placed his index finger on the trigger of his Glock pistol and pointed it directly at his sleeping grandson's head.

The man, dressed in brown, had quietly entered the mansion's back door behind the old bird woman and Claire. After observing the old woman, and also one of the four men, tossing meat to the dangerous dogs from both sides of the backyard, he felt safe traveling past the trained canines. Through the darkness, making no noise, he followed Claire and the old lady directly to the study. He crept in and hid behind the massive desk, clutching a thick wooden club in his hand, desperately trying to make sense of the scenario in the dark.

At that very instant, the four vigilantes rushed into the room, weapons gleaming.

Confusion set in as a disquieting jumble of sounds resonated simultaneously throughout the room. Claire could not be certain what was happening, nor could she make out the shadowy figures moving about in front of her.

Unexpectedly, the lights came back on in all their brightness, exposing all parties and weapons in the study. The back-up power system had activated.

Four men were dressed in black, wearing night-vision glasses and black facemasks. The quartet stood in the center of the room, each grasping a hunting knife.

Nikos Zenonakis stood firmly in his position behind the sofa, brandishing his pistol.

The man dressed in brown paced near the desk, his two hands clutching the wooden club.

But all eyes fell upon the old bird woman.

Sitting on the floor near the sofa, the old woman had pulled

George halfway up onto her lap. She cradled him on her left upper torso, and with her left arm held him securely in place. Leaning toward him, she hummed a childhood lullaby in his ear and stroked his forehead repeatedly with the bent and horribly twisted fingers of her right hand. George opened his eyes ever so slightly and uttered a word that sounded like, *Mama*, before his eyelids closed and he drifted into eternal sleep.

The handle of a seven-inch blade stuck out of his chest. There was no doubt that he was dead. The only remaining question was: Who had inflicted the fatal stab wound?

The confession followed in short order.

"I am his mother, Lia," the old woman said quietly. "I followed his life all of these many years. He had to be stopped. The courts were unable to do it, so it was left to me." She sighed deeply. "The destruction he meted out upon others had to end."

All action halted momentarily as the shocking revelation set in: Lia—known to the Cretans as *the old woman who feeds the birds*—was none other than the birth mother of George Zenonakis. And it was she who had taken his life.

Nikos had slipped from the room and quickly returned with an injured man.

Despite Gaston Lombard's condition, Judge Lastner recognized the well-known Miami-prosecuting-attorney-turned-private-investigator at once and called out to his men, "Let's get out of here." The unidentified men in black raced from the room, knives flashing.

Claire took one look at Guy and her heart sank. She ran to him, threw her arms around his upper body, and began to sob. "You're alive, my darling. You're alive." She kissed his face over and over again. "We'll be home soon. I promise." She helped him into a chair. "Do you have water?" she asked Nikos. She motioned as if she were holding a glass and drinking. He understood, and immediately fetched a cup of the cool liquid. Claire grabbed it and carefully placed it to Guy's lips, asking him to sip slowly. Guy would correctly surmise later on that it had been Nikos who had smuggled water to him during his captivity.

It was clear that Guy had been roughed up considerably. A good amount of dried blood appeared near his lips, all over his cut and swollen face, and on the back of his head. His wrists and ankles dripped with fresh blood. He needed medical attention—that fact was clear. A dispirited look possessed him, and he sat all but motionless. Hungry and weak, as hard as he tried, he could not seem to formulate words. But when he heard the voice directing the men in black to leave, a lucid moment of recognition pounded through his brain. It was the same voice he had heard in the Italian restaurant nights before—the voice emanating from the loudest chanter, the voice that predominated in the clandestine meeting, and a voice he had heard before. One day, he would recall to whom it belonged.

The sound of the wooden club dropping to the floor drew all attention to the man dressed in brown, standing near the desk. With a single hand, he ripped the false facial hair from his face to reveal a very satisfied Mr. Otto. "My only regret is that I did not kill him with my own bare hands," he uttered. "There is more than one way to die, and by killing everyone I loved, George Zenonakis killed me, too." His eyes misted, and he turned his attention to Gaston Lombard. "Mr. Lombard, I am so very sorry for what this thug did to you. I have followed the two of you since you first arrived in Crete. I wanted to be the one to do George in once you found him. And I knew you would." He sobbed tears of relief. "Your check will be waiting for you upon your return. You will find a healthy bonus for the work you did for me."

Nikos reached down and pulled George's lifeless body back onto the sofa. Gently, Nikos grasped the arm of the old woman and helped her up. "Lia, it's over," he said, speaking Cretan Greek. He had recognized George's mother at once when the lights had come back on. "I, too, was prepared to do the same thing tonight." He stared at her in disbelief as he continued to look upon the face of George's mother—a face he had not seen since George was a mere baby, and a face portraying a woman who had unquestionably lived a most difficult life. "*What* did we do to you?" He pondered the situation briefly before he continued to speak. "It's time you moved into the mansion, Lia. You will inherit all of this one day soon. I will see to it."

Lia dropped her head. "If I had been in my son's life, things may have turned out differently." She sat next to George's lifeless body and kissed him gently on the forehead.

Nikos leaned down and reached deep into George's pants pocket. He pulled out the spectacular red gem. He examined the stone carefully and held it up to the light to see, firsthand, its brilliant color. Slowly turning to Mr. Otto, he presented the supreme Burmese ruby to the broken man.

The money Mr. Otto would receive from the sale of the priceless gemstone could not bring Billy or Hillary back to life. But it would certainly eliminate his financial woes. He nodded his heartfelt thanks to Nikos. The insurance claim Mr. Otto had filed would soon be withdrawn.

Thereafter, Nikos walked behind the desk, inserted a key, and opened a lower drawer. He lifted a crumpled sheet of paper from it and handed it to Claire Caswell. With his hands, he motioned to his grandson and then to the paper, indicating that George had been the author of the sketch. Claire took a look at the drawing, saw the autograph, and immediately realized it was indisputable evidence. With his own hand, George Zenonakis created the drawing that proved he was responsible for the murder of Billy Otto, the theft of the millions from the safe, and the explosion of the Ottos' plastics factory. The shape of the building was unmistakable. She nodded to Nikos, folded the paper, and tucked it inside her purse. Upon returning to Miami, she would be certain to deliver the sketch to Sergeant Massey, Miami–Dade Police Department, so that it would be included in the department's file. The sergeant would also want a certified copy of the death certificate of George Zenonakis, aka George Zeppano, once it became available.

The magnitude of what just occurred started to sink in. George Zenonakis … George Zeppano … had been murdered. And while everyone in the room had been present when it occurred, not a tear was shed by anyone over his demise. In fact, with the exception of Claire Caswell and Guy Lombard, everyone else in the room had been prepared to kill the criminal that very night. It was a sad commentary on a human life that had come to an abrupt and violent end.

Despite Claire's knowledge that Lia had just committed murder, she left Guy briefly and approached the old bird woman. "Lia," she said. "Thank you for everything. You brought Guy Lombard back to me." She hugged her. "You have been through a lot in your life." For a split second, Claire recalled the accounting Lia had revealed to her earlier on their drive to Hania. The Zenonakis family had treated Lia cruelly after George was born, acted as if she had no value, and manipulated her out of her son's life forever. Things had gone from bad to worse after being cast away from her offspring at a young age. Her existence had been a series of challenges. Perhaps now she would finally have some peace.

The sleuth returned to Guy. She placed an arm around his shoulders as she helped him sip more water. "I love you," she whispered in his ear.

He grunted something back that only Claire could understand.

"My beauty." His eyes watered.

She kissed him on the cheek. "You're safe now. We're going home."

Claire helped him to his feet and braced his body against hers. Together, they walked slowly to the door. "Lean on me," she said. "You're not strong." She looked at him with a twinkle in her eyes and smiled a sweet smile. As they ambled, her thoughts went to Kostas and Martha. Maybe now—now that this entire ordeal was over—Kostas would be willing to talk to the Americans again. She hoped so. Both Claire and Guy were convinced he had acted out of fear for his life and that of his family. Certainly understandable under the circumstances; they did not blame him.

GEORGE ZENONAKIS would be given a proper burial the following morning and be laid to rest on the estate's property next to his father's grave. The Cretan police would never become involved in the internal affairs of the Zenonakis family; thus, the murder of George Zenonakis, aka George Zeppano, would not be investigated and his murderer would not be prosecuted. A death certificate would be issued without delay listing *natural causes* as the cause of death.

Three weeks later . . .
Miami Beach, Florida

HALF PAST midnight approached. Guy was exhausted, but could not sleep. He tossed and turned for a good hour, adjusting and re-adjusting his pillows, and throwing the covers on and off. He envisioned himself peacefully at rest under the hot Grand Cayman sun, sprawled out flat on a padded lounge chair covered by a large sun umbrella, with Claire by his side. And while that image usually helped him fall asleep on sleepless nights, tonight it did not do the trick. His mind would simply not turn off.

Then it hit him! The reason for his restlessness. *He knew*! *He knew whom the voice belonged to*! He had been before the man in court on a few occasions in prior years. That voice belonged to none other than the prestigious *Judge Thomas Lastner*!

He glanced over at Claire. She slept soundly. Trying his best not to awaken her, he inched and maneuvered his way out of bed. He dressed quickly and exited the condo, locking the door behind him. He took the elevator to the garage level and jumped into his late-model black BMW sedan. As he drove, he made a call on his cell phone. He pulled over and jotted something hurriedly on a small piece of paper.

"I owe you one, buddy," Guy said before disconnecting. "Sorry for the late call."

All of a sudden, another realization hit him right between the eyes. The name *Bradley Rentsal* was an alias. *Rentsal* backward spelled *Lastner*! How very clever!

Several miles down the road, Guy Lombard spotted a public telephone in the parking lot of a twenty-four-hour gasoline station. He drove in, parked near the phone, and walked toward it with a brisk gait. He pulled the crumpled note from his shirt pocket. Without delay, he grabbed the handset and dropped coins into the slot. He waited impatiently for the dial tone. When he heard it, he carefully punched in the unlisted home phone number of Judge Thomas Lastner.

After several rings, a man, seemingly disoriented after being awakened from heavy sleep, answered groggily. "Yeah?"

Guy covered the receiver with a cloth handkerchief doubled over several times, and chanted in a crisp, incisive rap.

We know who you are,
We know what you do.
And rest assured,
We are watching you.

"What? Who is this?" the judge boomed, snapping into an acute state of awareness. "Identify yourself!"

Guy repeated the chant one additional time.

The judge bellowed into the mouthpiece. "Identify yourself! *I demand to know who this is*!"

Guy did not respond. Instead, he smiled a triumphant smile.

Judge Lastner pounded his clenched fist into the mattress five times in rapid succession. "*Who is this?*" he screamed in a crazed voice.

Guy hung up the phone.

Highly agitated that he was not able to control the situation and get an answer to his question, Judge Lastner got up and stormed around the room, shouting a long list of obscenities at the walls. Then, suddenly, an undeniable feeling of raw fear overtook him, stopping him dead in his tracks. Someone outside of the group knew of the foursome's activities. *Someone knew*! And that created a very dangerous situation for all the members. He sat down on the bed and held his forehead in his hands. Alarm cloaked his being and nausea overtook him. An intense pain burst forth in his head. He fell back, paralyzed.

GUY RETURNED home and climbed back into bed beside his beloved, Claire. He listened to her breathing until his eyelids grew heavy. Nestled comfortably alongside the woman he adored more than life, he spoke softly, informing her of the call he had just made to Judge Thomas Lastner. He also verbalized his undying love for her. Claire remained motionless in her sleep and did not hear any of it; yet somehow, telling her both things made Guy feel better. Now he, too, could finally fall asleep.

"Marry me, my beauty," he whispered in her ear. "Marry me." This was the message he whispered into her ear each night after she fell asleep, hoping one day she would succumb to his subliminal nudging and say yes to his ever-present question. He kissed her gently on her back.

"Love you," Claire murmured in her sleep.

Guy's face looked calm as he fell into easy slumber.

LATER THAT same day, Judge Lastner's housekeeper found him dead in his bed. The Miami–Dade County Coroner's Office chief medical examiner would soon discover that a ruptured brain aneurysm had taken his life.

Bread gained by deceit is sweet
to a man,
But afterward his mouth will be
filled with gravel.

Proverbs 20:17